REDCAP

A Selection of Titles by Brian Callison

CROCODILE TRAPP
FERRY DOWN
THE STOLLENBERG LEGACY
TRAPP'S PEACE
TRAPP'S WAR
THE TROJAN HEARSE

Warwickshire County Council

2 7 APR 2018			
1 7 FEB 2023			

This item is to be returned or renewed before the latest date above. It may be borrowed for a further period if not in demand. **To renew your books:**

- **Phone the 24/7 Renewal Line 01926 499273 or**
- **Visit www.warwickshire.gov.uk/libraries**

Discover • Imagine • Learn • *with libraries*

Working for
Warwickshire

REDCAP

Brian Callison

This first world edition published in Great Britain 2006 by
SEVERN HOUSE PUBLISHERS LTD of
9–15 High Street, Sutton, Surrey SM1 1DF.
This first world edition published in the USA 2006 by
SEVERN HOUSE PUBLISHERS INC of
595 Madison Avenue, New York, N.Y. 10022.

British Library Cataloguing in Publication Data

Callison, Brian
    Redcap
    1.   Military police - Fiction
    2.   Cyprus - History - War for Union with Greece,
         1955-1959 - Fiction
    3.   Germany - History - 1945-1990 - Fiction
    4.   War stories
    I.   Title
    823.9'14 [F]

    ISBN-13: 978-0-7278-6434-5 (cased)
    ISBN-10: 0-7278-6434-3   (cased)
    ISBN-13: 978-0-7278-9179-2 (paper)
    ISBN-10: 0-7278-9179-0   (paper)

Except where actual historical events and characters are being
described for the storyline of this novel, all situations in this
publication are fictitious and any resemblance to living persons
is purely coincidental.

All Severn House titles are printed on acid-free paper.

Typeset by Palimpsest Book Production Ltd.,
Polmont, Stirlingshire, Scotland.
Printed and bound in Great Britain by
MPG Books Ltd., Bodmin, Cornwall.

CYPRUS, 1957

One

When the quarter-tonner's windscreen imploded I assumed, for a moment, we'd hit a low-flying bird in the darkness. Then Corporal Fox began screaming and I realized the birds were nine-millimetre parabellum, probably from a Sten or Schmeisser sub-machine gun.

While the back of the bench seat between us erupted in a cloud of intestinal sorbo, a disembodied wiper blade plucked at the shoulder strap of my battledress. Foxie's cap tipped forward over his eyes and as he doubled over the wheel clawing at his groin I registered a spatter of blood under his left ear where the shattering Triplex had gashed him.

Abruptly the Land Rover's headlights scribed a tight bucketing arc across the Cyprus mountainside as we careered downwards and off the road. My desperate lunge to reach the handbrake became like trying to grab a door handle on a capsizing ship. Broadsiding on two wheels along the rocky verge at forty miles an hour, we could have doubled as highly paid stuntmen in a movie.

Only me, I'm no showman and don't consider myself even moderately rewarded. Stuntmen don't get shot at by their bloody audience for a start, while it's the British Army, not ABC Pics, signs my pay cheques.

As Foxie slid down the seat on top of me I tried to squeeze his avalanching bulk below the dash under mine. Or maybe it was mine under Foxie's if I was completely truthful. Motivated by sheer terror, I'd probably have managed it if we hadn't hit the tree so soon. But I didn't . . . and we did, if you see what I mean?

That's when the door ripped off. Canvas-topped military

Land Rover doors are flimsy at the best of times: this one just kept going when the rest of the vehicle had stopped.

So did Corporal Fox.

So did I.

In what are understatedly referred to as moments of stress they, whoever 'they' are, claim that episodes of one's life flash kaleidoscopically before one's eyes. Yeah, right – assuming one's granted time for such leisurely preoccupation. All I remember thinking was what a *bloody* undignified way for a Royal Military Police staff sergeant to depart this mortal coil, ramrod-backed in the drill manual's approved sit-to-attention posture – only airborne, and travelling at thirty-odd feet per second. A regimented witch on her first solo, ex-broomstick.

Unless, of course, I included the Rover door and Corporal Fox, still keening monotonously in a high key, flying as my wing-men.

When I came round I was pleasantly surprised to find myself in bed. Everything felt wonderfully soft and springy . . . until I stretched luxuriously. That was when I fell out of the bush onto a bloody hard, rock-strewn piece of Cyprus.

With a battle-hardened soldier's presence of mind I quickly evaluated the situation and decided my first tactic was to be sick. Rolling over I tried hard to bring up the bile making a determined attempt to choke me. All I succeeded in doing was to discover muscles I'd never suspected I had. My whole body ached. Dozens of tiny, and a few not-so-tiny scratches transmitted electric shocks to my nerve ends and when I peered apprehensively through the gloom to confirm my hands had travelled the whole way with me, I observed they were shaking violently.

Groaning miserably I flopped back. Then realization dawned and I jerked up nervously again, accompanied by a hundred thousand bursting lights. The cerebral pyrotechnics made me flop back a lot quicker. Slowly the nausea passed and, more gingerly this time, I struggled up again feeling like one of those little men with weighted bottoms that just won't lie down, except I was equally terrified to sit upright because somebody or other nearby was still shooting, and maybe at me and Foxie. I could make a combat-qualified evaluation like that 'cause I could hear the weapon slamming not very far from where I lay.

I frowned . . . where the hell *was* Foxie, anyway? Couldn't hear him screaming anymore. In fact I couldn't hear anything except for the erratic stuttering of that bloody light-machine gun. Swallowing uneasily I peered around.

And found Foxie.

As well as solving the mystery of why Corporal Fox wasn't screaming any longer. Well, to be chillingly precise: why Corporal Fox wasn't doing anything any longer. While I'd been lucky enough to crash-land in a convenient thorn bush at the expense of a few minor abrasions, Foxie's flight plan had followed a less benign parabola. The stubby branch of a traditionally blasted somethin' or other had spitted him clean through the throat. Now he hung, oscillating from side to side: a bit like a Santa doll on a skeletal Christmas tree.

I think I whimpered a little as I stumbled over to the festive tableau. It was creepy Gothic up there in the mountains with the stark fingers of other long-dead trees pointing accusingly to the darkness of a wind-ripped sky. The tentacles of what, for all I knew, could have been British-soldier-eating plants clawed at my gaitered ankles as I forced myself to move closer to the patiently dangling Redcap while all the time frantically hoping that maybe the branch hadn't taken him through the throat after all. That maybe, just maybe, it was an optical illusion brought on by the crash.

I halted under the tree and looked up at Foxie. He grinned down at me in a curiously reassuring manner, almost apologetically as if to say it didn't really matter that he was suspended by the larynx on some foreign mountainside. Then I, too, saw what he seemed to be indicating. That it didn't really matter, at that.

Not that the discovery made me feel any better.

The sub-machine-gun round that penetrated the offside door before taking Provost Corporal Fox in the groin would have flattened further on impact with his hip joint. Slowing down, but still travelling at over one thousand feet per second with a propellant energy of nearly two hundred foot-pounds, it had then ripped through his genitals and spleen before, in its final act of disembowelment, carrying away his lower stomach.

I remember standing there with a million slimy things dragging over my skin, yet with a curiously floating sense of detachment. It was the oddest thing, really. The way I'd found myself critically inspecting Foxie's boots. They swung in front of me at just about head height, and I even found myself nodding approvingly as the sheen of moonlight caught the gleaming toecaps. Only a military police NCO could bull a pair of boots like that, I reflected. Only a real army copper or, somewhat grudgingly, maybe just a few of the Brigade of Guards mob. The real old sweats, that was.

I recalled Foxie the night he was issued with them: that same pair. First he'd heated a mess spoon till it was damn near red hot then, with tongue protruding from the corner of his mouth, he'd laboriously burnished the chromed leather heels and toecaps flat and smooth as a baby's backside. Hours later, and about three pints of spit and Cherry Blossom, he'd casually held them out to me.

'What d'yer reckon, Staff?' he'd said, poker-faced but sort of proud inside.

I'd looked them over sourly, thinking what a bloody good soldier Foxie was. Then handed them back. 'Suppose they're OK for football,' I'd sniffed, 'but what're you goin' to wear to look smart in, Corporal?'

He'd laughed good-naturedly at the time but later, catching a glimpse of him bulling them some more, I'd felt a bit guilty because you can't improve on perfection.

Anyway, I just stood there for what must have been quite a long time, gazing at Foxie's boots. I frowned a little when I registered a smear of something alien on his left instep and, raising my eyes, saw that the remaining viscera had ever so slowly started to follow the razor-sharp creases of his trousers.

The last thing I registered before finally vomiting was how shiny his brasses were against the snowy-white blanco that coated what was left of his web belt.

Like I said. He was a bloody good soldier, was Corporal Fox.

The gun started firing again, from a little higher up the mountain, just before I passed out again. But I wasn't frightened this time. Not with Foxie watching over me, so to speak.

I don't know how long I lay there but I don't suppose Foxie objected to hanging around, not all that much anyway. I vaguely recollect the spanging concerto of a light-weapons duel from a distance, and a flat, cracking echo that sounded like a British Mills grenade doing someone or other a bit of unpleasantness. Then Foxie winked down at me in his reassuring way, and I passed out again.

The next time I came round I tried not to look at him. It didn't really seem decent, somehow. He'd always been a bullshit merchant as I've already said, smart as a Toledo sword hilt. Even his fancy pyjamas, the ones he'd bought in Hong Kong, sported creases that threatened to lay his shin bones open while he was asleep. And anyhow, the way my mind was wandering then, I felt Fox would have been dead unchuffed at me, his staff sergeant, catching him off guard with his guts spilling out so untidily.

So instead I just lay for a few moments, ears straining to catch noises that didn't seem to be there anymore, and glowering at the silhouette of the wrecked Land Rover crouching a few yards away, looking as if it was trying to embrace the skeleton tree which had finally arrested it. From what little I could make out, we must have careered downhill for some way, breasting that dimly seen rise that concealed us from the road before brought to a halt in this dehydrated and desolate copse.

Trying not to reflect too deeply on why I'd lived while Fox had died, I wondered gloomily where the rest of my section had got to. I'd signed out four vehicles for the patrol and didn't reckon whoever ambushed us could have been sharp enough to take out all three quarter-tonners following mine. So where *were* they, for Christ's sake? Twelve armed Redcaps didn't just disappear up their own whistle barrels, especially if they had to reach out again and drag three Rovers in as well. Then reflected that there were only eleven men actually missing if I discounted Corporal Fox, who was roughly ninety per cent present and accounted for.

Cautiously lifting my head, I listened. Nothing moved; not even a bird. If birds really do go out after the proverbial worm at 0400 hours on a Cypriot winter's morning. I frowned again. Having received such an impressive display of bloody-mindedness from what I assumed was our local EOKA terror group, my mob should've been making the gunfight at the OK Corral sound like a public reading room after closing time, but instead . . .? Silence.

I let my head flop back with a groan. Not a loud enough groan to make anybody angry, mind you. Just a secret sigh of despair as I asked myself for the thousandth time why I'd ever joined the British bloody Army in the first place.

I'm Walker, Bill Walker. Rank: Staff Sergeant, Corps of Royal Military Police. Army number 34277368. Blood type AB. Height, six two-a-half. Born – far too long ago to derive any sense of adventure from the career path I was currently pursuing. Lucky number, thirteen. Shirt-collar size, seventeen. Likes . . .? Sociable barmaids, disserting at length on Queen's Regulations to captive audiences of squaddies, crispy-charred sausages and being admired. Dislikes . . .? Pickled walnuts, bad soldiers, members of the public who shout *Redcap bastard* then scuttle furtively away, and the Assistant Provost Marshal. Particularly the Assistant Provost Marshal. Not that I feel any great affection for anyone else holding the Queen's Commission, for that matter, which is partly why I'm still only a staff sergeant.

I have an external image which is nothing like the real me, but which keeps forcing me into doing things a real hard action-soldier would do. Usually at the wrong time and in the wrong place, which further helps to explain why I'm still only a staff sergeant.

I'm a good military policeman, I think. I try to blend just the right quantities of square-dealing and sadism – the square-dealing bit to pacify large private soldiers who might other-

wise feel tempted to smash my face in, and the sadism partly
'cause it keeps you in solid with regimental sergeant majors
but, more so, because the rank and file of the British Army
expects it of me.

I'm also a coward, but usually I'm more scared of being
seen to be scared than of the actual thing I should be scared
about . . . if you see what I mean?

I'm ruggedly handsome too, by the way. As well as shameless about telling lies when not under oath.

Passing a trembling hand over a bloodied but hopefully, as
far as I could feel, still ruggedly handsome face, I struggled
to recall the circumstances leading to Walker reclining flako
under the drawn cadaver of one of our best NCOs. Glancing
up involuntarily, I noted that Foxie's brasses were already
beginning to tarnish in the damp night air.

'Good rub up with a soft cloth before you go on parade,
mate,' I thought distantly. Then the sickness welled up inside
me again as Foxie jiggled a little in the breeze, as if to assure
me he was big enough to take a little unfair criticism.

I got a bit angry with Corporal Fox then: always feeling
driven to act the hard man, as I am. Now Foxie was doing
a pretty efficient job of dismantling that image so carefully
fabricated over years. Abruptly I turned from him in childish
pique. You maybe think it was more in revulsion but, to a
hard soldier like me, it was just irritation. Anyway, that's
my explanation.

Apprehensively I peered around. Still no movement, no
sound; not even the click of a safety catch. Shivering involuntarily as the chill Mediterranean night air seeped through
my battledress, I tried desperately to figure it all out.

We'd left around 0200, ostensibly to patrol the mountain
road from Limassol. It wasn't really my section or even my
duty as such, but Sergeant O'Feely had spent the past two
weeks and three pay days' worth of alcohol on impressing
his latest target with his evergreen line about how nice it
would be to marry a British field marshal and spend the rest
of her life sipping pink gins and laying about around swimming pools on exotic foreign postings. Mind you, I knew

9

bloody well that wasn't the sort of laying O'Feely had in mind, so when he pleaded with me in the mess to stand in for him on tonight's patrol, I confess to having appeared a tad unsympathetic.

'Staff,' O'Feely had announced breezily, 'Staff Sergeant, tonight is *the* night. Tonight I make the Hit.'

'No you bloody don't, O'Feely,' I'd growled. 'Tonight is the night you take your section out to keep the Zorbas on the path of British righteousness.'

His battered face creased into a lascivious grin. 'Staff, I'm needed here too badly. I got one local bike primed to be so naughty I might even have to arrest myself as well.'

I sniffed. 'O'Feely, you have the morals of an alley cat. You should've been ejected the moment you stepped through the recruiting-centre door. Particularly with a name like yours.'

O'Feely smiled irrepressibly. 'It so happens the recruiting bloke sussed I was too intellectual to waste on the navy. Now, how about you standin' in for me tonight and I promise to tell you all about it in the morning?'

'No.'

'I'll take Lance Corporal Butterworth's Polaroid. Bring you back some pictures?'

'No,' I said again.

'Last offer,' he countered without a trace of embarrassment. 'Tomorrow night I take you with me and *you* can use Butterworth's Polaroid.'

I rose from the table, hurt by O'Feely's automatic assumption that I could be vulnerable to bribery. Especially bribery of such a depraved nature.

'You're also an insulting bastard, O'Feely,' I retorted loftily. 'Jus' remember next time that I'm a provost staff sergeant, not a bloody pimp.'

If it hadn't been for the moist glint of disappointment his eyes, I would never have relented. Not after that. But I always was a bit soft about hurting other people's feelings. It was my one weakness, and enough to make me hesitate at the door.

'Tell you what, O'Feely,' I conceded generously. 'Take

10

me tomorrow night – and *you* can use Butterworth's Polaroid!'

. . . so here I was in charge of O'Feely's section of twelve men, with Corporal Fox as my driver in the lead Rover. The patrol to that point had been cold and monotonous as per usual. My only problem, and I couldn't prevent it from niggling at the back of my mind, was how the hell did O'Feely manage to persuade the local scrubbers he was a field marshal? Especially with three tapes sewn on his sleeve.

I'd just reached a decision to turn the screws a bit harder on Sergeant O'Feely for more instructional technique in the secrets of courting ladies, when the screen caved in and Foxie took a hundred and twenty-five grains of metal-encased lead in his lower gut.

While I lost twel— no, *eleven* men and three army-issue quarter-ton Land Rovers.

I groaned again. Louder this time, not even caring too much if a Cypriot insurgent's ear was cocked or not. I mean, hell – the Rovers I could maybe cover for at a pinch, but eleven coppers? Bloody near a ton of Military Police lance corporals? They were almost certain to be missed by someone. Eventually.

Pressured into risking the possible presence of olive-skinned bad guys bent on placing me in harm's way, I set my jaw grimly and clambered shakily to my feet. Walker was fast becoming unchuffed. Walker was, in fact, bloody well steaming! Warmed by anticipation of the retribution I intended to hand out to the next bastard – ours, theirs or anyone else's – who strayed out of line with Staff Sergeant Walker RMP, I strode briskly, and ruggedly, off into the gloom.

. . . it's hard to be specific about how long I lay unconscious the next time. Like I said, one moment I'd stepped briskly off my mark, yet on next opening my eyes the night had given way to the delicate pink wash of a Mediterranean dawn. Blinking hard, I tried to focus.

Reliable old Foxie was still there: still above and watching over me like God. Or certainly his boots were. They swung gently from side to side, with little strands of dried grass protruding from the right angle formed where the heel pieces met the bright-studded soles. I could even see under the bottoms of his anklets where white blanco dust had powdered off onto the chromed leather.

Nervously licking cracked lips, I allowed my eyelids to shutter down again. Foxie's boots were fast becoming an obsession. Walker's image was deconstructing in too many places for Walker's liking, and all because of a pair of size-eleven-a-half boots, black chromed field pattern, other ranks for the use of. Distantly I heard myself lapsing into a sing-song ramble while my tear ducts filled with apprehensive moisture.

Ruggedly handsome 34277368 Staff Sergeant Walker W, Royal Military Police, was sobbing. And singing hysterically. And needing to be sick again. The image finally shattered into a million terrified splinters.

Boots! Boots! LOTSA pairsa boots, in the store . . . HIN the store! There wus boots . . . boots! Thousandsa pairsa boots, in the Quar-ter BASTARD'S stooooore!

Wearily I raised a leaden hand to smear away a tear before it trickled down my cheek to plop into my right ear. The facial lacerations smarted painfully where the ductile salt had penetrated. I sniffed. A long, shuddering, ever-so-miserable sniff.

'*Staff?*'

. . . The shock of which marked the instant when I froze. Outwardly, anyway. Inwardly my bodily functions performed involuntarily. There's a crude service expression to describe such reaction but, right then, I was feeling more sort of delicate than crude, so I just froze. Bloody rigid.

A discreet cough. 'Staff Walker?'

The million slimy things on my skin all decided to change places at once. Shuddering, I allowed one eyelid to climb fractionally open. The vision that swam fuzzily into view was almost less bearable than the eviscerated Corporal Fox.

Acting Lance Corporal Tosh stared down at me with brow-furrowed concern. And I detested Tosh more than anyone else I can think of. Except for the Assistant Provost Marshal, that is . . . and pickled walnuts. But they're not people, either of 'em. Closing my eye again I prayed the spectre would dematerialise. But it didn't intend to.

An agitated hand shook my shoulder violently, followed by a frustrated squeak. 'Staff! Staff Sergeant Walker . . .? It's *me*.'

Abandoning hope I glared up at him.

'Who in Christ's name is *me*, Tosh? And how many times have you been told never to touch a wounded man till you're sure of what's wrong with him?'

The fat youth drew his hand back quick, as if I had leprosy or one of the recreationally acquired social diseases. Marshalling what was left of my splintered image, I gazed at him critically. He dropped his eyes guiltily. It was one of the countless things I couldn't abide about Tosh: the way he always contrived to look guilty somehow. Even bringing a prisoner in under close arrest, you couldn't help but get the impression there'd been a miscarriage of justice somewhere – that really it was Lance Corporal Tosh who should be locked in the slammer and his prisoner sat down at the duty desk to fill in the committal receipt.

Raising a grimy hand I furtively brushed away the tell-tale streaks that some insensitive observer might have interpreted as tear marks. Tosh watched with deep interest. I could almost hear the little wheels grinding away in his bullet-shaped head and hated him even more then.

'What're you grinnin' at, Corporal?' I demanded furiously. 'Or have you forgotten the whole fuckin' area's crawling with Yolkie terrorists? Dammit, lad, a mob of them jumped mc a fcw minutes back and clobbered me good. Probably in platoon strength.'

Tosh waved airily. 'S'all right, Staff Sar'nt. We're safe as the Bank of England 'ere.'

I let the rather ill-chosen comparison slide. 'Don't bloody argue, Tosh. Get layin' down on your big fat gut like you bin ordered to.'

Tosh still didn't move, just squatted there cross-legged like one those little plaster Buddhas you sometimes see on people's mantelpieces. Only slightly less useful. I registered a mole on the side of his chin and wished I could do something to help him remove it. Like shoot it off.

He smiled proudly. 'They was me, Staff.'

I blinked as a nasty suspicion formed. 'Whaddyou mean – *they* was *me*?'

Tosh was foolish enough to beam indiscreetly. 'Them terrorists, Staff: the ones you said was in platoon strength? Well – they wus me. I clobbered you . . . er, Staff Sergeant.'

He must have registered a glint in my eye poisonous enough to make him draw back from committing total suicide. 'O' course,' he qualified hastily, 'course I di'n't *know* it was you. Not until I got a proper chance to look.'

'Oh,' I muttered faintly. 'Oh well, that's all right then, innit? So long as you didn't know it was me you were beltin' over the back of the bloody skull I can't very well have you charged with assaulting a superior rank, can I?'

He grinned. A little overconfidently, I thought uneasily, levering myself up on one arm and sniffing. Tosh was getting a bit too much on me for my liking. Like I said, I'd worked hard on building the legend of Staff Walker. Hard as nails, debonair, nerveless in a pinch and, generally speaking, the finest thing that had happened to the British Army since gunpowder. Now this tubby little bastard Tosh was beaming down at me with enough knowledge of the Other Walker to blow my whole myth.

'You went down like a log,' he supplemented, impressed.

'Not surprised . . . shell shock,' I probed experimentally, albeit slightly digressing from the point at issue. 'Copped shell shock at Tobruk.'

Tosh looked sceptical. 'Shell shock? Dunno about that, Staff. I thought you were just crying. You know – 'cause you was scared bloody rigid?'

He frowned then, reaching deep down into the slimy crevasses of his mini-intellect. 'Anyhow, where's that Tow Brook you're speakin' about? I never heard of any place called Tow Brook.'

I guess a lot of my closest mates spun in their sandy graves right then. After what Tosh had said about Tobruk, I mean.

I didn't feel mad though: just sad. Don't forget, this was back in the halcyon days of National Service when conscripted morons like Tosh were all too often the rule rather than the exception, even in Provost. Understanding their problems, trying to guide them the right way, was all part of the duty I was charged with. Being there for them, and acting as their mentor. Sort of, well, *helping* them become better people, if you see what I'm getting at?

So I guided him.

'Lissen, you khaki-coloured fucking spawn of an illegitimate union between a eunuch an' a dyke,' I said, enunciating with great precision, 'if you so much as breathe a *word* of what you jus' thought you saw, then not only will I kick the fuck outa your fat arse, I shall also see to it that, when they clamp you in the can for attempted murder of a senior rank, they don't jus' throw away the key – they bloody MELT IT DOWN F'R SCRAP . . . ! *Savvy?*'

Tosh yelped like a tail-docked puppy as the guilty look returned while his fleshy cheeks wobbled: nodding violently to assure me he'd got the message loud and clear. I glared at him suspiciously, then, recalling our situation, went back to peering nervously around. I wasn't exactly guilt free myself, seeing I'd been so preoccupied with mentoring Lance Corporal Tosh that neither of us had kept any kind of guard. For all I knew, every EOKA terrorist in Cyprus could have been closing in through the surrounding undergrowth. Walker was definitely slipping this morning.

'I don't suppose,' I asked heavily, 'I don't *suppose* you thought to bring a gun with you did you, Lance Corporal?'

He started nervously, then began ferreting in the withered grass.

'Got my Sten somewhere, Staff,' he stammered placatingly. I shuddered while he patted under clumps of weed, and wished I hadn't left my own side arm in its webbing holster hanging over the back of the Rover seat on account of Messrs Webley and Scott's product having a tendency to dig uncomfortably into my groin and keep me awake on patrols.

Tosh suddenly sat back, uttered a pleased grunt and

tendered what may well have been a Mark III Sten sub-machine gun at one time. Ugly, mass-produced by the yard and costing roughly the price of two jamjars, it was still frighteningly effective at killing people when fired in their general direction. Meaning the weapon suited Tosh's capabilities to a tee. With just his kind of soldier in mind, the British Army called it the Woolworth gun or, even more caustically, the Plumber's Delight.

Ignoring the fact that he'd apparently forgotten to insert a charged magazine when he'd gone terrorist-hunting, I watched gloomily as, with enormous concentration, he laboriously picked bits of dried grass and dirt from the barrel before blowing critically down it. I remember reflecting wistfully on how much better my morning could have felt if he'd pulled the trigger by mistake, assuming even Tosh would have carried it ready-cocked to fire under the circumstances.

Leaning over I extended a distasteful index finger and prodded Tosh's battledress blouse. His brows met again in a baffled vee as I removed a charged magazine from an ammunition pocket apparently otherwise stuffed with bits of string, fluff, a packet of army-issue contraceptives and a photograph of his mother.

Glaring at him spitefully, I snatched the Sten and smacked the magazine into place; cocking the weapon sharply but, as it turned out, irresponsibly. A catapult made from a twig and elastic band could well have proved a lethal weapon in Tosh's hands.

'You oughter be bloody ashamed of yourself, Tosh. Keepin' photos of your mum alongside those things.'

He flushed proudly. 'Ackshully that's Helena, Staff. My girlfriend.'

I studied the picture again, bit my tongue out of sympathy, and shoved the Sten back at him. 'Go on, Corporal. Pretend you're a real soldier for a few minutes. Look after Corporal Fox and I'll go scout round for the rest of the section.'

Hurriedly I began to crawl on my hands and knees, hoping the bottle of brandy I'd secreted in the Rover hadn't followed the same route as the door. And Foxie. A sibilant hiss from astern made me freeze in my tracks, reactivating the million

16

slimy dwellers in the hairs on the nape of my neck until I realized it was Tosh trying to attract my attention – as well as that of every gunman around the bloody Mediterranean.

He still squatted there clutching his Sten like a stick of Blackpool rock. It was broad daylight by now and the trees and drought-stunted bushes stood motionless in the yellow warmth of the early morning sun. The wind had dropped altogether and everything was so quiet it seemed even more unnatural than when it was dark. Still not a bird or an insect moved and I shivered uneasily, deciding to look for my Smith and Wesson first, then the brandy.

'Christ, Tosh. Can't you do anythin' quiet?'

'Sorry, Staff, but did you say to look after Corporal Fox?'

I blinked and glanced uncertainly up at the corpse dangling almost directly above him. Its brasses were so tarnished by now that they hardly glinted at all. Quickly I dropped my gaze again, preferring even to look at Tosh than at the unidentifiable streamers beginning to dry out above him.

I nodded confirmation. Quite tolerantly, for once. Whatever else one thought about Lance Corporal Tosh, one had to admire his aplomb. The way he could wait there so casually, quite undeterred by the prospect of being left all alone on a hostile foreign field with a bulled-up cadaver. Not that I imagined being temporary custodian of Corporal Fox would present too many challenges over the next few minutes; not even for him.

Not until he shrugged sheepishly. 'Yeah, well . . . where *is* he, then? Corporal Fox, I mean.'

I suppose, deep down, I derived great joy from his saying that. The fact that an unmilitary little bastard like Tosh had a strong enough stomach not to reveal even a flicker of emotion at the horrific demobilization of one of his section: well, frankly, it had been needling me. I'd even begun to feel a grudging respect for him, which I resented.

I didn't say anything. Just indicated above his head with a most pleasurable feeling of anticipation.

I don't reckon it was the hysterical scream that brought about the lumbering arrival of Sergeant O'Feely so much as that, when Tosh finally did discover Foxie, he involuntarily loosed off the entire thirty-two-round magazine from his Sten.

After the first three I'd prostrated myself on Cyprus with hands clasped over my head. Only when I eventually screwed up the courage to lift it again was I greeted by the sight of O'Feely standing over me, legs apart and weapon at the ready, grinning like the Cheshire Cat in *Alice*.

'Good morning, Staff Sergeant Walker,' he greeted with obvious relish.

Scrambling awkwardly to my feet I made a half-hearted attempt to dust myself off yet again, then gave up: sick and tired of people catching me lying down.

'Don't you know enough not to come chargin' up like the Fifth bloody Cavalry, O'Feely? Anyway, how d'you know all that yellin' and firing wasn't the Zorbas, stupid? You coulda got your big fat head blown off.'

My fellow NCO shook his head reassuringly. 'Soon as me and the lads heard the row we knew it wasn't proper soldiers makin' it.'

I decided there and then it was the last favour I was ever going to do for O'Feely. I felt a little better at the implication that the section wasn't so much lost as mislaid, but nevertheless ... I opened my mouth to make a defensive retort, but O'Feely wasn't listening.

His mouth had tightened and the weather-beaten features perceptibly blanched as he, too, caught sight of Foxie. His adam's apple jerked convulsively while he swallowed hard, then dropped his eyes to the still retching Tosh. Walking over he shook the young lance corporal by the shoulder.

'Come on, lad,' he muttered, carefully trying to avoid looking up. Tosh didn't move, though. Just lay there heaving and crying spasmodically, with bits of leaves and grass sticking to the rough khaki serge of his battledress. O'Feely shook him again, a little harder, but Tosh simply drew his convulsing body into a tighter ball, still clinging to the same foetal posture. O'Feely looked over to me grimly. He didn't need to ask.

I shrugged, struggling to project the image again. 'Took one in the gut and crashed the Rover.'

He smiled unexpectedly. 'Glad you're OK, Bill.'

I blinked a little, then shook myself hard. That kind of remark didn't make me feel any tougher and I was just beginning to realize exactly how shaken up I really was with the night's events. Time for rearguard action.

'What're you doing here, anyway?' I retorted aggressively. 'Thought you were supposed to be demonstrating your eighth wonder of the world to some local boot at my expense.'

He grinned the O'Feely grin. 'Her old man wasn't so accommodating as you. Had to make a sharp strategic withdrawal – out of her and the back window both. Then just as I got back to the billet the balloon went up about this mess you'd got yourself into so the Major grabbed me as 'is driver.'

'Steadman?' I said, suddenly apprehensive again. 'Here?'

O'Feely nodded. 'Sergeant O'Feely, he says to me, I need a man I can rely on to get Staff Walker out of the shit. You're the only senior NCO in the company worth a toss, so you come along with me . . . so here I am. You been saved.'

I nodded dumbly. Steadman. The cop with attitude. If he was here things couldn't get much worse. Then Corporal Fox's boots pirouetted in the periphery of my vision and I hastily changed my mind. But not entirely. The recently appointed commanding officer of 368 Provost Company, Cyprus, was the worst thing that had happened to me in twenty years of service. And O'Feely reckoned I'd been saved?

'Better get back to the section,' O'Feely urged.

He knelt on one knee beside the boy and shook him again. 'Up you get, lad,' he encouraged gently but Tosh just stayed curled up tight, moaning between sobs. O'Feely glanced up at me queryingly, and I shrugged. We couldn't just leave him there, tempting as the thought was, but the kid wasn't helping himself much either.

'On your FEET, Corporal!' I barked. The thought of Steadman waiting impatiently, almost certainly fondling that scar of his, was undermining my slowly returning confidence. And anyway, it wasn't decent to leave Corporal Fox any longer than necessary. Not the way his brasses were tarnishing like that.

O'Feely stood up while I turned away deliberately, ostensibly to retrieve Tosh's Sten lying abandoned in a scatter of glittering cartridge cases. We didn't have time to wet-nurse a reluctant National Serviceman but I still winced as I heard O'Feely's boot slamming into Tosh's ribs. A lot of people were getting hurt this morning.

The boy sobbed and I turned just in time to see O'Feely kick him again. Tosh clutched at his ribs in agony, well on his way to forgetting about Foxie. O'Feely drew his boot back and I could tell he was sweating. I didn't feel too good about it either.

'On your feet, you gutless little maggot!' Sergeant O'Feely snarled, at the same time glancing covertly round the clearing to make sure we weren't being observed. Tosh whimpered, rolled over and raised his backside the way a camel does when it gets up, although his tear-stained face still stayed on the ground and I could see little bits of earth adhering under his screwed-up eyes. I'd never noticed what long lashes he had until then. Camels had them too.

O'Feely kicked him a third time. 'Get UP, Tosh! Gerrup or I'll boot your fuckin' spine clear through the top of your bloody skull.'

Tosh slowly clawed his way to his feet then just stood there crying quietly while sort of turning his head to one side so's he wouldn't accidentally catch sight of Corporal Fox. I walked back to join Sergeant O'Feely and together we made a half-hearted effort to square him up. The youngster's blouse had bunched up and pulled out of the top of his belt while the bottom of one trouser leg hung down over the grubby white gaiter. O'Feely retrieved Tosh's cap with its creased red cover and, dusting it with his elbow, placed it firmly on his head, pulling the peak well down over his eyes. Then he squared away the red RMP duty armband, tugged the uniform about a little and Tosh looked almost military again.

'Right, lad,' he said quietly. 'Don't look up: just about turn and we'll all get out of here.'

We walked up through the skeleton trees, past the wrecked Land Rover and towards the road where the rest of the section waited. Before we crested the rise I let the other two go ahead, then turned to look back at Foxie. And didn't flinch at all.

'Don't go away, mate,' I whispered softly. 'We'll be back for you soon.'

I knew he wouldn't ignore the order. Like I said: he was a bloody good soldier, was Corporal Fox.

Two

As we came up to the section I searched apprehensively for Steadman but couldn't sight his immaculate figure anywhere.

On the way back O'Feely had told me there'd been no casualties on our side, not even a minor injury. Other than Foxie, that was. And Tosh's bruised ribs. Nevertheless I still frowned concernedly round the troops as they sat cleaning their weapons. They all looked tired and dusty but I was surprised to see pleased looks being furtively directed at me, almost as though they were glad to see me back.

But I knew I was far too hard a martinet for that, and no one loves a Redcap staff sar'nt, so I just glowered at them and reminded them they wasn't on a bloody mystery tour so they should get up off of their fat backsides an' kid on they was proper soldiers. They didn't even seem to resent that bit of mentoring either: just wiped grubby hands over sweating faces and grinned inanely at each other.

I left O'Feely and Tosh and walked curiously back to the ambush spot. Bullet scars had chopped up the surface of the track as my eyes followed the churned-up skid marks leading over and down to where Foxie had died. I noted the blackened cancer of a grenade burst, probably the one I'd heard through my earlier terror. Making sure no one could see me I closed my eyes momentarily and thanked God for the miracle that meant only one mother would grieve tomorrow.

I spat into the dust and chewed my lower lip pensively . . . where the hell *had* the Major got to? The three remaining patrol Rovers still lay canted in the ditch where their drivers had abandoned them soon as Fox and I had launched into our hell-driving act. The CO's vehicle, on the other hand, sat supercilious and gleaming, smack dead centre on the crown of the road: the legend ROYAL MILITARY POLICE neatly picked out in red letters on a whiter-than-white board mounted above the aluminium-painted front fender. I grinned to myself and thought how keen Steadman must have been to get away, wherever he was, otherwise he'd have detailed off some poor sod to clean it again anyway.

Provost Corporal Davidson was sprawled over the flat bonnet of the lead vehicle, cleaning his Sten with a piece of four by two and wearing a frown of intense concentration. It was hot by now, with the sun well up in the sky. Davidson's BD blouse lay over the back of the seat and runnels of sweat channelled down through the dust on his face. He looked up and quickly levered himself erect as I approached. I thought he looked tired and drawn, but his eyes still lit up when he saw me.

'Staff?' he said. 'You're OK, then? Christ but we were worried when we saw you and Foxie go into the ditch.'

'Yeah, I noticed, Corporal,' I retorted bitterly. He winced.

'I couldn't do a fuckin' thing, Staff. The Zorbas were throwin' the bloody lot at us and all I could think of was to get the lads under cover. We returned fire for maybe twenty minutes, then the bastards just vanished.' He shrugged. 'Then the CO and Sar'nt O'Feely arrived and told us to stay here, rather than risk gettin' picked off in the trees.'

'Sorry, Davidson: you did the right thing.' A sudden thought struck me. 'But in that case – how in God's name did Tosh get lost? You surely din't send him off on his tod, did you?'

The corporal looked a bit uncomfortable at that, and glanced resentfully over at the recuperated Tosh currently surrounded by an admiring circle of his mates. 'The thick little bastard kept on about goin' to look for you and Foxie. Next thing I knew, he'd vanished.'

I stared at him speechlessly. Tosh? That podgy conscript with a mole on his chin. The boy I'd judged as a gutless skiver of the first water. The boy who'd gone to try and rescue his patrol commander with a Sten gun stuffed with grass and not even loaded. I remembered the way O'Feely had deployed his boot with my furtive sanction, and felt

23

guilty again. It was getting to be a habit. Feeling guilty, I mean – not kicking Lance Corporal Tosh.

Davidson turned to gaze searchingly across at the group.

'Where's Foxie, Staff? I lost half a quid to 'im at pontoon yesterday. Got to break it to him he'll have to wait till next pay parade.'

'Reinvest it, Davidson,' I said gruffly, then turned quickly on my heel and walked away. I sensed Davidson watching me go with a puzzled expression on his face, and hesitated: swung back.

'Fox is dead, Corporal!'

Davidson's legs gave way and he sort of slumped back against the Rover wing. I heard the brasses of his belt scrape across the painted metal. Fox and he had been inseparable muckers. They'd enlisted at the same time, got their second tapes at the same time, gone drinking, whoring and policing together in every base from Singapore to Catterick. And now Davidson would be alone. My bloody eyes started to smart again but, true to the image, I seized the opportunity to restore my reputation.

'Get a detail. Three men. Take a field stretcher. Lance Corporal Tosh will lead you down to Fox . . .' I gulped, then pressed on brutally. 'You'll need a sack with you.'

I didn't stay. Davidson would need a few minutes of privacy. Soldiers can grieve too, and cry. And Davidson was a career soldier. Like Foxie.

O'Feely looked up as I approached. 'Where's the CO, Sar'nt O'Feely?'

He jerked his head up at the mountain. 'Gone climbing. The men say he wouldn't take anyone with 'im. Jus' went off, pistol in hand like Wild Bill bloody Hitchcock.'

'Hickock,' I muttered absently.

'Yeah, him too. Well, he headed off on 'is own, anyway. Told Davidson to wait down here. Probably gone looking for clues. A great one for clues, is Steadman.'

Resignedly I picked up O'Feely's Sten and cocked it. 'He'll be trying to suss where they were waiting for us. Nosy bastard.'

'*Now* where're you going?' O'Feely demanded, looking at me as though I'd had a bump on the head. Which I'd had.

'I got enough problems without having a dead boss to account for.'

Stuffing three spare mags into my ammo pocket I hefted the weapon experimentally. It felt like a dead weight and I'd developed a blinding headache, but I had a bad feeling about Steadman which I couldn't shake off. Why *had* he gone off on his own like that? It didn't make sense: not with a whole section of men raring to go, only to be uncharacteristically stood down. Not unless he was even more eccentric than I already suspected him to be. The once handsome, now irreparably ravaged features of the Redcap officer had to have affected him inside, somehow. One thing was certain. Major Eric K. Steadman MM, Corps of Royal Military Police, was displaying a reckless disregard for his own safety. Or maybe he didn't care about dying. I'd seen it in battle-scarred casualties before, and I knew.

O'Feely drew his Webley and Scott and flicked the chambers open. I shook my head. 'Not this time, O'Feely. You stay here and daddy the section. Davidson's getting a detail together to bring in Fox's body. He'll need support with this one. I'll take a quick shufti round for Steadman myself. Check?'

He wasn't happy about it but, shrugging, he unhooked his webbing belt and silently held it out to me. I felt a bit guilty at being reminded that my own .38 was still in the crashed Rover: hopefully in company with the brandy. Again the weight of the side arm dragged my hand down as I took it. Buckling the belt round my waist with an effort, I pulled my SD cap down low over the bridge of my nose in best MP tradition.

O'Feely watched anxiously as I frowned up at the towering mountain, and I knew he couldn't decide whether I was slightly more or marginally less crazy than our boss in going without backup. I couldn't either, for that matter. I just sensed, somehow, that destiny had shaped events to be this way.

He gestured at the Sten as I turned away. 'Remember that's a grown-up's gun. Try not to shoot yourself, Staff Sergeant.'

I stuck two fingers up at him and jumped stiffly across the narrow ditch. After a few steps I suddenly remembered the thing that had been nagging at me all night. I halted and looked back. Davidson and Tosh were rigging the stretcher while the rest of the men watched uncomfortably in the sun. O'Feely was still staring after me with a concerned expression, quickly erased when he saw me turn.

'By the way, O'Feely – just how the hell *do* you con those scrubbers of yours into believin' you're a field marshal?'

The irrepressible Redcap pretended to unbutton his flies. 'So who can tell a bollock-naked field marshal from a bollock-naked sergeant?' he yelled coarsely.

I turned again and started to climb the mountain.

It proved a nerve-racking challenge from the onset, clambering up that boulder-strewn slope alone. Several times I thought I detected movement ahead and halted nervously, index finger caressing the Sten's trigger. Once I heard the rattle of avalanching scree and threw myself flat just as one of those skinny Cypriot mountain goats went bounding away like a kangaroo, over to my left. Yet despite that, I wasn't fully able to concentrate on the task I'd set myself. I couldn't stop dwelling on Corporal Fox, and the agonies he'd suffered before he died. I hoped, if I ever got hit, that it would be nice and clean in the head so's I wouldn't scream like an animal and embarrass everybody.

After half an hour I simply ground to a halt. I'd already taken too great a physical and psychological beating. My legs wouldn't stop jerking involuntarily as I flopped under cover of a rock face to gaze wistfully back down at the road. The quarter-tonners appeared as Dinky toys and, as I watched, the windscreen of one flashed briefly as they hauled it out of the ditch. Now the sun hung directly above, beating down with such intensity that I had to handle the blued metal stock of the Sten gingerly to avoid being burned. Even the arid, scented air seemed bent on suffocating all who breathed it, while nothing stirred beneath its cloying embrace. Only the invisible whirring and twittering of thousands of tiny dried-grass-bound insects disturbed what was fast becoming an all too familiar and lonely silence.

The headache had expanded to migraine ferocity while my throat worked spasmodically to bring saliva into my rancid mouth. I cursed for not having had the foresight to bring a water bottle and thought gloomily of the abandoned brandy. I remembered a couple of aspirins left in my pocket after a particularly heavy night, but I couldn't face chewing them dry. Miserably I sank back, questioning why I always had to attempt one bridge too far, constantly fall prey to my own self-generated myth of Walker the Indomitable Soldier, because, in this instance, the myth was fast running out of control. Like Frankenstein's monster, it was proving too powerful for its creator.

Five minutes of unrestrained self-pity and I'd virtually thrown in my hand. Didn't even stir when a blob of guano splashed on my sleeve: just stared hollow-eyed up at the carrion congregating high above me, slowly wheeling against the crystal blue sky. Vultures, I reflected morosely. Probably vultures, waiting for dinner time. I giggled at that. Dinner time . . . Death time. Come and get it! *Walker with White Sauce.* Bird-shit white. Coward white. RMP-gaiter-white. Suddenly I was laughing outright . . . *Provost Pudding à la Viscera . . .?* Foxie winked down at me again: lugubriously polishing his boots while I floated comfortably just off the ground.

O'Feely materialized then: standing above me wearing the dog-collared uniform of a field marshal in the Corps – Corpse? – of Padres. I frowned: his fly buttons were undone. Was it within my policeman's authority to book an ecumenical field officer for being improperly dressed on parade . . .? He began to intone sonorously from the Provost Training Manual. *When thou liest down and thus avoid all duty and responsibility, thou shalt not be afraid, Staff. Yea, even though thou doth lie down and throw in thine hand, thy sleep shall nevertheless be sweet . . .*

O'Feely took a long swig of my brandy, then, just as I was licking cracked lips in anticipation, jumped out of some scrubber's back window while, all the time, Foxie just hung around grinning reassuringly.

27

I closed my eyes.

Until the shot smashed through the silence.

I'd rolled over on my belly with the stubby, colandered barrel of the Sten vectoring ahead of me before the crack of the small arm finished echoing across the shimmering slopes. Above, Vulture Squadron began wheeling and squawking in outraged protest and I grimaced wryly. Whatever else the shot had done, it had postponed the mental disintegration of Walker for another day.

If there *was* to be another day?

I lay doggo for a few moments, every already-aching muscle in my body tensed for the smashing impact of a second round. It didn't come. Nothing moved. Inch by inch I removed my service cap before ever so cautiously raising my head. A nervous tic at the corner of my mouth began twitching and, digging my thumb at it savagely, I started to get irritated. Bloody irritated!

Roughly two hundred yards ahead and above loomed a massive ochre-coloured rock formation reminiscent of a Dartmoor tor. I glowered at it, almost willing it to disgorge hordes of EOKA assassins so's I could finally deploy the weapon that sat hotly gleaming in my dirt-encrusted hands. But the Yolkies were terrorists, and terrorists are shadowy men. They didn't come out and fight: especially when taking on the British Army. Cyprus, Palestine, Aden, Malaya: terrorists, nationalists, partitionists ... they were all the bloody same. Bombs in married quarters targeting squaddies' wives and kids: the odd sniper from long range or, as had happened to my patrol, a brief fusillade of nine-millimetre bullets under cover of night followed by a hasty withdrawal to hide within the bosom of the family. That was Ethniki Organosis Kipriakou Agonos – their National Organization of Cypriot Struggle – in '57.

I decided I'd no option but to go for broke and the hell with it.

Thumbing the Sten to automatic I started to crawl uphill again, towards the mass of tumbled stone. It was tough going as spiky brown needles of dried grass whipped at my face.

I was getting angrier and angrier but, at the same time, more and more apprehensive as my backside waved in the air. What a *bloody* embarrassing place to get shot, I reflected morosely. And who was goin' to believe Walker got hit in the arse when he was advancing?

The lanyard of my ... no – *O'Feely*'s ... Webley and Scott snagged in a clump of unyielding vegetation and dragged me to a halt. I lay panting for a moment to find myself glaring at one of those little insects that sit about all day in balls of spit on long grasses. The insect glared back with matching hostility and gave me a soldier's farewell with its feelers. Now even their bloody insects fancied themselves as wannabe terrorists ... I couldn't handle the tension, the corrosive fear of being picked off by an unseen enemy a moment longer. Swearing bitterly, I got up and ran like hell for the safety of the rocks.

I hadn't even made it halfway before deciding getting angry had been a bad idea, so I gave up being mad and just stayed scared which was, at least, a familiar emotion. Every sucking breath dragged like cottonwool down my throat and I could hear myself sobbing with frustration as, twice, I nearly stumbled full length. How the *hell* did those bloody mountain goats do it?

Only after what seemed an eternity did I sense the protective shadow close around me. Terror gave way to the euphoria of realizing I'd run the gauntlet and so far survived. Buoyed by that small victory, I charged round the bulbous rock shoulder, boots kicking up little spurts of shale and the Sten at a ready-for-anything present. Warrior Walker had arrived. Bad people – prepare to die!

The pistol barrel that slammed into my midriff expelled what little wind I had left . . .

I vaguely recall retching as I hit the deck like a self-propelled dustbin while watching the Sten skitter away in a flurry of stone chips. Frantically attempting to draw my holstered side arm, I was still fumbling when a boot smashed brutally down to pin my wrist and preclude that alternative ploy.

I had one tactical option left.

'BASTaaaard!' I yelled in terrified frustration: rolled over, covered the back of my head with my hands, screwed my eyes tight shut and waited for the bullet engraved with my name.

I didn't have long to wait. Nor was my risk assessment that far off the mark. Fate had certainly got my name right: only the method of its delivery was at variance. Not necessarily more welcome – just different. Not when I recognized the icy voice that cut through my disintegrating consciousness.

'For Christ's sake, get *up*, Walker!'

Gingerly I hauled myself erect and looked sheepish.

Steadman leaned languidly back against the rock face, Browning pistol dangling casually from its trigger guard. Even for a provost major his turnout was immaculate. Officer's service cap pulled down to shield piercing blue eyes at just the right angle of depression; corps badges glinting against the lapels of a Gieves-cut, double-diagonal cloth battledress blouse expressly tailored in the pursuit of elegance.

Grudgingly I had to concede his appearance almost matched Foxie's: albeit Corporal Fox's off-the-shelf army issue BD had been rough khaki serge looking like it'd been tailored by a myopic quartermaster sergeant with sheep shears, before Foxie performed his own re-stitching magic.

But above all they did share one thing in common, the major and the other rank. The triumph of their boots . . . I swallowed uncomfortably: the evaluation of boots seemed to be rapidly becoming my singular – sole? – obsession. Certainly I couldn't prevent staff-sergeant-critical eyes from noting Steadman's revealed barely a hint of grime despite his having recently climbed a bloody mountain. Gave the impression that dust, even hostile terrain dust, wouldn't dare settle on them. Brown of course, with them being officer issue, but still boots that glinted like freshly lacquered enamel below the weighted bottoms of trousers hanging low over snow-white gaiters.

Only difference was that Foxie had been human: capable of emotion. The jury was still out on Steadman. I'd never been able to shake off that inexplicable apprehension I'd felt from the moment he'd assumed command of 368 Provost, Cyprus. But he was still my CO. Dragging a bleeding hand to the salute, I belatedly recalled having left my cap somewhere down the mountain and ended by according him a feeble, appropriately medieval tug of the forelock.

He didn't bother to return it, just smiled bleakly: the casual response causing the left side of his face to distort into a plastic surgeon's nightmare. Each time I'd encountered that blue-gashed deformity I couldn't help but marvel, not without sympathy, how anyone afflicted by such a traumatic wound could still appear as satanically handsome as the major.

It was the last time I would ever feel anything other than a fearful hatred for the man.

'We're hardly on parade, Staff,' he said. 'For which you should be damn grateful, considering the appalling state you're in.'

Recovering my Sten he eased the action before tossing it back to me. 'Next time you attempt to storm an objective single-handedly, Walker, take a little more care. Otherwise you'll end up with a bloody sight more than a thump in the gut.'

But I hadn't expect appreciation for having pushed myself to the limit in coming up to check on him. That's the army. *Big fleas have little fleas upon their backs to bite them, And little fleas have littler fleas, and so ad infinitum . . .* I myself had levelled much the same sort of criticism at O'Feely a million years ago. And I certainly didn't propose to correct Steadman's assumption that my gung-ho charge had been a valiant, if ill-considered assault: that to me, a few minutes ago this particular strategic target had presented more of a sanctuary than a military objective.

Muttering a weak 'Yessir,' I kept my counsel.

'So present your sitrep, Staff Sar'nt. Presumably you've had ample time to prepare your version,' he jerked his head in the direction of the road, 'of that shambles you appear to have supervised down there?'

Invariably the CO showed a facility for making you out to be a bloody fool even when you'd done all the right things.

31

Then I remembered I'd largely done all the wrong things anyway, and decided to await a more favourable climate in which to display injured innocence. Instead I simply told him what had happened, omitting the unfortunate instances when the image had broken down and I'd given way to tearful hysteria. And the bit about O'Feely's having kicked the shit out of Lance Corporal Tosh.

Give Steadman his due, he listened attentively and without comment until I'd finished presenting Walker's case for the defence.

'Corporal Fox was killed instantly?'

I thought bleakly of the way Foxie had screamed for such a long time, but that was a confidence that would always remain between him and me.

'Affirmative.'

'But Fox was our only casualty?'

As an epitaph from his commanding officer, the emphasis on *only* came as an overly casual diminishment of a soldier's passing but I kept my expression neutral, being way too army-wise to risk laying myself open to a charge of dumb insolence. Just nodded curtly without betraying open resentment.

'Only one casualty, eh?' he repeated with evident satisfaction.

. . . Which marked the moment in which the most extraordinary event occurred. The most chilling response I'd ever witnessed to the news of a campaign comrade's death.

As Steadman grinned broadly and added, 'That's excellent, Walker. Then we're even!'

I'd stared at the Redcap officer uncomprehendingly for what seemed a very long time. No – I *had* to be mistaken. The bloody man couldn't actually be *grinning* . . .? Not so openly. Not with such evident self-satisfaction that the scar sort of crinkled up to compress his left eye socket until satanically handsome became overwhelmed, and only Satan remained?

I was trying to persuade myself I'd simply misheard Steadman – that this could only be some bizarre distortion of tendon and tissue brought about by his affliction – when he proved me wrong again; this time by reaching to grasp my arm. Such a gesture in itself was hardly the form of contact any prudent senior officer would risk making with a subordinate. And certainly not conspiratorially like that: the intimate invitation of a confidant to his peer. The way an errant schoolboy might act when anxious to demonstrate how naughty he'd been.

'There's something I want you to see.'

Involuntarily I'd recoiled from his touch, still repelled at imagining what kind of leader could construe humour out of another rank's death. Steadman didn't seem to notice. Just kept urging me round the rock before indicating with the blued foresight of his weapon.

'Snap!' he said incongruously.

I didn't move, fully preoccupied by trying to figure what had suddenly caused his behaviour to become so out of character. Steadman had spent the last weeks since becoming our commanding officer in establishing himself as an unpredictable sod – every 368 Provost NCO would sourly endorse that – but at least he'd been consistent in such unpredictability: cold-eyed, undemonstrative and quick to seize any opportunity to convey the image of being a hard bastard. A bit like me, I suppose. Only I didn't carry the rank to be quite as convincing with it.

I continued to hang back, eyeing our elegant major with growing unease while he, in turn, remained focused intently on a cleft between the rocks. Until he waved the pistol impatiently in a manner that brooked no delay.

'Here, Walker. Come over *here*!'

So I gloomed, 'Oh, fuck it – jus' go along with the bloody man.'

And I did.

The child lay in a foetal position, all hunched up and drawn back into the stone cavity as far as he could retreat. Bony knees, already beginning to adopt a waxen sheen, protruded from under a pair of ragged short trousers about three sizes too big for him, while little hands on the end of stick arms remained outstretched, grubby palms held towards us in terrified supplication.

The bottom of the threadbare shirt was frayed, too, and I couldn't help feeling sorry for him because it didn't look as though he'd had much of a mum – not when she allowed him to go out like that. Mind you, I suppose he looked pretty much like any other nine-, ten-year-old Cypriot kid in this poverty-stricken area.

. . . Apart from the entry wound, that was. Precisely nine millimetres of a British Army-issue Mark I FN Browning high-power automatic pistol round in diameter.

Fired from close range through the child's cordite-pitted cheek. Just below his still-disbelieving left eye.

Three

The next eternity passed in a welter of horror-filled images. I didn't stay with the destroyed child. I couldn't. Just turned around and stumbled back down the mountain with the Major watching me go. Watching, yet not lifting a finger to stop me.

Stooping numbly to recover my cap lying where I'd abandoned it, I found myself glancing involuntarily back up at the rocks expecting – maybe even hoping – that Steadman would call me to heel and flay the hell out of me for such an act of crass insubordination. That way, at least, would re-establish a pattern of behaviour I could understand that would, in turn, help drag me out of the twilight zone of revulsion I was foundering in.

But he didn't. Just stood, pistol in hand, silhouetted against the skyline like a great rogue stag: motionless but emanating a near-tangible menace. I got scared then, as well as sick and, swinging round, scrambled headlong towards the Lilliputian army below.

O'Feely was waiting for me, the rest of the section watching curiously as I approached. Pulling my gut in and sticking my chest out like a pouter pigeon, I jumped heavily across the ditch onto the road, staggering a little as twelve earnest faces doubled to twenty-four and began to swim before my eyes. Then the image locked into staff-sergeant mode and the other Walker glared at them aggressively.

'When the lady an' the donkey arrive to start the act, I'll bloody let you know. Until then, get fell in over there with your weapons.'

They grinned furtively like a bunch of schoolgirls and shuffled into a straggling line. O'Feely excused himself politely and wandered over as any dad might do, to helpfully suggest they might care to square the formation up a bit 'cause any putty-brained bastard gettin' hisself more than a millimetre outa kilter would need 'is mum to sew a zip fastener in the arse of his battledress to permit the butt of his BLOODY STEN to project!

Then sauntered back to where I'd sought refuge behind the lead quarter-tonner. 'You look terrible.'

. . . And thank you too, for your sensitivity, mate! He never mentioned Steadman, although his curiosity must have been killing him.

'Shut up, O'Feely.' I looked anxiously around. 'What've you done with my bloody brandy.'

'I'm under orders to keep quiet.'

'O'FEELY!'

He smiled beatifically and leaned into the vehicle before holding up what could well have been a full bottle a very long time ago. I frowned.

'It's evaporated one hell of a quick.'

He belched contentedly. 'Proven law of physics. Lemonade evaporates with lightning speed. And it *must* have been lemonade, mus'n't it. Cause you wouldn't dream of contravening Queen's Regulations by having personal spirits stashed in a military vehicle, would you? Not with you bein' a staff sergeant and everything.'

I snatched the bottle and up-ended it. O'Feely observed sadly as I allowed the five-star soft drink to bite into the back of my parched throat. When I finally doubled forward, coughing painfully, he drew a deep breath of admiration.

I felt a bit better. At least the tears in my eyes were self-induced this time. Sergeant O'Feely jerked his head up towards the shimmering crag of rock.

'Do I take it you found the Major, then?' he finally hazarded, eyeing the bottle but too proud to ask for another swig, or maybe he didn't have the nerve to after the job of demolition he'd already done on it. I choked on another mouthful then handed it to him without a word. His head tilted back and I watched gloomily while what was left evaporated at the rate of two bob a second. Turning away, I gingerly began to remove my webbing.

I could ... I *should* have said more, then. About Steadman, I mean. And the corpse of a pitifully under-nourished child with the back of its head blown away. I don't know yet what stopped me but, somehow, I couldn't. Maybe it was a lifetime of service-instilled reticence: the unquestioning acceptance that whatever a superior officer does is beyond criticism other than between equal ranks, and off the record. Pretty well all armies work that way. It's undemocratic, feudal in its origins, but also a bloody good out for anyone involved in a cock-up – except for the bloke who gave the order in the first place, which is why the system is perpetuated. Blind obedience to any man with a tape more than you and a cynical disregard for the consciences of all who stand lower in the chain of command.

Either way, historically a lot of blokes had relied on it. Like the men in black uniforms who'd offered that line of mitigation for their obedience to 'orders' in a scruffy little courtroom at a place called Nuremberg.

Mind you, we hanged a lot of them, on reflection.

But then, they lost the war.

'Yeah, I found him,' I muttered cryptically. 'Davidson back yet?'

He didn't say anything; just jerked his head down the road and, tossing the bottle into the ditch, spat after it.

Silently we watched as the weary crocodile tramped heavily towards us, Corporal Davidson bringing up the rear. The lad's eyes never left the stretcher and its irregular, blanket-shrouded load bumping and swaying between two sweating lance corporals. Tosh headed the file, gingerly carrying an ammunition box by its green webbing strap.

I frowned, momentarily shelving the other problem I had. The one up the mountain. Foxy shouldn't be returning to barracks this way: wearily and almost furtively. Foxy had been the original bullshit merchant and, by God, Corporal Fox was going to finish his last patrol with all the spit and ceremony it was within my power to accord him.

37

'Companaaay . . . Company hatten-SHUN! Company will present arms . . . *Presennnnt* HARMS!'

Whatever else it did, it worked a small miracle for Corporal Davidson. His head came up, his shoulders straightened and he marched past the rigid section like a Sandhurst cadet on his passing-out parade . . . or a military policeman.

And Foxie was back with his lads.

Admittedly it was all a bit Errol Flynn and Hollywood on reflection. And somewhat diminished by the recipient of the salute having been hidden under a soiled grey blanket. Most of him, anyway. The rest of Corporal Fox was marching ten feet ahead of himself in a battered army-green ammo box. I hoped, when they laid him to rest with full military honours, that they wouldn't request the Jocks to provide a regimental piper. Foxy never did like the lament on the pipes: always used to say it was too sad.

'One recovered,' I turned away, wishing I hadn't been so bloody generous by letting O'Feely finish the brandy '. . . one still to come. Detail another party of volunteers – but excuse Corporal Davidson.'

O'Feely followed my gaze up the mountain as incredulity dawned. 'He din't *get* one, did he – a terrorist? The way this lot fucked up, I'd figured they was like grouse. Out of season.'

'Oh, he got one all right. He's probably tapping an impatient foot now, expectin' me to detail a team of bulled-up gamekeepers to bring down his bird.'

'I'll head it myself,' O'Feely beamed, suddenly revitalized. 'This I got to see.'

I turned on him savagely. 'Yeah, you jus' bloody *do* that, Sergeant! You just go up there and take a good hard look at a terrorist with a bullet in the face. Treat yourself to a great big bastard celebration . . .'

I walked away, feeling his hurt burning the back of my neck. I swung back again. The corners of his mouth betrayed a shocked whiteness but I was past giving a damn.

'. . . Then come an' spew your fuckin' ring alongside of me.'

O'Feely and his four lance corporals had begun cursing before they'd clambered fifty yards from the road. I watched them go until they'd reduced to sweating khaki dolls almost un-detectable against the shimmering brown mountain. Carrion Squadron still afforded them air cover but from further uphill now: wheeling and squawking and defecating directly above the rocks where, presumably, Steadman still waited.

I couldn't help hoping that O'Feely might prove to have more guts than I, and maybe ask a pointed question or two. But I didn't hope too hard. Even though the irreverent NCO had all the makings of a rebel, he was still just a sergeant. And he'd only got that far by cultivating a well-honed desire for self-preservation to match that which I myself had devel-oped from bitter experience.

My prediction was to prove correct.

To give O'Feely his due, it wasn't a straightforward matter of having bottled out at pointing the finger at his own CO – more a case of the Major's having manipulated O'Feely's perception of events. I was to discover later that Steadman had made a few alterations to the set by the time the recovery detail got there. And of course, when I'd gone up initially I hadn't thought to carry the section's forensic camera with me. Not to record a scene of crime I'd never, at that junc-ture, suspected I would come across.

First, he'd dragged the little boy from his dead end of last refuge and laid him out neat and tidy: stick arms respect-fully folded across the skinny chest in an act of compassion typical of the British Tommy – as well as being one pre-empting any subsequent impression that the victim might just have been a retreating supplicant killed with cold delib-eration. Observing the decencies of death is commendable. Such reverence, if corrupted, can also be productive. It can convert a cowering corpse from a murdered child to a deeply regretted by-product of an anti-terrorist operation.

Next, Steadman had discovered heaven-sent evidence that would prove crucial to his claim that the nine-year-old had harboured hostile intent.

I'd never even noticed the small-calibre rifle and, I suspect, neither had he until long after he'd squeezed his trigger. A photograph would have preserved the scene. Either way, the gun hadn't been evident when I'd been present, suggesting it could only have lain concealed uselessly beneath the body at the instant of the child's dying. Even Steadman, for all his cold insouciance, must've felt damn relieved on finding it. The British Army had been taking hit-and-run casualties from EOKA for two years prior to that day on the mountain. They hated us, and we hated them. Even the hint of a weapon's existence was enough to provide any anti-terrorist soldier with justification for labelling murder as self-defence.

To me, that particular weapon wasn't justification so much as a little boy's toy, the kind the Cypriot goatherd children used to carry with fierce pride to warn all that one day they, too, would become men demanding respect. The kind of guns that were two generations ancient: all bound together with wire and hairy bits of string and which couldn't possibly have discharged anyway, because their firing pins had mostly crystallized and snapped off years ago . . . certainly not the five-hundred-rounds-per-minute kind that can take out a military vehicle from two hundred yards along with the entrails of its driver.

Finally Steadman had laboriously collected, from where his Browning high-power automatic pistol had scattered them, all the glistening white splinters red-glued with sun-bleached golden hair that, prior to his making the kill, had previously formed the posterior of the dead child's eggshell skull. Being a thorough policeman, and having a bit of time on his hands, he'd preserved them as trophies too; neatly bundled in an otherwise pristine handkerchief. A place for everything, and everything in its place – the military policeman's philosophy, and thus the Major's inflexible rule.

Even before Steadman's shooting party returned, I'd begun to form the unsettling impression that were I to speak out against him, not only would I be on my own, but that he would happily find a special pigeonhole for me, too.

Regulation size, of course. Approximately seven feet long by two feet wide. And precisely six feet deep.

Not much more to tell, really, about the afternoon of that endless day in which Foxie gained his discharge. It was nudging 1900 Cyprus time before the hunters returned from the hill bearing their trophy in triumph. Or was it triumph? Maybe only Steadman projected that impression, although he masked it well by adopting his usual taciturn disregard for his soldiers. None of the bearer lance corporals said much at all: not even when they were dismissed to go and join their mates.

Even O'Feely, a very hard copper indeed, vanished briefly before rematerializing, furtively dabbing at his mouth with a soiled khaki handkerchief. Other ranks were issued with khaki hankies, white ones being reserved for officers, and blown-away shards of children's' skulls.

They remained uncharacteristically subdued, particularly when sliding the little bundle into the back of a quarter-tonner beside Foxie. It was difficult to be gentle all the time because death tends to impose its own constraints on the smoothest of evolutions. The designers of the Land Rover's military variant had overlooked provision for accommodating rigor-stiffening corpses in an otherwise excellent British Army workhorse.

Look after him, Foxie, I remember thinking. He's far too young to be in there on his own . . .

As the sun slipped behind the parched mountain that had provided the backdrop to a good soldier's misfortune and a small goatherd's abruptly curtailed life, we made ready to begin our homeward journey leaving my, and Corporal Fox's, own crashed vehicle stripped of radio and other attractive items, for a sapper unit to recover.

I'd studiously avoided contact with Steadman until then, although I'd actually felt quite piqued by his ignoring me just as I was doing with him – largely because he'd carried the psychological stalemate off better than I, in that each time I'd sneaked a furtive glance in his direction, he'd given the impression of being a man who didn't give a shit.

It was only when I was about to settle wearily into my second, and by that time longingly awaited rocking chair of the day with Davidson as driver, when the Major appeared through the falling darkness, accompanied by Sergeant O'Feely. His approach was matter-of-fact, even polite.

'Be good enough to dismount, Staff Walker, and accompany

41

me back to barracks. Corporal Davidson will drive Sergeant O'Feely in this vehicle. They'll lead the column: you and I shall bring up the rear.'

I glanced at O'Feely in pointless appeal, but he just shrugged and looked uncomfortable. Though not half as uncomfortable as I'd suddenly become.

Preoccupied with speculating on Steadman's invitation, I even forgot to change sides while plodding reluctantly back to the CO's immaculate fighting machine. Only after I'd clambered into the Rover feeling a lot less relaxed than I'd initially figured on being, did I become aware of him still standing by the open door.

His censure was tolerant, even jokey. 'Correct me if I'm wrong, Walker, but I'm not aware of the regulation that requires majors to act as drivers to staff sergeants?'

I gloomed *ohhhh shit!* while levering myself sideways and under the wheel without a word. Steadman eased into the passenger seat beside me like a spider getting into bed with a fly, then leaned across the dash and flashed our headlights.

What had set off as a routine military police patrol, but was returning as a camouflaged funeral cortège, began to roll.

That trip back from the mountains recalled, for me, the tensions felt as a kid down in the front row when watching some scary horror film. It took us over an hour to retrace the tortuous road while, all that time, the Major sat half-turned and observing me, not saying a bloody word – just staring with those cold eyes of his until the sweat began to trickle between my shoulder blades with the nervous strain of it.

I knew all that because I could see his ghost before me. It was satin-black out there and all the time I couldn't ignore his faint reflection in the windscreen, illuminated by the eerie green glow of the dash illumination. I'd never felt so relieved to see the first prickle of Limassol's street lights punctuating the darkness ahead.

Naturally I got complacent then. All that gut-wrenching apprehension, and all to no account. I'd even begun to realize, with a faint stirring of pride, that I was hungry. The omens heralding the restoration of the Walker image were looking up again.

'How can you bring yourself to eat knowing Foxie's not comin' back, Staff?' the younger NCOs would respectfully marvel in the mess.

'Don't you worry 'bout Corporal Fox, son,' I'd casually reply. 'He's not got the stomach to face food no more.'

And thus another myth would be established to swell the Walker legend: the hardest Redcap in the Corps. I inhaled expansively, even cocking a jaunty, challenging eye at the spectral Major's reflection ahead.

. . . Which I shouldn't, of course. Not before analysing it a little more studiously. The reflection, I mean. Had I done so I might have registered that my fellow traveller's mirror image had acquired a significant addition.

Having been recently cleaned and oiled out of operational neccessity, the green-glow highlights made the personal side arm now in his hand clearly visible. As well as emphasizing the fact that it was levelled at the back of my skull. Only for a moment admittedly, but for a very *long* moment . . . before Steadman considerately inverted the FN Browning's squared-off muzzle and, almost absently, allowed it to trace down the scar on his cheek.

Considering it highly improbable that such a meticulous officer would so carelessly permit himself to contravene Queen's Regulations regarding the safe handling of weapons, I could only assume I was intended to read the gesture as a threat. Or a promise . . .? Either way I stopped relishing late supper in the mess, and went back to glooming about pigeon-holes again. Deep ones.

He indicated ahead. 'Pull into that entry, Walker.'

'What about the rest of the section?' I hazarded hopefully.

He made play of inspecting the magazine receiver in the butt of the Browning but, somehow, I didn't think he would have omitted to insert a recharged thirteen-cartridge clip. Not like Lance Corporal Tosh would've done.

'Sergeant O'Feely expects our return to be delayed. He's been briefed to take them straight back to the Provost lines.'

The green-ghost pistol gestured again. 'This one, Staff Sergeant.'

I decelerated, nosed into the alleyway then engaged the handbrake and sat stiffly, staring straight ahead. The scaley things under my hairline were slowly standing down again, reassured by his use of *our* and *return* in the same sentence. Thus emboldened, I got curious to discover how he intended to broach the subject that obviously preoccupied us both, although I'd already made up my mind to be as bloody obstinate as possible. Well, short of pushing him to construe such reticence as an open invitation, that was – to disregard the *our* part of returning to barracks.

'Switch off.'

I switched off. The Rover's engine kicked as its cylinder carbons cooled and died.

'Lights, Staff Sergeant.'

I switched the lights off.

A pale moon was rising now, dispelling the darkness enough to appraise our situation. The surrounding area was shadowed and still, and potentially lethal. Ahead loomed a high brick wall revealing we were in a cul de sac. The last person to have found himself alone with Steadman in such a literal dead end, I reflected grimly, had been the child.

Briefly a silhouette broke the line of the wallhead, then just as quickly vanished. Probably a cat, but I still shifted uneasily. This was fertile ground for the EOKA terrorist recruiters. British Army vehicles, particularly RMP patrols, parked off the beaten track extended an open invite to host an opportunist grenade.

Of course, being a slave to habit and the pursuit of personal comfort, before we'd set off I'd surreptitiously withdrawn my own service revolver from its webbing holster and posed it behind the seat, hadn't I? And I could hardly draw attention to that flagrant breach of regulations, what with Steadman still beside me. Ever so cautiously I extended my hand to feel for the butt stock of my Sten lying on the bench between us, not entirely certain of which of the two threats now hanging over me was likely to demand priority.

Steadman either didn't notice, or didn't care. Certainly he

44

didn't speak immediately, and I was damned if I was going to. Instead I continued to grope for the sub-machine gun while peering out warily, and listening to the creaking of the heat-stressed engine. When the Major did finally break the silence, it almost came as a relief.

'I gather you have something on your mind, Staff Sergeant.'

I gave up playing psychological games I wasn't equipped to win. 'Maybe I have.'

'Such as?'

'You know damn well. It'll be in my report.'

He raised a languid eyebrow; not that languid really worked for him, not the way that livid scar dragged up into his hairline. 'When addressed by your commanding officer, Walker, you will please observe the pleasantries of rank.'

I couldn't conceal my astonishment. It was so bloody bizarre. That Steadman should be concerned with military etiquette while parked up in a Cypriot slum playing hookey from the column like a couple of furtive gays.

'Damn well – *sir*!' I obliged tightly.

'Thank you, Staff. And what, in addition to your appraisal of the events leading to the death of Corporal Fox, will be in your report?'

'A statement regarding the incident that took place subsequently. On the mountain.'

'When you eventually followed to give me, ah . . . fire support?'

I liked that. Fire support. I took a mental note to include the phrase in my affidavit. 'Yeah.'

'Then we will discuss it.'

'Nothing to discuss, Major.'

'I said *will*, Staff Sergeant. It wasn't a suggestion.'

'Discussion might be interpreted as collusion. And collusion's not to my liking.'

'Collusion?' he queried, as if mystified by my use of the term. I hesitated, words had never been my strong point, and resolved to look it up when I got back. Always presuming I *was* still scheduled to get back, the size of the hole I was digging for myself.

'Call it what you want, the facts are plain enough. It's up to the Provost Marshal and Brigade to interpret them.'

'Facts?' He spread his hands deprecatingly. Or had he merely done that to ensure the Browning continued to glint mindfully in the moonlight? 'Don't you mean assumptions?'

'Witness evidence. Persuasive enough to justify Brigade convening a court martial for murder.'

'Murder?' I wished he'd stop repeating everything. Not that he seemed too put out: more amused, really. 'Now that's an extraordinary allegation, Staff. Please state your grounds for making it.'

I slammed a palm awkwardly against the wheel – *Jesus*, that hurt! But I hadn't intended to be so impulsive.

'You know bloody *well* what grounds!'

Steadman simply waggled the gun mindfully while I wished to God he'd holster it, then we could have a proper fall out. 'The pleasantries, Staff Sergeant. Don't forget the pleasantries.'

This was a very chilling man to sit beside in the middle of a hostile alleyway in the middle of the night. Such a tolerant reproach for a subordinate's open insolence: as if cautioning a recalcitrant child. He was so sure of himself, so bloody certain I couldn't do a single effective thing to harm him. Which I probably couldn't. The nervous tic at the corner of my mouth started to pull again but I ignored it.

'OK, you want grounds, Major – then I'll give you grounds. Try a Cypriot kid with half his face shot away! I'd say that presents bloody strong grounds, for starters.'

The scar whitened perceptibly at that. It seemed I was getting under his skin at last. 'He was a terrorist, Walker.'

'He was a wee laddie playing soldiers with a home-made gun. You shoulda spanked his backside – not slaughtered him!'

This time he abandoned languid: each word directed with the malevolence of a poisoned dart. 'He ... was ... a ... *terrorist*! Damn it, he'd tried to kill you too, Walker. What the hell d'you think ripped Corporal Fox's guts out – a kiddie's catapult?'

'Probably a nine-mill Schmeisser. Certainly not a boy's

46

toy.' The tic at the corner of my mouth slammed into active mode again. 'You must've seen that was all he carried, Steadman, yet you still executed him without a shred of compassion.'

'I took him out before he shot me. No more than that, Walker.'

'CRAP!' I snarled, then felt briefly euphoric. First time ever I'd actually said that to a field officer. Out loud, anyway.

Now he was tense as well: a second small victory for me – or a potentially terminal one. I was still unprepared. By then I'd only closed my hand around the butt stock of the Sten and, ever so discreetly, begun to ease it across my knees while trying, at the same time, to swivel the barrel towards him. He didn't seem to notice, and I prayed desperately that he wouldn't: not before I could slip my finger through the trigger guard. The front bench seat of a Land Rover is a somewhat cramped forum for Quick Draw McGraw gun play, and Steadman was odds-on favourite at that moment. He already held his pistol pointed in my general direction.

'You're forgetting I saw the kid in the cleft,' I pressed to hold his attention. 'He hadn't been trying to shoot you, Major – he was tryin' to get away from you. He could see what was coming . . . Christ, man: that child must've died a thousand deaths in the space of time it took you to pull the trigger.'

'And that's your evidence – a presumption? That you *thought* he hadn't intended to shoot me first?' Steadman actually chuckled. 'Grow up, Walker: you've been a Redcap long enough. You know only the dumbest of bloody squaddies would dare press charges on the unsupported allegation of one witness.'

'Not one witness. O'Feely and his bearer party also attended.'

'And witnessed what . . .? An RMP senior officer engaged in recovering the body of an armed thug – *armed*, Staff Sergeant! They'd already been ambushed in that area, with one NCO killed. Do you seriously imagine Brigade's going to take action on such a flimsy conclusion?'

And he was right. Come to that, maybe I'd never really wanted to win the argument anyway. Maybe I'd always wanted him to persuade me to disregard the whole brutal affair. I was bleakly conscious that my alternative was to put my head above the parapet: take on a military establishment that would use every pressure in the book to dissuade an NCO from rocking the boat. Particularly if he was trying to prove that one of their close brotherhood of officers and gentlemen, just wasn't.

Still, I wasn't going to concede defeat that easy. The gung-ho sword-for-justice image in me pushed me into having one more tilt at Walker's Windmill: the bloody-minded one that had long ago ensured I'd never make sergeant major.

But I'd gained confidence by then: felt I could afford to indulge in a last, albeit futile, pop at him. I'd finally succeeded in dragging the Sten across my knees without his knowing. Fumbling in the darkness, I ever so gently eased the safety handle downwards out of its slot while slipping my forefinger around the trigger. On target, and ready cocked to fire at will, the reassuring weight of the sub-machine gun afforded me great comfort.

'Yeah, I do reckon Brigade will pursue you, Major,' I lied. 'A Redcap officer killing children makes bad press for the Corps: calls for boards of inquiry, statements from the Defence Minister. They'll hang you out to dry by civil trial if necessary and, deep down, you'll never be certain they won't do so. A kid nine, ten years old – packing a string gun? Put yourself in the place of a civvie jury.'

And that was that. Now I was prepared to concede, yet still feel vindicated. I'd taken the moral high ground even if I'd lost the argument. Only one niggling uncertainty still remained. Thanks to my persistent baiting, did *Steadman* appreciate I was only persisting in a spiteful bluff? That I no longer intended to land him in it?

It seemed he didn't.

A barely perceptible movement of the hand and the nine-millimetre railway tunnel that was the muzzle of his FN high-power Browning had lifted fractionally.

Like the eye of a malevolent Cyclops, it now stared intently at the underside of my chin.

Four

To Steadman's credit he had seemed genuinely concerned to alleviate my out-going, betraying no hint of the unstable menace that lay below the surface. 'At least you can take some consolation, Staff Sergeant. From having ensured I'll be court-martialled.'

The proprieties up to the last, then. I had to accord him his due for that. Say what you like about him, he was scrupulous in maintaining the pleasantries of rank.

'But only on a lesser charge of unlawful killing, eh, Major?' I concluded for him tightly, ever the smart one. 'Caused by the reckless discharge of a firearm.'

. . . Then I shut up fast when I detected the barrel of the Browning begin to pull slightly to the left, a deflection that could only be caused by the increasing pressure of his finger on the trigger.

The slimy things I thought I'd left behind on the mountain caught up with me again, multiplied by a factor of ten. Most of me froze rigid right away: only my mind continued to function, and at warp speed at that. Steadman's pistol had a trigger pull of, say, three and a half pounds . . .? I gulped. I was approximately three ounces away from a thousand foot-pound confrontation with a bullet. There was only one option left.

I had to shoot him first.

Then I decided not to.

. . . Because only then did it occur to me, albeit reprehensibly tardily, that there was no bloody *point* in doing so – that if I *had* intended to blow him in half, I should've done it five minutes ago! That my sub-machine gun was, for all its devastating superiority over a handgun at such point-blank range, actually of no comfort at all.

It was fruitless to try pre-empting his killing me by taking *him* out first with the Sten. The instant cadaverization of any animal causes the reflex contraction of muscles and sinews. It's why a hen can sometimes run halfway round the farm-yard even after its beady-eyed head's been chopped off. And the magnitude of reflex action generated in a much larger animal amounts to a hell of a lot more than a three-ounce squeeze.

Even dead, Steadman would still blow me away unless I instituted a *bloody* quick rethink of my future strategy for survival – all five milliseconds of it!

After four milliseconds, I resorted to the only tactic I could think of.

I yawned.

A great, luxurious, stretchity yawn. A yawn so vast my backside lifted clear off the seat and left me rigidly suspended with the back of my head against the roof support at one end, and the steel-capped heels of my boots forced against the foot pedals at the other. And do you know – I enjoyed it: I really did. There's only one activity I can think of that relieves nervous tension better, and even then O'Feely was better at it than I.

Collapsing back on the seat in a pretend-relaxed heap, I watched for Steadman's reaction from the corner of an appre-hensive eye. Have you ever sat on a late-night Tube train and yawned cavernously – then smiled inwardly as the same yawn travels right down the opposite row of faces and comes right back up to you on your own side? It can be amusing. Well, it *can* be if you're a sad bastard like me. Unless you happened to notice, in the interim, that one of them is a stary-eyed sort of fellow traveller with a loaded gun.

Anyhow, despite himself, the Major yawned as well. For all his cold self-control, he simply couldn't help it. It's another of those involuntary reflexes. And as he exhaled angrily, I inhaled with a great surge of relief on seeing the muzzle of the pistol waver. It seemed an opportune moment to forward my ambition of staying alive long enough to enjoy that late supper.

I lunged viciously and he doubled forward, grunting involuntarily as the cylindrical barrel of the Sten took him in the gut. I heard its Barleycorn foresight grate on the brass buckle of his webbing belt and thought savagely: *that'll* bloody give you somethin' to sort before parade tomorrow! Not that it would: his batman, Baggo Nialls, would've been fair pissed at me had he known, while he spent his drinking time on burnishing out the scratches.

I hesitated, frowing uncertainly: not quite sure of what to do next. Steadman had dropped the Browning, meaning he no longer posed an immediate threat. And he *had* made an important point when reminding me of my responsibilities. As a senior NCO in the Royal Military Police it *was* incumbent on me to observe the pleasantries of rank and not banjo my commanding officer unnecessarily.

. . . Then I remembered the dead child: thought, *Ohhhh fuck it!*, drew back the weapon, and speared again – this time mustering all the fear, all the loathing, all the resentment that he'd engendered in me during the last few hours. Steadman convulsed and began to retch. I sat and watched, yet took small consolation from his discomfort. It had been an inadequate revenge for his terminating such a tiny span of life, and I could only hope that, somehow, a little Cypriot boy with grubby knees and a frayed jersey might be looking down from whatever celestial mountain he now tended his flock on.

And maybe understand that we weren't all monsters in the British Army.

I knew it wasn't over: that it would never be over. But the critical momentum so essential to the act of killing had surely been dissipated? I kept a wary eye on the slumped Steadman though, while I waited to find out.

I'd begun to feel hungry again, and the cat had reappeared to crouch on top of the wall; had even sat long enough to drop a grenade on us had it been an EOKA cat, by the time the Major straightened up stiffly. He'd been unaware of my watching him, so far as I could make out.

I reached for the ignition key.

Steadman said, 'I haven't ordered you to move yet, Staff Sergeant.'

51

Oh, for *fuc* . . .?

'You seemed fascinated by this, ah . . . embarrassment,' he indicated his ravaged cheek. 'Are you curious to learn how I acquired it?'

I would've dyed my hair green to know, but I was even more anxious to divest myself of the man afflicted by it: a caution made doubly acute on realizing he'd been perfectly aware of my furtive scrutiny. Almost certainly lying doggo while taking his turn to review his options. Yet again I'd underestimated him.

I shrugged with an insouciance I didn't feel. 'Not particularly. Asking would imply I give a shit.'

It was a gratuitously cruel response, and childish of me. For all I knew, the scar had something to do with what had happened on the mountain: helped explain why he'd climbed up there alone, fully aware he was offering himself as a sniper's target, and ended up murdering a child. Maybe he was even seeking some gesture of absolution? But I was in no mood to provide psychoanalytical comfort to mentally disturbed majors. I'd been on the go for over thirty-six hours by then, discounting those periods best overlooked which I'd spent lying prone below Foxie or shit-scared halfway up the slopes.

Deep down, I still was. I'd only dared risk that one final, rebellious reply 'cause the Sten still lay reassuringly to hand across my lap, and I'd already checked carefully to make sure his gun was lying below the dash.

Oddly enough, he let it go.

So I relented. Marginally.

'OK, I notice you'd earned the Military Medal. I thought officers usually bagged themselves an MC.'

The scar tightened perceptibly. ' Don't be so bloody supercilious, Walker. Back in '40 I was just a CMP lance-jack with the Expeditionary Force in France. You're not the only man to have come in through the squaddies' barrack room.'

Now that revelation *did* impress me. It takes an extra-special breed of man to rise from recruit to major in the British Army, though war accelerates promotion for a lot of people: some of them not worthy. But I'd already had cause to appreciate that Steadman was the product of *some* special breed.

And like I said, I'd only relented marginally.

'So what are you trying to prove, Major? That you were a bloody good Joe in those days? I've had to lock plenty of good Joes in cells in my ti . . .'

I ground to a halt when I saw he wasn't listening. He still gazed ahead, but I got the feeling he wasn't seeing anything. Even when he did speak, it was with an unsettling, detached air.

'My section were retreating to Dunkirk, one step ahead of the Bosch push. All roads to the beaches were choc-a-bloc with heavy transport, horse wagons, staff cars, artillery pieces, half the French and Belgian armies as well as our own. We Redcaps were mostly doing traffic control, route signing – trying to keep things moving. You can imagine the chaos.'

I couldn't resist a dig. 'You're not the only soldier to have been at Dunkirk, Major.'

He smiled fleetingly at that. But not in a resentful way.

'Touché, Staff! Anyway, the transport was snarled at a little crossroads east of St-Valéry. A Redcap sergeant was struggling to untangle the snafu. He'd been seriously wounded by shell splinters but, rather than desert his post and hold up the retreat, he'd lashed himself to a stake in the middle of the road. If anyone deserved this medal, it was he.'

Steadman lost it momentarily, and I guessed he was back on that crater-pitted road to Dunkirk. I'd passed along it too, and suddenly I felt closer to the strange, volatile officer than I would have believed possible two minutes before. Perhaps, somewhere in this recounting of a battle-damaged soldier's past glories, I might divine some reason for a child's death seventeen years later.

'Go on – sir.' I forced the courtesy out, though I could've bit my tongue off soon as I'd said it.

'I managed to persuade him that bleeding to death wasn't helping anyone but Jerry, so I bundled him into the next vehicle – a NAAFI wagon it was, still handing out tea and wads on the move – then took over the point. Around two hours later a brigade major came by in a three-tonner and ordered me to get out – said the Panzers were right on his tail. Asked me to rig up a direction board showing the route to the embarkation beaches before I left, as a sapper unit covered by a Jock infantry company were blowing the last bridge before pulling back like scalded bloody cats.'

I had to grin. 'I can believe.'

They say one smile makes two, and so it proved. Involuntarily Steadman returned the grin and, for a fleeting moment, the ravaged side of his face was masked by shadow. In that fleeting moment he struck me as being equilaterally handsome again. Even looked like a good Joe.

But like I said.

It *was* only for a fleeting moment.

He stirred. 'We'd been warned to be alert for Jerry fifth-columnists misdirecting our movement signs. I decided to wait for the rearguard, then take off in the last truck.'

This was a man I could have respected under different circumstances: a Military Medal is only earned the hard way. Cynicism comes easier for me. 'A decision like that – you needed a doctor, not a medal.'

'I got both, Staff !' This time the wry distortion was unmistakable. 'A few minutes later I saw the column approaching from the bridge. I was very young then – still devoured the *Boy's Own Paper* whenever I got the chance – so I put on my best London bobby act. I can still recall how enormously proud I felt: ramrod stiff to attention, one arm in the air and the other flat across my chest, directing them to the beach . . .'

I didn't doubt it. He would've looked good as co-star in an Errol Flynn movie, only better-looking than Flynn. Once upon a time, anyway. Before whatever, presumably, happened to him in France in 1940.

'All the vehicle crews laughed to me, and saluted as they passed. For the first time since we'd been ordered to retreat I began to feel I was fighting a winner's war.' He broke off momentarily in sardonic reflection.

'. . . Until I registered the swastikas painted on the trucks!'

My first reaction was to laugh. Not *at* him. Hell, no. More the kind of response you'd make to a mate in the mess to ease his discomfiture at revealing an embarrassing secret – but I had neither the inclination nor the guts. We weren't mates and, anyway, that eerie distance in his eyes was disturbing enough to dispel any false impression of togetherness.

'Shit happens, Major. And the scar?'

He blinked oddly at me. 'A joke, Staff Sergeant – a Teutonic bloody joke! Some of the old-school Prussian cavalry officers still carried sabres in those days, even in action. While I stood there, staring uncomprehendingly up at that Jerry column rumbling past, one of them – an SS *Obersturmbannführer* – leaned from his staff car and . . .'

Steadman began to knead the purple wound viciously then, as if trying to squeeze out the memory. When he started doing that I could see he was losing it again, didn't know how to handle it, and finished up wishing desperately that my reluctant curiosity hadn't got the better of me: that I'd started the Rover and driven us both back to barracks while he was still groggy.

'And . . .?' I prompted warily.

'. . . And slashed me right across the goddam FACE!'

'*Jesus!*' I muttered, blanching.

'The bastards laughed, Walker. Eighteen years old, terrified, swallowing my own fucking blood and sensing the whole side of my face hanging off – and they *laughed*! Didn't even bother to take me out. The way they had it figured, there was a whole shooting gallery of us penned in and waiting to be slaughtered on the beaches. One already neutralized Brit *feldpolizie* more or less wasn't worth a bullet.'

Steadman's voice had sunk to a dull, flat monotone. And he wasn't talking to me any longer: only to whatever demons had been trapped within him for seventeen years. 'The last thing I can remember was that SS colonel looking back at me – still brandishing his bloodied sabre and roaring with amusement.'

55

By then I could barely decipher the hate-impregnated mouthings. 'That *fucking* colonel. He could . . .'

OK, so it was against my better judgement that I found myself leaning closer to hear. Not recklessly, mind you: not without having taken the precaution of easing the Sten's cocking handle from its safe slot again and laying the muzzle just short of his chest. The creepy-crawlies had recommenced their creepy-crawling through the short hairs at the back of my neck, but this time I didn't need a reminder to shoot at the first indication of threat.

'. . . Could *what*, Major?'

He ignored me: fist now clenched white and knuckling the scar with a masochistic disregard that made me shift uneasily in the seat. Despite hiding behind a sub-machine gun, I'd've still felt more secure sitting on a barrel of nitro while driving off a cliff. I *had* to snap him out of it. I mean, what else can you do with a gibbering, homicidally inclined senior officer in a space six foot by three?

'Get a bloody GRIP, sir!'

'He could so easily have shot me – but he played a *joke*, Walker! The bastard took my face away instead.'

'Major *Steadman*!'

Fingers locked together now, clasping the back of his head while he began to rock back and forward like a freaked-out child.

'He took . . . my . . . fucking . . . FACE away instead.'

So there I had it. Psychoanalysis the hard-soldier Walker way. Almost certainly the key to why a battle-scarred veteran would set himself up as a terrorist sniper's target of opportunity.

Christ, but I was scared bloody rigid even despite the solace afforded by the nine-mil Plumber's Delight. I'd been a military copper since . . . I dunno – since the last ptero-dactyl fell off its perch, it seemed. I'd handled regiments of potentially murderous brown jobs in my time: soldiers and NCOs so crazed with drink or domestic pressures or combat shock that King Kong hisself wouldn't've relished taking 'em on, not even with a bloody field gun. But this was different – this was above my punching weight. Dead man walking . . . with a major's crown on his shoulder, the weight of the British Army behind him, an impeccable hero's record and an already clearly demonstrated desire to kill me.

Even the EOKA cat had prudently removed itself from its ambush point on top of the wall by then. My stomach constricted with revulsion while, involuntarily, I found myself pulling as far as I could from the khaki-clad thing that uttered foul gibberish beside me.

OK, so I would have coped eventually. I always did.

Well . . . I *would* have done.

. . . If I hadn't dropped the bastard Sten.

I don't know yet how I managed it. I think probably its webbing sling got snarled in the gear lever and pulled it out of my hands as I shrank away.

Meaning the shooting-him option was out. So what else could I do, apart from legging it after the cat . . .? Then I remembered an old military axiom from way back. *The best means of defence is attack.* I didn't think to wonder whether that included lunatics as well as armies, but maybe that's an added reason for why I'm still only a staff sergeant.

'Is that why you shot the boy, Major? Did you take *his* face away too, did you?'

I waited apprehensively, not daring to reach below the dash to retrieve the Sten as Steadman slowly raised his head and looked at me in bewilderment.

'The boy?'

'That kid on the mountain. Did you shoot him in the face deliberately, Steadman – or did you just get lucky with your first round?'

The haunted man frowned: slowly began to focus on the present. I noted how he drew his hands down the ravaged features to leave white bloodless traces where his fingers had pressured each cheek. Thank Christ for *that*, I thought hopefully – tomato or Daddy's Own sauce with your crispy-charred bangers, Walker?

I should have had the sense to stop there, but I didn't. I'd finally gained the psychological upper hand. Maybe I could grasp this one last opportunity, before we reverted to our small-cog, big-wheel military status to make the pursuit of justice at least possible.

I knew that if I could get the Major to admit premeditation, even verbally, then I'd have evidence holding far greater significance in law than an uncorroborated assumption. Certainly it would afford me enough ammunition to go to the Assistant Provost Marshal's office. For all our historic antipathy towards each other, Lieutenant Colonel Slake would be first to give weight to an affidavit sworn by a veteran staff sergeant of the Corps of Royal Military Police, prepared to state under oath in court that his CO had confessed to the murder of a child.

At the least, even should my determination fail in the cold light of dawn, I would still have brought Major Eric Steadman RMP, MM, to *some* small, albeit totally inadequate account. Ensured he'd never sleep easy again, burdened by a nagging anxiety that maybe tomorrow, next week – maybe even next year, I might just get reckless enough or drunk enough to take on the military establishment after all.

It was now or never. Setting my jaw to conform with best interrogation practice, I went in for the kill.

'DID you, Steadman – did you *enjoy* putting a hole in his face like that Nazi *Obersturmbannführer* did to you? Square the circle of degradation, did it . . .? And that solo of yours up the mountain, knowing the Yolkies could still have been keeping obbo . . . does your disfigurement haunt you so much you'd welcome gettin' yourself blown away – or did you deliberately go hunting for a victim?'

But he *still* didn't respond in the way I'd anticipated – goddammit, he *never* responded like an ordinary lunatic might reasonably be expected to! When he did finally reply, it was with cold dispassion. In other words, situation bloody normal. In the CO's case, anyway.

'I've been foolish to confide in you, Walker. You'll forget everything you've heard. Do you understand?'

. . . And I knew I'd lost the initiative. The adrenalin of rage subsided instantly and I just felt weary and frustrated by the whole monstrous affair. You've blown your last chance, Walker. Time to go home.

Leaning awkwardly below the dash, I groped around the

and set my jaw. This time I could definitely afford to, what with his pistol safe in its holster and me having pre-planned enough, for once, to bring the Sten up along with my reprieved head.

Raising the muzzle, I placed it where the Corps badges glinted dully in his lapels. 'You're psycho, Steadman. That obscenity has corrupted your mind.'

The white bat fluttered again. And ever so deliberately pushed the barrel aside!

I blinked disconcertedly. Maybe I should've tried that approach with *his* gun?

'Don't try to understand me, Walker,' he advised flatly. 'Just jump when I order you to, and we'll get along well with each other.'

'In your fuckin' dreams, Major,' I retorted weakly, acutely mindful by then to observe the pleasantries. 'You executed that kid and one day, I swear to God, I'm going to bring you to book for it.'

I won't pretend he quaked with apprehension. In actual fact he just stuck one derisive middle finger up to me, then leaned forward and flipped the switch so that the glow of our side lamps burnished the wall ahead us. Hardly a breakthrough of Holmesian proportions, and certainly not the confession I'd so desperately tried to elicit, but at least I'd succeeded in proving *some*thing.

That Steadman *had* been a lance-jack. Once.

'Negative your last, Walker. By the time I've finished, you won't be able to prove you're a bloody soldier: not even a bad one.' The purple scar tissue tightened perceptibly. 'I shall throw the book at you every time you blink without my sayso, Staff Sergeant. A military policeman must be above reproach. I intend to see to it that you are reproached with monotonous regularity.'

The peak of his cap cast an impenetrable shadow across his eyes but I knew, with a wave of empty despair, that the spooky Major hadn't finished with me. The spider had just begun to sidle across the web, while I buzzed ineffectually in sticky impotence.

'I intend to take out insurance, Walker. No matter where

you hide in the army, I shall destroy your character so completely that you will never be listened to. Not by any court of law.'

The punchline came almost as an afterthought. '. . . Or alternatively – I may decide to kill you.'

By the time we'd arrived back at the Limassol Provost lines, I'd decided against bangers and mash.

Five

Slumped disconsolately at the plastic-topped scratch-proof table, I gloomily traced the slashes that legions of British Army-issue clasp knives had carved to belie the maker's claim. Across from me, Charlie settled more comfortably into his chair and popped another can of Export. His beret slipped from his shoulder strap to the drink-slopped table, but he wrung it out fastidiously then stuffed it back in place. Teetering dangerously astern, he clomped his heavy ammunition boots amongst the litter of empty cans on the table and belched with deep contentment. I glared irritably at him.

Charlie Parrish. Or 71532291 Colour Sergeant Charles Parrish MM and Bar, to give him his Sunday name, of Her Majesty's Lancashire Fusiliers. The hardest soldier I'd ever met: small, but perfectly formed, mad as a box of frogs and probably the closest mucker I would ever have outside the Corps.

I'd first met Charlie at Dunkirk, probably on the same day that Steadman was traffic-policing an SS Panzer column. I hadn't been quite so close to collecting a medal as the Major, though. In actual fact I'd been making a determined attempt on the world land-speed record in an ancient commandeered 1929 Citroën when the-then Fusilier Parrish had pleaded with me to give him a lift as far as the beaches. I hadn't liked to refuse his appeal under the circumstances. Especially as he was holding the muzzle of his .303 Lee-Enfield under my chin when he'd made it.

We were together on the poor bloody paddle-steamer *Princess Irene* when she went down with a Stuka bomb in her boilers a thousand yards off Bray Dunes, but Charlie and myself had avoided being counted among the nine-hundred-plus troops who went down with her. Charlie won his first gong then, and I was the bloke largely responsible for his being awarded it. Well, when I say *responsible*, I mean I was probably the most vocal of the survivors he helped to save, and you can't be a hero without someone to give you a reason, can you?

The next time we met, we both had two tapes up. Parrish was earning the Bar to his Military Medal fighting Rommel's Afrika Korps at Tobruk, while I'd been trying to maintain as strict a neutrality as my uniform would allow. They even gave me a medal too, following that lot, but largely through a misunderstanding. The real motive I had for carting that unexploded bomb out of the ammo store was that it also contained the only two cases of illicit whisky left in the besieged city, and I'd been the one who stashed them there. If I'd thought a bit smarter at the time, I would've moved the Scotch and left the bloody UXB . . .

Anyway, now the Lancashires had been deployed to Cyprus, and me and Charlie had got together again. I liked him a lot, Charlie Parrish. Considering he wasn't a Redcap.

I hadn't told anyone about my bizarre confrontation with Steadman three months before, not even O'Feely, but that night, meeting up with Charlie after several years, I'd been unable to suppress it any longer. I'd told him the lot: all about my apprehensions and concerns for the future. Parrish hadn't said anything, just sat and listened and absorbed cans of Export like a camel preparing for a long distance voyage. Only when I'd finished blowing off steam did he drain his current tinnie and look beerily reflective.

'Now you, mate,' he summed-up, scalpel-sharp in his perception, 'now *you* are one staffy with a real problem.'

'Oh, *very* helpful and supportive,' I growled, a bit needled by the quality of his counsel. 'Especially considerin' it's got a major's crown on its shoulder.'

He shrugged: we both knew the score. There wasn't much else he could do other than offer an experienced ear and self-evident advice. 'So I say keep well clear of 'im, and always have a bloody witness handy, mate. Even in the crapper.'

I didn't know it then but Charlie, poor bastard, should

have been taking his own advice to heart. Not that either of us could, at that time, have anticipated what was to follow.

I gazed half-heartedly round the smoke-fogged room. The place was one of those lower end of the leisure market establishments where not very nice girls worked and the licentious soldiery played – and paid. Normally Charlie and I appreciated that sort of atmosphere: it made us feel at one with our natural environment, and was a hell of a lot more fun than moodily poking a billiard ball around the ploughed green baize of a NAAFI table. I benefited from the additional frisson of knowing that, being a Redcap senior NCO, the APM would've gone ape if he'd found out.

But I wasn't at my social best that night, although I'd felt bound to make the gesture. Charlie hadn't drunk himself into a stupor since he flew in, and he'd been in Limassol nearly eight hours. Involuntarily my gaze fell to his gaitered ammunition boots stuck up on the table in front of me. The gleaming leather reminded me of Provost Lance Corporal Fox again, and I took an uncharacteristically hasty pull of Newcastle Brown ... Brigade *had* insisted on the Jocks' regimental piper playing the Lament, by the way, ignoring the risk of courting Foxie's celestial disapproval. I hope he hadn't felt too sad up there, still looking after a small child with grubby knees like I'd asked him to.

Charlie beamed in critical appreciation as a couple of Turkish scrubbers with vermilion-glossed lips bore down on us. Being his host for the night, I groaned and felt for my wallet. Upstairs they had the British armed forces' version of Hitler's strength-through-joy cubicles, each flanked by floor-to-ceiling mirrors with sliding curtains – drawing them aside during the biz was an optional extra. The mirrors were one-way glass and for an extra couple of notes, those in the know – sad bastards like O'Feely, for instance – could squeeze in behind and view the contractual gymnastics from the other side. Taking your Kodak Brownie in with you cost a trio more. From the deprived look in Charlie's eye, I reckoned one glance in the mirror and he would save himself the physical hassle.

Being a toff, he'd swung his boots off the table soon as

the girls sat down, then clomped them up again and beamed at the expanse of fishnet-covered leg on display. Both presented bosoms that would have demanded bras manufactured in an Istanbul shipyard. It didn't matter here, though: they weren't wearing any. The more mature lady of the night turned predatorily to tackle me while I leaned apprehensively back to avert collision. I could tell by the skin-tight cling of the satin skirt that she hadn't contracted to the other half of the set either.

Even white teeth flashed in a regulation smile. 'My name, it ees Pedal, Sergeant Major Captain. And my bes' frien' here, she ees Jasmine.'

Not for the first time, I saluted the originality of British industry. Every brothel from Yokohama to the North Pole hosts one performer called Petal and one called Jasmine. Apart from Blighty. In UK garrison towns they revel in such exotica as Flo, Aggie, Slack Alice . . . maybe the odd Sophie if the establishment is dead class.

'Pleestermeetchew,' Charlie said happily, already in love.

Jasmine the Marginally Younger enhanced his mood romantic by immediately placing her hand on his gaiter and commencing to work expertly up towards his Blanco Number Nine-encrusted webbing belt. Love may have been a many-splendoured thing to Charlie but, to a working girl, time is money. Like the spectre at the wedding, I merely observed Parrish sourly. Judging by the expression of weather-beaten ecstasy on his face, I reckoned to see the razor sharp creases in his BD trousers steam flat any moment, under the deftly ironing hand.

Just before her oppo triggered blast-off, Petal blew me a vino-scented moue while raising a pencilled eyebrow suggestively. 'You weesh to come upstair, Sargeant Colonel?'

'*He's* goin' to come down here in a minnit,' I growled, watching the wriggling Charlie aprehensively.

She signalled to the enthusiastic apprentice with a sharp elbow, *Don't handle the goods till they've paid for 'em*, and the breasts bobbed as she heaved her ample bulk to the vertical. Reluctantly I turned on the cruelly deflating Parrish. His beret had slipped from his shoulder strap again and I irritably dredged it out of the brewer's puddle and shoved it at him. The two girls had gone on ahead and Charlie hobbled after them in an agony of frustrated impatience, one hand clutching his groin. I'd already found I couldn't get Foxie out of my head that night. That sort of gesture wasn't helping.

They awaited us impatiently at the bottom of the Stairway to Paradise. The managing director turned and flashed like a lighthouse again.

'You want short time, Sergeant Captain? Or per'aps an exhibition?'

Charlie awaited my response with baited breath, a liquid-eyed cocker spaniel impatient for the guns to blast.

'Depends on the house tariff,' I said cruelly.

Charlie jiggled impatiently. It was like buying a kid an ice cream. Pedal moved suggestively against me. She'd done the marketing course. 'Two pound English short time: five pound for exhibition.'

I stared at her in outrage. 'Five *quid*?' I yelped. 'Christ, missis, we only want to rent 'em, not bloody buy 'em!'

Fusilier Colour Sergeant Parrish shot me a glance of disgust and suggested my wallet must be even smaller than some-thin' or other else. But Charlie was both sexually mal-adjusted and potless, and anyway, it was my treat so I had the executive authority. And I was no virgin conscript pushover.

'This randy little bastard here, he's not goin' to last out for more than half a quid's worth even at the full union ra—!'

Petal suddenly extended a practised hand and engaged me. It was a totally improper and below-the-belt negotiating technique. I still can't recall quite how she did it, but it sure as hell put the offered price up to the contract tender.

It wasn't until next morning I discovered O'Feely had gone for five notes' worth at the same time. From the other side of the mirror. Using Lance Corporal Butterworth's Polaroid.

Two nights later and I was still browned off: this time on account of my being provost duty guard commander at Post

Baker, or *Bravo* as I kept forgetting to call it. I'd never got the hang of the new NATO phonetic alphabet, though I conceded some aides-memoires came easier from the change. *Romeo* had replaced *Roger*, which brought O'Feely easily to mind, while for *W* now read *Whiskey*. Which made me think of Charlie Parrish.

Completing my third paper aeroplane, I launched it across the room to where Corporal Davidson scribbled industriously at the duty desk. Nothing much was happening and it was shaping to be a ten-aeroplane night. The origami airframe pancaked on the RMP Training Manual, skittered off and finally nose-dived into the geometrically squared folds of the grey blanket on the duty NCO's bunk.

'Zeeeeooooow . . . keeers-PLAT!'

Davidson ignored my reporting the incident. 'Army Form Missile Mark Four, sah . . . ! Yessah – out of control, sah . . . ! Destruct, destruct, destruct . . .'

Gloomily I sniffed and looked appealingly at the clock – still only 0420: the wee sma' 'oors, as they say in the Black Watch. A time when sensible people are asleep; when villains take to their nocturnal professions. The time when madmen go mad and terminally sick people die. I shivered. It got bloody cold at four in the morning.

Lighting a Capstan Full Strength, I wandered over to the duty desk. The new day's standing orders caught my eye and my finger traced idly down the list, hesitating on the signature beneath – *Major Eric K Steadman, Officer Commanding*. I'd never discovered what the K stood for.

Killer? Krazy man – Knut . . .? I permitted myself a wry smile. Whatever he was, so far he hadn't been anything but your average, reasonably courteous CO when I'd been around. That bizarre incident on our way back from the mountain: now a good twelve, thirteen weeks ago, was it? Maybe he, too, had come to conclude that we'd reached a mutual stand-off. Maybe he'd even erased it from his mind?

Then I recalled the manner by which he'd revealed the actual state of that mind, and my smile faded.

Corporal Davidson chucked his ballpoint onto the desk

and leaned back victoriously. 'That's the lost and founds done, Staff. What's next for the worker?'

I yawned. 'Finished checking that accident report, have you?'

'The Fusilier truck and the civvie? Yes Staff.'

'And the AB 170s?'

'Yes, Staff.'

'And all them little pink forms?'

'Yes, Staff. And the blue ones too.'

I was impressed. I should have done most of them myself, as it so happened, but there's no point in having a dog et cetera. I tossed him a Capstan and he lit up gratefully.

'You do get through forms like a dose of civil servants, Davidson,' I granted expansively. 'Given time, you might even learn to be a copper as well.'

He grinned. 'You know what they say, Staff. Get the facts, straight from a soldier.'

'Wouldn't know. Haven't got any in this company.'

Another yawn overtook me and I gazed longingly at the bunk before deciding it wasn't worth it. I could never be sure of what tricks Steadman might try to pull, no matter how much I tried to reassure myself. Walker in his kip on duty . . .? The Major would have my head on a plate with my sweetbreads as garnish. Stubbing the Capstan in the tin lid that did service as an ashtray, I lifted my cap from the hook on the back of the door, tugging its slashed peak firmly down in regulation Redcap staffy-on-the-prowl fashion.

'Goin' to take a shufti round, Corporal. Stay near the phone.'

Stepping into the still cold night air, I closed the door behind me so's he wouldn't notice before hunching down into my collar. Debating on whether or not to nip over to the billet for my greatcoat, I decided it would do more for the image to be seen striding out briskly, scorning the elements . . . mind you, a sneaky extra vest slipped under my shirt wouldn't be noticed? Walker the Rugged moved sharply off towards the sergeants' quarters, muscles tensed like piano wires as the scorned elements bit into his cast-iron frame.

69

On the way I got to wondering whereabouts Charlie might be. The Lancashires were on perimeter guard duty that night, and I'd noted the orders listed Colour Sergeant Parrish as guard commander. I peered keenly into the dawn half-light. I hadn't seen him since our reunion – well, not apart from his likeness staring, bleary but utterly ecstatic, from O'Feely's candid camera pics – and was more than keen to find out exactly what the delectable Jasmine had done to bring about such graphic expression.

Well, it *had* been my ten quid, and our shared love tryst had done sod all for me. That Petal hadn't been lying: not when she'd referred to herself as Pedal.

Over to the east, the concrete silhouette of the arms store stood etched against the faint pink glow of the stirring sun. It was very quiet: a still, eerie sort of dawn like on the morning Foxie died: only the slightest movement on the skyline betraying the slouched disenchantment of a lonely sentry. In the foreground a row of Nissen cookhouses merged into the blackness and as I watched, a door opened briefly, allowing a shaft of yellow light and the rattle of slop-buckets to escape. Skirting the white-painted rocks marking the edge of the parade ground, I didn't envy the ACC cooks and fatigue men their endless, and traditionally thankless, task of feeding an unappreciative British Army.

I'd almost reached the dim blue light marking the entrance to the sergeants' mess when the burst of nine-millimetre rounds stitched their way across the parade square towards me.

Paralysed by the suddenness of it, all I remember was registering a geyser of whitewashed stone chips suspended in mid-air as if captured by electronic flash, then something bit a piece out of the side of my boot. In the ensuing silence – and about twenty seconds past death time – I hurled myself prone before attempting to shrivel down to the size of a clump of weed.

The whole camp fell dark and quiet again. It was plain spooky, huddled there with everyone else apparently either asleep – or dead? I shook my head firmly: no way could you kill eleven hundred troops with one burst of sub-machine-gun fire. Always assuming, that is, you *wanted* to kill eleven hundred troops?

. . . As opposed, maybe, to just *one*? The creepy-crawlies suddenly returned in battalion strength to the nape of my neck – Steadman? I shook my head even more firmly. Not the calculating Major. Not even he would be crazy enough to hope to get away with such a high-profile assassination attempt in-house.

So what the *hell* . . .?

. . . Which marked the point when the whole camp erupted in a frenetic display of panic, disbelief and shambolic in-efficiency, and I realized only a few moments had actually passed since some person or persons unknown had shot a ha'penny-sized half-moon out of the edge of my boot sole. And then I realized what it was, the only thing it could possibly be – that EOKA had got cheeky. They'd crawled out of their holes and hit the camp, probably trying for the arms store or ammo dump.

Lights started to blossom all over the area and I snorted in disgust. National bloody Servicemen! That's the ticket, lads – switch on all the bastard stage lights! Make bloody sure you don't make it too difficult for the gunmen.

As if on cue, the cookhouse door jerked open again to vomit black silhouettes framed like celluloid ducks in a popgun shooting arcade. Momentarily overlooking the fact that I was supposed to be a weed, I rose and began running while screaming a horrified warning.

The terrorist with the Schmeisser or whatever was quicker off his mark than I was.

Cook Corporal Donovan was smashed off his feet as the second burst went into his chest: careering backwards across the preparation table like a white-aproned squid to crash-land on the red-hot cooking range. Trays of bacon rashers and already solidified fried eggs clattered to the deck on top of now prudently grovelling fatigue men. I started to divert towards the blood-spattered shambles then, remembering with a clutch of panic that the gunman was still working, just kept on running past the colandered cookhouse door to hurl myself into the sanctuary of a latrine entrance. I retained a sickening image of Donovan's barrel chest opened like an obscene crimson flower as he slowly roasted at gas mark 6 on his own range, while the scattered eggs and bacon reminded me it was a Sunday morning – the one bloody day I could've looked forward to a half-decent breakfast.

By now the camp was wide awake. The rattle of small-arms fire seemed to come from everywhere around me, some of it even aimed *at* the terrorists. From the MT section vehicle park rose the spluttering roar of hastily started engines while over towards the arms store all hell was breaking loose. A dull explosion made me realize this was no spontaneous gesture of anti-British resentment, this was a well-planned and coordinated attack: they'd even acquired a Bangalore torpedo to blow a gap through the wire. I crouched a bit lower and listened to the chorus of screams and conflicting orders as sleep-dulled National Servicemen were dragged into the service of their mother country.

'Sergeant Kennedy – where the blazes is Sergeant *Kennedy* . . .?': 'Get outa that fuckin' BILLET, Private . . . !': 'Where's me rifle gone, for Chrissake . . .?': 'Did you see Bertie, Spider – Jeeeezus, he must still've been in 'is kip when they caught 'im . . .': 'Who the fuck's been cleanin' his gear with the bastard fire extinguisher again . . .?'

A flickering glow slowly grew in intensity from the blitzed cookhouse. Something was burning. I wondered momentarily whether it was Cook Corporal Donovan or my Sunday break-fast, then a petrol-injected roar made me swing round. A Ferret scout car whined across the parade ground, turret clamped tight shut and the vicious-looking main armament traversing hungrily. I bloody nearly cheered . . . at least the armoured boys were getting their act together. As it approached I cautiously stuck my head around the edge of the latrine door. Nobody shot me so I stepped out and waved my arms frantically. The turret swivelled optimistically towards me then, disappointed, continued its frustrated search for a target. A tousled head wearing a black Corps beret topping a gaily striped pyjama jacket sprouted enquiringly from the bowels of the machine. Dressed in jim-jams like that, I knew the head had to belong to an officer.

'Provost Guard Room, sir?' I yelled nervously. 'Can you drop me off there?'

The head considered for a moment. 'Affirmative, Staff Sergeant: nip up on the arse of the old cow, there's a good chap.'

I clambered aboard, still fearfully conscious of the proximity of the Schmeisser virtuoso, discarding my weed impression and trying now to imitate a piece of rust as the Ferret's driver engaged the clutch and we shot off like a wad of blotting paper propelled by an elastic band. Grabbing hold of a ringbolt I clung on grimly as my ten-ton taxi headed at terrifying speed down the main camp drag.

The head turned towards me and grinned cheerily. 'Jolly exciting don't you think, Staff?'

I nodded emphatically. *Bloody* emphatically! It was all right for *him* dressed in his inch-thick steel battledress, whereas I hadn't even made it as far as collecting my extra vest. The dawn was slowly becoming brighter as I peered round the stippled sand paint of the turre . . .?

Ohhhhh – SHIT!

A massive Fusilier three-tonner was careering towards us, canvas canopy blazing like a torch. One horrified glance was enough to register the line of bullet holes spattering the windscreen in a scenario reminiscent of Corporal Fox's previous departure . . . I closed my eyes and clung even more leech-like, feeling the Ferret swerve drunkenly as the flaming truck clanged glancingly against our flank, then the three-tonner's nearside front wheel ran up on the veranda outside the Regimental Office and the whole bloody rig cartwheeled in a tumble-weed ball of flame.

The head in the turret moved sharply and we skidded to a halt. I got sick of motorized transport, fell off and lay winded, glaring up at the grit-impregnated tyres that loomed above me.

A matching pair of oily boots and gaiters landed heavily on my outstretched hand. I howled and agonizingly reflected that Walker and army-issue boots, whether bulled to a glass finish or marinated in Castrol, just weren't compatible. Even while I debated whether or not to charge them with aggravated assault on a military policeman, their wearer bent down and, as he dragged me to my feet, I saw it was the corporal driver of the Ferret. He flashed a nervously apologetic smile at me – like he hadn't noticed I was a Redcap – then ran off after the pyjama-clad subaltern already struggling to open the now-horizontal offside cab door of the blazing truck. I followed a bit less enthusiastically, trying to rub six aching places at once.

It took the two of us to haul the young officer away from the wrecked and twisted cab. White twists of skin stripped from the palms of his hands still hung from the red-hot door handle as we dragged him, sobbing with delayed agony, to the shelter of the Ferret. Like he'd said: jolly exciting.

I went back again but only 'cause the image made me. I'd known it was useless even before levering myself up beside the smoking, still-spinning front wheel. The door's Plexiglas had caved in and, as I looked down into the inferno where the anonymous RCT conscript was still dying, a lick of fire stroked me almost gently across the face. I fell backwards carrying an image of a black-huddled monkey-like thing still moving spasmodically within a cocoon of orange and blue swirling flame.

. . . Then someone started shooting again and I hurled myself back under the comforting bulk of the armoured vehicle.

Most of the firing had died down by the time I'd decided to forgo the dubious hospitality offered by the Armoured Corps, and settled for crawling back to the provost duty room on my hands and knees instead.

The window had imploded under a burst of fire that had also brought most of the ceiling to floor level. Davidson, looking doubly pallid what with the plaster dust and everything, crouched behind the purely psychological shelter of his desk, revolver in one hand and telephone in the other. I looked at the clock, which had so far survived. It told me it was 0442 hours. I checked to make sure the red second hand hadn't stopped, but it hadn't. It suggested that less than twenty minutes had passed since the first burst chased me across the parade ground, which was a bit demoralizing 'cause I thought we'd been at war all bloody day, the way I felt.

Davidson swung round jumpily when he heard me and waved the big Webley in a most aggressive manner. I hastily shot up a restraining hand while he shouted into the phone, 'Here's Staff Walker now . . . well, go FIND the bloody Major, you stupid bastard! Tell 'im all the duty men are over at the arms store . . . I don't give a monkey's, Lance Corporal – jus' you get off of your fat arse and get lookin' for 'im at the DOUBLE!'

'Talking to Tosh?' I divined.

He slammed the phone down and waved the revolver at me again. 'You coulda got your fuckin' head blown off, Staff.'

'Next time I'll have my secretary ring for an appointment. And anyway, I was in the safest place, Davidson. You'd've missed.'

I stayed on my knees and reached up gingerly to where my own service revolver hung in its webbing holster. Being a soldier highly trained and lowly paid to kill people, I really *had* to get into the habit of carrying it. Buckling the white-blancoed belt around my waist, I felt a little more secure. Then I remembered Acting Lance Corporal Tosh's minor oversight in forgetting to load *his* bloody gun before he went looking for an enemy, and drew the Webley and Scott as an afterthought. Flicking the chamber open I made doubly sure six shiny brass cartridge heads winked up at me.

We both ducked involuntarily as a stray round scored a supersonic groove along the wall to precipitate a further snowstorm of atomized plaster onto the duty desk – probably a friendly British bullet any-bloody-way. Particularly as this was the RMP guard room, and impossible-to-prove targets of opportunity don't arise for disgruntled squaddies every day.

Acting on the principle that lightning never strikes twice in the same place, I elbow-crawled over to join Davidson, then sat panting with my back against the desk. It must've been one of the last shots fired because after that a shocked hush fell over the camp.

We eyed each other uncertainly.

'You'd better get over to the arms store,' I said. 'See if the CO's there. If he is, ask him to come here soon he can get away. Right?'

Davidson nodded dubiously as I yanked a Sten from the rack and shoved it at him while unlocking the ready use ammo cupboard. He stuffed four mags into his pockets and slammed a full clip into the weapon. Yanking the cocking handle back he walked – somewhat overcautiously, I thought – over to the door. Standing prudently behind him, I peered over his shoulder. It was light enough to make out detail now and we watched as a long black column of smoke rose vertically from the still-flaming three-tonner over by the regimental office. A bit farther away the cookhouse had included itself in the menu for today, and was grilling nicely. I wondered if they'd managed to get Cook Corporal Donovan's body out before the place erupted. Glanced back to the cluster of men around the burning truck, I saw that the Ferret had moved carnivorously on, and hoped the pyjama-clad subaltern hadn't damaged his hands too badly . . . which reminded me of the flame-encased, still convulsing monkey-thing, and suddenly I didn't resent missing out on bacon and eggs for breakfast.

A platoon of Lancashires moved briskly past at the double, rifles held loosely at the trail. I scanned the strained faces to see if I could recognize Parrish but he wasn't with them. Lighting another full strength, I stepped back into the room after Corporal Davidson moved off. To be honest, I was worried about Charlie. He'd have been dead unchuffed to have survived the last lot, only to terminate his service engagement with a terrorist's bullet hole providing the full stop to his medal ribbons.

I needn't have worried. Ten minutes later the door slammed back on its hinges, and Charlie Parrish arrived.

Though it wasn't so much Charlie arriving first, as the prisoner he was escorting.

The little guy shot into the room like a human cannonball before smashing into the wall on the opposite side with a

76

thump that made me wince. Most of the plaster that was left fell off and lodged in the oil-matted hair of my unexpected visitor. I surveyed the high-speed arrival with interest as Charlie followed in rather more leisurely fashion.

He was around thirty years old – the prisoner; not Charlie. Dark surly eyes glared at me like a trapped animal, which he was, come to that. Blood from a deep gash above one eyebrow dripped onto pseudo-commando black trousers and jersey. His face had been camouflage-blackened too, looked like charcoal had been used, in preparation for the hit-and-run attack they'd just completed although, in his case, the running part had seemingly been overtaken by events and a Lee-Enfield rifle butt. I wondered if he'd been the bloke who'd tried to ventilate me with the Schmeisser and, more successfully, to cook the cook corporal.

'Mornin', Charlie,' I said. 'What you got there, then?'

Parrish looked a bit breathless, I thought: not at all like me, fit as a butcher's dog seeing I tended to spend a lot of my working days lying flat out like one. Spatters of earth clung to his battledress as though he'd been taking cover under a bush, which he probably had under the circumstances. Dragging his beret off he stuffed it into an ammo pocket, then ran dirty fingers through tousled hair before finishing up with a bout of violent scratching.

'Suppose you'd call 'im an undesirable alien, mate. Part of the shower that come through the wire after the Bangalore went off. One of my C-platoon sentries copped it, though . . .' He walked over and prodded the little man spitefully in the chest with the muzzle of his rifle. 'Who done it, Greasy – you, or one of your muckers?'

The Cypriot flattened himself against the wall, eyes liquid black and big as those of a frightened calf. He could still draw on a reserve of courage nevertheless because, without warning, he spat right in Charlie Parrish's face. Charlie stood there a long moment while the mucus slithered down his cheek, simply sizing the guy up without any expression at all. When he did react, he moved so quick I hardly saw it happen.

Reversing his rifle, he drove the butt viciously into the

prisoner's midriff. The bloke screamed in agony and buckled to his knees, arms clutched tight across his middle. Parrish drew his foot back but I shouted just in time, 'EASY there, Charlie! Not on provost property.'

He glanced at me a bit bolshie then, before shrugging and lowering the weapon. I stepped over and looked down at the detainee while Parrish slowly wiped his face with the back of a hand. I stubbed the retching man none too kindly with the toe of my boot. 'We got the Mad Major comin' over in a few minutes, Zorba. He'll be keen to have a nice chat with you, soon as he's filled his little rubber hose with sand and put his Gestapo suit on.'

'Bastard,' Charlie ground, with feeling.

'He is too. You and me enjoy ale and women. Steadman gets his rocks off hurtin' people.'

'I mean them – those EOKA. That sentry, Bill? Eighteen years old, he was. Only called up last month. They slit his bloody throat from ear to ear. *Eighteen* for Chri— Bastards!'

I retorted, largely for the benefit of the prisoner. 'He don't know what a bastard is, Colour Sar'nt Parrish: not till he's met the Major. You ever had your fingers broken one by one with pliers, lad? Or your teeth cut out of your gums with a razorblade?'

The little feller paled considerably at that, which gave away the fact he spoke English. I felt a twinge of sympathy: it didn't leave him much to plan his immediate future on. Anyway, I'd started feeling a bit queasy as well by that time, just thinking about it. And *I* knew I was only kidding about Steadman.

I think?

The black-and-white minstrel at our feet forced a defiant sneer. 'Your officer like you, huh? Fuggin' English Nazi.'

I stuck my face as near to his as the stench of garlic would allow. 'You watch your mouth, Greasy. Call the Major a fuckin' Scots Nazi if you feel so inclined, but not English. He's a regular nationalist, like you lot.'

The guy was a battler, if nothing else. Being short of a machine gun he hawked and spat at us again with ideologically committed hatred. This time Charlie took it in much better humour. Just smiled back amiably and wagged an admonishing finger.

'Now that's not a nice thing to do, is it?' he said reasonably. 'That's a *very* unpleasant habit, that is.'

. . . Then kicked the prisoner full in the face! The man's head smashed back against the wall and as it rebounded I could see where his skull had left a concave indentation in the only bit of green distempered plaster left.

I gazed at him with shocked concern as he lay whimpering on the floor. I couldn't just ignore the incident and do nothing – not with his nose shattered and lip split open like that, and me a responsible Redcap senior rank. Suddenly I had the solution and, crossing to the duty desk, grabbed a couple of wads of blotting paper and hastily shoved them under the Cypriot's head. I mean, have *you* ever tried to remove bloodstains from pristine, white-scrubbed wooden planking?

Then, despite my clearly signalled concern, Parrish went and put the boot in for a second time.

'Bloody cut it OUT!' I yelled, stooping irritably to shift the blotting paper over a bit. 'Has he been searched yet?'

Charlie shook his head, feeling a bit better.

'Questioned him at all?'

'Sounded Greek to me, mate.'

I heaved the semiconscious prisoner over on his stomach while Parrish moved to stand over him, legs straddled. He screwed the muzzle of his rifle hard into the soft flesh at the base of the now-bloodied skull while I cautiously spread the man's arm and legs till he lay, face down, splayed like a tide-abandoned starfish. He was too far gone to stand him straddle-legged against the wall, although searching potentially violent suspects that way is generally more prudent: they've no balance, and any intended move is telegraphed a long time before it happens.

'I could shoot the little bastard now,' Charlie volunteered helpfully. 'Save you gettin' your hands dirty, you being a staff sergeant and a pretend Redcap and everything.'

'Not on my floor, you won't,' I retorted hastily, not quite certain if *he* was saying that for the terrorist's benefit too, or meaning it.

Apart from the occasional shouted command and the revving of a truck engine, everything was still quiet outside. If you listened carefully you could just catch the hum of a Coventry Climax fire pump from the direction of the burning cookhouse and a dog barking in the distance. Running my hands up the man's legs, I felt distastefully around his crotch then patted him all the way up his well-muscled torso. He was clean . . . well, as far as weapons were concerned anyway.

I'd emptied his pockets and was examining my intelligence haul – a pack of Wrigley's gum, an old Famagusta to Nicosia bus ticket and two rounds of what looked like Czechoslovakian SMG ammo – when Steadman arrived.

Rising stiffly, I stamped briefly to attention as he surveyed the spread-eagled Cypriot, all the while measuredly tapping the seam of his khaki-trousered leg with his officer's bamboo cane. Apart from a few smears of soot on one sleeve he looked as languidly immaculate as ever.

Even his smile was most pleasant. 'Good morning, gentlemen. I see you have a guest.'

Parrish deferred to the pleasantries only to the extent of straightening his back fractionally. We responded in chorus. 'Yessir!'

The Major sauntered over and gazed down, chewing a pensive lip. It was the first time Charlie had the pleasure of making Steadman's acquaintance, and I could tell he was surreptitiously weighing him up. But there was something else there, too: a kind of . . .? I dunno – some intangible bond that gave me cause to feel a bit apprehensive for the prisoner. Parrish had lost one of his young lads, and had never been reticent when it came to the rough stuff. I wondered uneasily if the EOKA man wouldn't have been better advised to let himself get shot at the wire and taken the easy way out.

Then I shrugged inwardly. You can always fall back on the Nuremberg defence, Walker, and the soldier's obeisance to 'orders', I thought. I wasn't in charge. The Major carried the rank, and therefore the responsibility. Didn't he?

It was shaping to get nasty, though: I could sense it in the air.

The CO's eyes flickered as he saw the blood-soaked blotting paper then took in the shiny smears on the patch of wall plaster above: especially the indentation where the Cypriot's skull had been slammed against it, and . . .?

. . . and ohhhh, *shit*!

I suddenly felt sick as I realized that Charlie Parrish had unwittingly landed me right in it.

A detainee, given over to the custody of the Royal Military Police, subsequently suffers a serious assault? Clear evidence exists, quite literally in the shape of the injured man's skull, to prove that said assault took place in an RMP holding area . . . only that time the Nuremberg defence, however tenuous, placed *me* square in the frame! *I'd* been the senior – in fact, the only – RMP man present during the incident.

So Steadman had me. Bang to rights! I was finished. Just as he'd promised I would be.

. . . And then, dammit, the unpredictability of the man caught me unawares yet again when the Major's mouth just twitched a bit at the corners, and the scar crinkled faintly. 'I see you've been making him comfortable, Staff Sergeant Walker?'

The image made me grin tightly. Either that, or windy pains did.

'As a baby in its cot, sir.'

'Anything on him – his ID? Anything that might indicate the names of his associates?'

I encompassed the pathetic few things on the table. 'Negative, apart from that lot. Otherwise he's clean.'

The aquiline nose wrinkled distastefully. 'Figuratively speaking.'

I grinned again, more confidently. 'Yessir, he does stink a bit at that.'

The penetrating blue eyes flickered to rest enquiringly on Charlie, still massaging the back of the prisoner's neck with the rifle foresight. Parrish gazed steadily back, almost like he was accepting a challenge to enter one of those staring contests we used to play in school, then lifted his chin fractionally in response to the unspoken question. 'Colour Sar'nt Parrish, sir. Lancashires.'

Almost imperceptibly that something – I still couldn't identify exactly what it was – but that curious affinity appeared to pass between them again. I can't describe it better than that. Maybe a mutual consensus: a rapport . . .? All I know is that I suddenly felt I was being sidelined: that I was excluded from the mental net.

But then, I hadn't just lost one of my baby-faced National Service kids to an assassin's blade, and had already witnessed how the rage was burning Parrish up inside.

That's when I really began to feel concern for my friend. Drop his guard, permit himself to think, even for one moment, that they had anything in common, and Charlie Parrish was entering the big league. With Steadman, I mean.

Because Charlie didn't possess the crazy guile, and certainly not the rank, to compete.

Six

The Cypriot groaned and tried to lift his head. Parrish shoved a bit harder and the damaged face went down into the gore-soaked blotting paper again. Steadman produced a gold-embossed Benson and Hedges pack and lit one without offering them round. Not that we expected him to; other ranks were only assumed to smoke Woodbines or roll-ups anyway.

He blew a reflective trail of smoke. 'Did he give anything away at all when apprehended, Colour Sergeant Parrish?'

'No, sir. Not much of a conversationalist, sir.'

Steadman moved closer and Charlie stepped back a pace, grudgingly withdrawing the rifle. Beads of fear-sweat glistened in the detainee's short black hair as the Major prodded gently between the man's shoulder blades with his cane. He sounded almost regretful at inflicting such inconvenience.

'What is your name, please?'

Charlie looked a bit disappointed. His service-conditioned image of us Redcaps had taken a step back. Probably he'd assumed any proper professional sadist in RMP would come up with a more imaginative prelude to the interrogation, like a stirrup pump inserted in the rectum. But there was plenty of time, and anyway, the stirrup pumps were all in use right then.

The split lips moved with difficulty. 'Fuggin' Scotch bastard.'

I glanced guiltily at Charlie as Steadman raised a quizzical eyebrow. 'Wrong answer – though their intelligence is damn accurate.'

Then his expression suddenly hardened and I was unpleasantly reminded of his fleeting changes of mood on that night in the Range Rover. 'I will ask you once more – what is your *name*?'

No response. The yellow cane began to tap, tap . . . tap again with metronomic precision against one snowy-white gaiter. Give him something, I silently urged the little guy. For Christ's sake, give him *something* to take the heat off!

When the man's head did come up it was as defiantly as ever: blood and mucus mingling with boot polish and sweat. 'Fuggin' *scarfaced* Scotch bastard!'

There was silence for a very long moment. I remember thinking anxiously, *Oh, dear. Ohhhh dear, oh dear . . .* while tensing for the explosion but, typically contrary, the Major didn't appear offended in the slightest. Just inverted his cane reflectively, and traced the seventeen-year-old wound that had already triggered the death of a child. I'd swear he even smiled a little. Or his mouth did, at least.

. . . Before he stepped forward and, ever so deliberately, placed the steel-rimmed heel piece of his right boot on the prisoner's outstretched right hand. He was very precise about it: selecting the point where five fingers conjoined with the dirty palm.

Following which meticulous action, Steadman then raised his other foot clear of the floor.

And pivoted!

The Cypriot's middle finger came off clean, having provided the fulcrum for a size nine-and-a-half British Army-issue guillotine. I had no concept of the pressure exerted by the full weight of a thirteen-stone male swivelling on his heel, but I did recall the pain when a slightly built slip of a lass in stiletto heels once stepped back on my leather-protected foot on a crowded bus. And inwardly I gagged.

Outwardly I just feigned stony-faced tough, conscious of Charlie watching covertly for my reaction. Even he looked stunned – or did he? He was bitter enough, certainly hard enough, to have done it himself if he'd thought he could get away with it, so maybe he was only seeking a pointer to RMP etiquette. The view from which window should we take in, presumably? During what he, in common with the rest of the bloody army, knew for a *fact* was standard practice for us Redcaps when pressed to fill our cells quota? His lead should come from me: it was my factory, my environment, and I should have acted there and then.

. . . Only there was no *and*. I let Charlie down in that shocked moment, as well as myself. I *didn't* give him a guide to how he should respond when, with cold premeditation, a military police major amputates a suspect's body part. Instead of protesting, I actually found myself observing the whimpering gunman with detached interest once I'd got my initial revulsion under control. I even started to feel a bit pleased in fact, because, whatever happened from now on, Major Eric K. Steadman, RMP, MM, had made his first and last mistake: he'd sawn his own branch off on the wrong side without any help from me, and this time there were *two* witnesses: both senior non-commissioned officers, and a prisoner's severed finger as Exhibit A. Even without Parrish's evidence, I'd got him off my back for good. I'd see Steadman put away where he could never, ever pose a threat to Walker's future again.

Closing my eyes momentarily I recalled the Mad Major's previous atrocity on the mountain. And hoped that perhaps, just perhaps, a child's spirit would rest a little more easily too, in the knowledge that there was, indeed, some balance to the scales of justice.

I opened them damn quick again when the whimpering prisoner became a screaming prisoner: screaming just like Foxie had done before he . . .?

Jesus!

Steadman hadn't stopped. He was still grinding away with his steel-capped heel, crushing the man's hand. But he wasn't without expression now: merely without feeling. The scar had turned rage-purple, and the look in his eyes terrifying: trancelike.

'Your name? Tell me your *name*! What . . . is . . . your . . . NAME?'

'Kondoyiannis . . . !' the little guy stopped shrieking long enough to blurt. 'Stavros Kondoyiannis!'

Then went back to screaming, while the Major carried on

grinding. *Jesus!* I began to panic – looked appealing at Charlie for support but he continued to stand there feet apart and rifle still levelled at the prisoner, the only sign of tension betrayed by a slight chewing movement of his jawbone under the ear.

When blood, bright crimson blood, blood the colour of Jasmine and Petal's lipstick, began to spurt from under the Cypriot's remaining fingernails, I couldn't sanction such brutality any longer. Apprehensive even then of Steadman's possible reaction, I placed a tentative hand on the Major's shoulder. The last time we'd shared such rank-inappropriate intimacy had been in a limestone cave on top of a mountain.

'Major?' I shook the shoulder firmly. 'Major *Steadman*, sir!'

It took quite a long time, before he finally blinked and looked dazedly at me – and probably seemed a bloody sight longer than that for the poor wretch on the floor who, by then, had subsided into crooning animal-like whimpers. But at least this time he didn't disappoint. This time his response *was* predictable.

The Major lifted his boot sharply before, swinging round, he struck my restraining hand from his shoulder. The scar changed colour from purple to a deathly white as his cheeks suffused and his pent-up hatred for me flooded out.

'Take your filthy hands *off* me, Walker – get them OFF, damn you!'

I drew back, shaken. 'Sir, you were going to . . .'

Steadman's voice rose to a shriek and I caught a glimpse of Charlie Parrish gaping white-faced: his normally stoic features frozen in incredulity.

'Shut your fucking MOUTH, Staff Sar'nt, or by *God* I'll bloody crucify you!'

Stamping to attention, I riveted my eyes on the line of bullet holes decorating the far wall of the room. The MoD standard-issue portrait of Her Majesty the Queen still hung with true British pluck, albeit slightly askew. Her Royal Highness now wore a terrorist's bullet hole right through her forehead. I remember hoping Steadman wouldn't notice and get any ideas.

'SAH!' I bellowed, rigidly erect but, at the same time, mentally giving thanks for the fact that Charlie had allowed the muzzle of his rifle to swing casually across the Major's back. As I said, Charlie was no powder puff, either.

Steadman swung abruptly, suddenly conscious of Charlie's scrutiny, but Charlie just stared stone-faced back. His rifle deflected slightly, but only very slightly: the challenge had been issued. The Major saw it, hesitated, then permitted a faint smile of acknowledgement for a self-elected opponent as unscrupulously hard as himself.

'Colour Sergeant Parrish, isn't it?'

'Yessir, Parrish. With a double R.'

Steadman looked at me pointedly, then switched back to Charlie. 'And can *you* carry out orders when given, Parrish?'

Charlie hesitated. I knew he was trying to ensure he wouldn't say anything to land me in it, but the Major was a major, when all was said and done.

'Yessir,' he answered cautiously.

The terrorist, Kondoyiannis, began to move slightly, starting to come round again. His mutilated hand slowly withdrew from its late, already maggot-white finger, leaving a thin trail of blood soaking steadily into my previously bulled floor. Steadman stubbed him sharply with the gleaming toe of his boot and the man tried unsuccessfully to roll away in his twilight of terror. Charlie stopped him, though. He rammed the .303 into the nape of the man's neck again, and the little terrorist froze. Trapped between the two soldiers he'd found himself in a dead end with no way out. It sounded familiar.

'Strip him,' Steadman said.

Charlie blinked. 'Naked, sir?'

'Down to the buff, Colour Sarn't: not even a jock strap.' Steadman smiled jovially, the chameleon had changed colour yet again. 'Especially not a jock strap.'

I shuffled uncertainly. I could – I *should* – have walked out there and then: gone straight to the APM and laid my complaint. Whatever game Steadman intended to play next, it wasn't one I proposed to be a part of, although he'd already conveyed the distinct impression I wasn't even getting dealt a hand. But I still had Charlie bloody Parrish and his big mouth to worry about. He'd been more or less offered an excuse to get out, but he hadn't taken it. Like I said, he should've listened to his own advice about staying well clear of Steadman.

I kept glancing appealingly at the door, willing someone else to knock and enter. O'Feely preferably, or Davidson: even Acting Lance Corporal Tosh – may God forgive me for wishing such terrible misfortune upon myself – and break it up.

Fortunately Steadman himself came to my rescue: helped me find a solution to my quandary. Or to put it another way, the spider decided I was gumming up the web, and prepared to evict me.

'Staff Walker,' he purred, placid as a mill pond again, and deceptively polite. 'Would you please be good enough to go and find the Fusiliers adjutant? Give him my compliments and ask if he wouldn't mind stepping over. But not too quickly, eh?'

Charlie looked up sharply at that, and I could see he'd been caught with his pants down already – well, with the prisoner's pants down in actual fact, seeing he was just dragging them off the unconscious terrorist, Kondoyiannis having passed out again either from pain or fear. But no doubt the CO had an antidote for everything, even a senseless mind.

I made a last attempt to remain as close protection for my mate. 'I'll phone over, sir. The duty room shouldn't be left unattended—'

Steadman stepped close to me then. I could see his knuckles gripping white around the cane. When he spoke his voice was hard and low, every syllable spat as if frozen in ice. 'But it won't be unattended, will it, you bloody fool?'

The scar tightened: purple tissue over a throbbing wound. 'When I give you an order, Walker, you will obey it without question, and at once. Do you underSTAND me, Staff Sergeant?'

My heels crashed together again. Like jackboots. 'SAH!'

'Then – get *out*!'

Dragging my cap savagely down over my eyes I saluted,

about turned, marched out into the now blinding early morning sun. The last image I carried with me was of a set-faced Parrish dragging the jersey off over a bloodied, mangled hand. It promised to be a terrible day for terrorists.

Forty-five minutes later Charlie was in the cells. It was a terrible day for colour sergeants, too.

Seven

The summary inquiry took place a few days later. The Assistant Provost Marshal conducted it himself. Lieutenant Colonel Philip Slake, MC, MM, Royal Military Police: referred to covertly by the Corps officers as Fillet Steak and, even less affectionately by other ranks, as Bull's Bum.

In my jaundiced view, Slake was the best leader you could ever hope to have your enemy serve under. I should know; he'd been my section commander in the sandy days of '42 and I'd often thought that, had I been taken POW, I would have been persecuted by a much nicer class of officer in the Afrika Korps.

Charlie Parrish didn't stand a snowball's chance in hell, right from the start. Oh, not through any fault of the inquiry, or the manner by which Slake conducted it. Whatever my personal opinion of the APM, both he, and the army, went to some pains to get at the real truth of the matter. It wasn't any reflection on them that the wrong conclusions were drawn from the evidence presented, or from Steadman's statement, or the medical officer's damning indictment.

Mind you, the Cypriot prisoner could have proved key to altering their perception of what had actually taken place in that duty room on the morning of the attack. Stavros Kondoyiannis would have been the best person to – in a manner of speaking – finger his persecutor.

But they didn't consider much would be gained by citing Kondoyiannis as a witness.

Largely because he was dead.

The Colonel had convened his inquiry in accordance with the elementary principles laid down by the Judges of the

90

Queen's Bench Division in what are known, predictably, as the Judges' Rules: the first of which states: *When a police officer is endeavouring to discover the author of a crime, there is no objection to his putting questions in respect thereof to any person or persons, whether suspected or not, from whom he thinks useful information can be obtained.*

In short, Bull's Bum considered the quickest way forward would be to set up a rolling interview with every such person or persons with useful information, in order to decide whether or not to recommend Charlie be court-martialled and, if so, what charges should be pursued. It was an open secret he'd been told that the Provost Marshal's office wanted the whole incident done, dusted and swept under the carpet soon as possible. That Redcap personnel had been involved, and that They Who Controlled RMP Career Officer Advancements weren't at all happy about it.

The first witness called was the camp regimental surgeon, who testified that the injuries sustained by the late Stavros Kondoyiannis, EOKA Terrorist Retired, were comprehensive, most comprehensive, and furthermore that – damningly for Charlie – most, if not all, appeared to have arisen from systematic and deliberate assault upon the victim's person . . . or, in plain language: torture.

Seemingly the prisoner had ended up with fractures of the skull, clavicle, nose, both cheekbones, two ribs and three fingers excluding the one he'd mislaid on my duty room floor. His genitalia hadn't been overlooked for said systematic treatment either, while, in a revelation that caused me more than a passing twinge of unease, his face also *did suffer severe wounding: evidencing deep lacerations and impact lesions consistent with the application to his person of a boot or similar instrument.*

Fortunately for Parrish, the surgeon also testified to the fact that the injuries, while grievous, had not been considered life-threatening, and confirmed that one terrorist had finally left the camp en route to British Military Hospital, Cyprus, in a still-alive condition, albeit more kicked than kicking. But at least that meant Charlie was spared a murder charge.

The next witnesses were the still-shaken RAMC driver and attendant medic of the military ambulance which had been ambushed less than a quarter of a mile from the camp gates. They told of a burst of anonymous gunfire that had ripped through the Red Cross target-marker on the side of the mercy vehicle, and how said gunfire had persuaded the unhappy Stavros to finally abandon his quest for clean white sheets and morphine-aided relief on account of his having absorbed eight British SMG parabellum rounds.

I had wondered where the Major had disappeared to for nearly three-quarters of an hour that morning. Only during the inquiry did I discover that so did everyone else I'd assumed he was with at the time – *they'd* all been under the distinct impression he'd been with me! Ultimately it was Acting Lance Corporal Tosh who'd provided Steadman with an unshakeable alibi: swore blind he'd 'bin spoken to by the CO within the camp area during the critical time-frame, your warship sah!'. Call me a cynic, but the Board didn't know Tosh. If I'd been questioning the fat maggot he'd've finished up confirming with equal conviction he'd also chatted to Napoleon, Julius Caesar an' Rupert the Bear hand-in-hand with Minnie Mouse, at around that same time.

Mind you, I accept it couldn't have been him – Steadman, I mean: not Tosh – who did the ambulance job, because that night both the BBC World Service and British Forces Radio Cyprus said reliable sources close to the Ministry of Defence had revealed it was EOKA again and nothing to do with the British Army: implying that Stavros had been taken out to prevent him from spilling the beans on their terror network – EOKA's, this time: not the British Army's.

Either way, the hit on the mercy vehicle represented a set-back. I was pretty unchuffed – OK, not as unchuffed as Kondoyiannis, seeing he was the one who got shot – but still very disenchanted by it nevertheless. Apart from Charlie in the cells, whose credibility was automatically in question with him being the accused, the dead Cypriot had been the only bloke present in the duty room who could have confirmed that Staff Sergeant Walker had never . . .

well, hardly ever, touched him. That I'd been an absolute gem, who just happened to wear the wrong colour of cap cover.

After hearing the medics' evidence, the three officers constituting the Inquiry Board adjourned for lunch in the officers' mess. At precisely fourteen hundred plus one brandy and two pink gins later, Bull's Bum and Co. arrived back accompanied by a newcomer to the Inquisition: a young RMP captain called Timms.

Now Timms worried me a bit. No doubt he worried Slake even more. He looked a pretty tough cookie, and it was generally rumoured he'd been flown in from London to keep a watching brief on Slake's inquiry at the instigation of the Adjutant General himself who, in a Redcap's bible, ranks one crossed baton higher than God.

The Colonel, however, was an adversary to be reckoned with, make no mistake about it. Don't let my personal prejudice fool you in thinking he wasn't. Any man who rises to half-colonel in the British Army, and certainly in provost, can be nothing less than a ruthlessly dedicated soldier. Slake had both of those attributes in spades but, whether by design or stupidity, he'd acquired an unfortunate image too, a Colonel Blimpish veneer which positively smacked of bigotry and plain boorishness to lesser onlookers, although, on reflection, having served under him through shit, shot and shell I'm being overly charitable. Far as I'm concerned, the bloody man's veneer went right through to the sap. Bull's Bum was, and always would be, bigoted and boorish.

But equally, he was a political animal. Army-wise enough not only to appreciate the sensitivity of the proceedings but also to be aware, first and foremost, of the need to protect his own flank. He would have been acutely mindful that the alleged assault took place on military police premises within his own patch, arguably under military police responsibility for the victim's safe holding and, most contentiously, immediately following a visit to the duty room by the self-same military police officer who had subsequently processed the charges against Fusilier Colour Sergeant Charles Parrish.

93

While I think he did sincerely believe that Charlie's arrest had been justified on the basis of the prima-facie evidence, Lieutenant Colonel Slake would have been equally aware that heads, particularly his, were liable to fall if the Kondoyiannis affair wasn't put to bed discreetly, and that nothing contentious – like the officially sanctioned torturing of terrorist suspects – was allowed to surface that might embarrass the British government should the world press pick up on it.

. . . And *that* was where sensitive got doubly sensitive. Where the APM's judicial ice got thinner and thinner.

Because he knew damn well the world press *would* pick up on it. While he'd so far managed to contain the incident largely within the army family, families can fall out with each other. The RMP, RAMC and Lancashire Fusiliers each had a vested interest in protecting themselves from criticism, while leaks to the press by aggrieved officers determined to defend their own, weren't unheard of. Add to that equation the near certainty of some pro-Greek Unionist whistle-blower in Cyprus CID picking up a phone, and the APM courted treble trouble. Were he to allow one snowflake of suspicion to rest on his Corps's tailored shoulders without absolute justification or, conversely, turn the screws too tight on the Lancashires' reputation by sanctioning Charlie's martyrdom without a scrupulously fair hearing, then Bull's Bum would be well advised to order his bowler hat as the torture of Stavros Kondoyiannis blew into the biggest politico-military scandal since the Frogs mishandled the Dreyfus Affair.

But he'd have handled it. Handling sensitive Redcaps-versus-the-rest-of-the British Army issues was what he did.

Well, he would have done. If Fusilier Colour Sergeant Charles *Parrish* hadn't gone and rocked his boat.

Certainly the first of the several charges against Charlie was relatively straightforward. In isolation, it wouldn't even have been considered a prosecutable disciplinary matter. All said and done, we'd been reacting in a defensive role, and we were the British not the Salvation Army. If we opted to play football with an enemy's head rather than shoot a hole through it, that wasn't an atrocity: it was an act of compassion.

So Charge One was really down to deciding if premeditation had been a factor. Whether the prisoner's face did suffer severe wounding, evidencing deep lacerations and impact lesions consistent with the application to his person of a boot or similar instrument in the heat of battle – or at a later time, as the result of a deliberate and gratuitous assault by Fusilier Colour Sergeant Parrish?

Charlie hadn't even bothered to deny he dunnit. In fact he'd freely admitted to putting the boot into Kondoyiannis: defiantly insisting that said action had properly reflected the use of reasonable and necessary force on his part to subdue a violent hostile who'd already been at least complicit in, if not directly responsible for, the murder of his sentry.

Good one, Charlie, I'd thought when I heard that. A little stretching of the truth by me and you might just get away with that porkie. And I was happy to stretch the truth thin as cat gut if I had to. Especially when it was the only injury sustained by the Cypriot detainee that still threatened to place me, Walker RMP, between a rock and a hard place – or more accurately, between Charlie's ammunition boot and a plaster wall.

I say *still threatened* because there was also the Case of the Amputated Finger to be considered by the Board, and in that regard I'd become very much indebted to my closest friend. Nuremberg defence or not, Charlie could have landed me right in it by revealing I'd also been present in the duty room when Steadman had committed his act of sheer barbarism, but he didn't. He was in trouble enough, and had obviously figured the odd severed digit here and there wasn't going to make any difference to the outcome. So to protect me, he'd selflessly developed amnesia about the precise sequence of that particular atrocity.

OK, supporting him by massaging the truth wasn't much of a quid pro quo, but I was limited in what else I could do to repay Charlie. The rest of the charges listed, I couldn't help him with. They were irrefutable: the ones destined to put Parrish away, and the bloody idiot *had* given the prisoner a savage kicking, all said and done. The proof was plain for Bull's Bum and his Board to consider in depth before they recommended a court martial prior to banging him up where the media can't hear and the sun only shines between bars – the fractures, the lacerations, the abuse of parts private. They'd even produced Stavros's finger, lying somewhat macabrely in an RAMC glass Petri dish on the table, labelled *Exhibit Baker* . . . or was that *bravo* now?

Obviously all down to Charlie's account: an open-and-shut case judged solely on the prima-facie evidence. Parrish had been caught blood-red-handed while, as far as the Board knew, no one in RMP had spoken with the prisoner prior to the Lancashires adjutant's arrival on the scene, other than to politely ask for his name and address.

But *that's* where Fusilier Colour Sergeant Parrish begged to differ: had really gone and upset the army's apple cart and thus, by definition, Slake's. Because according to Charlie's sworn statement, Kondoyiannis had *already* been interviewed before Captain Blacklock arrived at the duty room accompanied by me. Even more apple-cart-upsetting – that he'd not only been questioned, but had been questioned at length *and* by a senior officer of the Royal Military Police, at that.

Worse: Charlie was doggedly continuing to insist that the most serious injuries suffered by the little Cypriot had been inflicted *during*, NOT following, said period of questioning and, most damningly of all – that they hadn't been inflicted by him, Colour Parrish, anyway, but by the Redcap officer himself!

One Major Eric K. Steadman, MM: a decorated war hero with an impeccable record of service.

A ludicrous defence, obviously. But potentially, political dynamite.

Eight

Ludicrous or not, therein lay the quandary of Lieutenant Colonel Philip Slake. How to defuse Charlie's counter-allegation, then hang Charlie out to dry after giving him an eminently fair hearing.

In fact the only fortunate aspect for Bull's Bum was that the unhappy Stavros had subsequently suffered his collision with eight SMG rounds. It meant that while the ambulance hit muddied the quest for hard witness evidence, Kondoyiannis had, at least, been prevented from opening his big Greek-sympathetic mouth to the Cypriot media. In fact, that ambush was so convenient for everybody except Charlie that I resolved to check whether the APM himself had a boiler-plate alibi for that morning.

Come to that, the mysterious Captain Timms hovering in the background couldn't have been helping Slake's post-lunch digestion either. Big Flea being watched by Bigger Flea's Littler Flea? I knew the feeling well.

Anyway, at 1407 hours, after an impressive display of Important Paper shuffling followed by a concise if grudging résumé of the morning's evidence for Timms' benefit, the star witness for the prosecution was called.

Steadman marched the length of the room looking as immaculate as ever, halting to within a hair's breadth of the regulation three paces from the table before saluting with the faintly familiar ease that establishes that the person receiving the courtesy is, after all, only one pip higher in the pecking order. Colonel Slake nodded pleasantly, but I found it interesting that Timms merely surveyed Steadman with a noncommittal expression.

97

Bull's Bum waved what I'd long learned to recognize as a deceptively friendly hand. I'd seen it produce confessions more effectively than a priest with a loaded rubber truncheon.

'Please be seated should you so wish, Eric.'

It occurred to me it would be interesting to see if he called Charlie, Charlie, and invited *him* to sit down when it came to his turn on the rack. Our elegant CO wasn't, however, falling for the invitation to drop his guard, and relaxed only as far as the *at ease* posture; thereby managing to imply by disapproval that the whole thing was a complete waste of bloody time and why the hell didn't the Board simply accept the charges against Parrish as being already proven enough to justify Charlie's being banged up 'cause he, Steadman, had formulated them himself.

Slake ignored the intended message: the smile on the face of the tiger. 'An unfortunate necessity this, Eric. I'm sure you'll agree.'

Eric stared bleakly at a vanishing point some three inches above Slake's head. 'No, Colonel, I do not.'

'You don't?' The APM's bushy eyebrows climbed to merge with his hairline. 'Then please explain why you don't agree – Eric.'

'Because, sir, I consider that dealing with the actions of an allegedly over-zealous infantry NCO should remain within the routine scope of day-to-day policing. Notwithstanding this particular incident involved serious assault on a local civilian, I fail to see why it should be considered more contentious than any other crimes of violence suspected to have been committed by army personnel.'

Slake frowned. This was hardly the attitude he'd antici-pated. Steadman had Charlie Parrish's counter-allegation to refute, yet his tone was one of criticism rather than penitence. Caution here, Blimp – good old Eric was no junior subaltern. Half-colonels don't push majors around. Not unless they're dead certain of their facts, and the facts weren't clear yet.

'Then perhaps, Major,' he retorted sharply, noticeably dropping the *Eric*, 'you would care to place that reservation on record now. Before we turn to a detailed examination of the charges against Colour Sergeant Parrish.'

A good reply, that. To a pro-provost reader of the inquiry transcript it would read as though the Colonel was anxious to have all possible grounds for objection documented while, on the other hand, a Fusiliers' champion might figure the APM for a jolly fair bloke committed to exploring every avenue which might lead to Charlie's absolution. Either way, no one in the media would be able to make head nor tail of it.

Steadman nodded, unperturbed. 'Affirmative, sir. And with respect, let it be further recorded that, in my view, the fact that this inquiry has been convened at all implies a lack of confidence in my personal integrity.'

Bull's Bum leaned forward over the table, too old a campaigner to be hit twice by the same cannonball. 'Your objections are duly noted, Major Steadman. I would, however, draw your attention to the fact that this inquiry does not constitute a court martial, and that an appearance before it does not, in any way, carry implication of complicity, nor does it make any suggestion that the individuals called before it are called for any reason other than to further the cause of justice. I would draw your attention to Judges' Rule One, with which I am sure you are familiar?'

Steadman nodded bleak assent: he'd made his point and could afford to be magnanimous. 'While you will no doubt appreciate, Colonel Slake, that, as commanding officer, my concern must be to ensure that no undeserved discredit should fall upon 368 Provost Company.'

'Just as this Board will ensure that none shall, Major,' Slake assured him most gravely, albeit with as much warmth as a bottle of liquid oxygen. Before adding the sting in the tail. 'Unless, of course, such discredit proves not to be undeserved – but merited.'

If the ability to talk was to be the deciding factor then Charlie, never strong on the thespian skills, was as well staying right where he was. In the cells. I reflected on the result of my own attempt to turn defence into attack on that crazy night in the Rover, and wondered morosely why everything seemed to work better for majors.

'To continue, then,' growled the Colonel, obviously

irritated by that minor skirmish. 'A few points I wish to raise in connection with your deposition.'

He rustled through his papers until he found the document in question. As he held it up for Steadman's identification I half-expected its originator's signature to read *Hans Christian Andersen*. 'This is your formal statement, Major? Good! Now, in it you say that you left the duty room only minutes after your staff sergeant . . . ah – Walker, is it?'

Steadman nodded. 'Yes, sir.'

Walker is it, nothin'! Bull's Bum knew my name *bloody* well. Had never forgotten it since I'd declined his demand to hand over my case of Scotch at Tobruk. I claimed it'd got blown up by the German Army, but he'd discovered too late I'd been keeping it to ingratiate myself with field officers only. Slake had been a mere subaltern then. The second case, the one he never found out about, I'd ferreted away for the Afrika Korps: Walker's bargaining tool for quality treatment if the beseiged city fell.

'And you remained outside until Walker returned with the Fusilier adjutant, Captain Blacklock?'

'I did.'

'Forgive me, Major, but I fail to see why you felt it necessary to vacate your own duty room at that time?'

The CO allowed one hand to drift momentarily to caress the scar. 'I thought it politic.'

'In what way politic?'

'I considered that the detainee, Kondoyiannis, was still a Fusiliers' responsibility. While the regulations require all prisoners to be handed over to the Royal Military Police at the earliest possible time, no due process had been commenced at that point, no committal receipt issued. I felt, therefore, that in view of the grave charges the man would undoubtedly face, the informal presence of RMP personnel might have compromised future court proceedings. That is why I sent Staff Sergeant Walker to find Captain Blacklock, and why I then left the prisoner in the custody of an apparently capable infantry senior NCO.'

Nicely stated, Major. Almost credible. But it suited Slake's book.

100

'So you acted as you did to pre-empt any legal defence being mounted on the basis that the suspect had been questioned by provost before being formally committed and cautioned?'

'I felt it advisable that interrogation should be conducted at a later time, in the presence of a Joint Services Interrogation Unit officer, and strictly according to the laid-down rules of procedure – yes.'

Round Two to Steadman. I yearned for the good old days of 1241, when the feared first Sergeant of the Peace, the William of Cassingham, accompanied by his retinue of tipstaves, hangmen and priests, dealt out rough and ready punishment to all who contravened the military code. They didn't need rules of procedure then. Just a staunch yeoman head-banger called Parrish and a handy tree branch.

Mind you, the William probably had a few Toshes in his mob, too. And a lot more useful than mine. If nothing else, at least ye firste Redcap Tosh could've provided them with someone to practise on.

Bull's Bum turned, grudgingly paternal, to the young Adjutant General's nominee. 'Do you wish to put any questions at this juncture, Captain Timms?'

'You have greater experience in this field than I, sir,' Timms demurred politely. 'Perhaps I may be permitted to clarify points as they arise?'

A nice discreet rejoinder. Captain Timms would go far in the diplomatic service, never mind the army. Steadman eyed him warily, all the same. It seemed we all suspected there was more to the mysterious supernumerary than a neat knack of indicating respect without subservience.

'Very well.' The AMP cleared his throat. 'Then, when did you first see the prisoner Kondoyiannis, Major?'

'When I entered the duty room. At approximately 0530 hours on the morning of the attack.'

'And who was present at that time?'

'Colour Sergeant Parrish and Staff Sergeant Walker. It's in my statement before you.'

Bull's Bum leaned forward and pretended to study the paper a moment, though we all knew damn well he could've recited it by heart. 'And did the prisoner exhibit any signs of injury when you entered?'

I started to sweat, then. Questions like that, and Walker's kit was about to head for the glasshouse. Along with Private Walker. The mere fact that I'd been present while Charlie had been kicking seven bells out of the little Cypriot, but hadn't managed to prevent it, was in itself an indictment. I looked wistfully at the way out. Steadman had made a promise to me on the day the child died on the mountain. Now Slake was offering him his chance on a plate, to fulfil it.

But Steadman conceded only a wintry smile. 'The fighting had been short but fierce, Colonel. It naturally followed that any attacker would have suffered some marks and contusions.'

He was playing with me, the bastard. My collar became uncomfortably tight just then.

Captain Timms craned forward a little at that point, listening intently as Bull's Bum continued with some asperity. 'Perhaps you would elaborate, Major. Precisely *what* marks and contusions were evident when you first entered the duty room?'

How long have you got, Slake? I thought gloomily, recalling how I'd packed blotting paper around the little Cypriot's head to absorb the blood from his shattered nose and lips, and resolved to be a much kinder, more caring person. To put people before floorboards in future. Not that I anticipated much of a future: not after Steadman finally said his piece.

'The prisoner had minor abrasions, presumably caused when he crawled through the wire. His clothing was torn and dirty, as were the uniforms of the NCOs. He had sustained a serious laceration to his forehead, which was bleeding profusely. You will, however, find statements before you to the effect that this wound was observed by three other Fusiliers prior to Colour Sergeant Parrish having escorted Kondoyiannis to the provost duty room.'

'According to the evidence given by the camp surgeon, he'd also been kicked in the face, Major: a kick which fractured his nose and both cheekbones. Yet you refer only to a serious laceration.'

Steadman hesitated then, preparing himself for the kill. This was where Walker and the image separated for ever: the image to the mists of Corps mythology and Walker to the obscurity of the military prison service. Yet when he did answer, it was almost dismissively.

'Kondoyiannis's features were masked by blood, Colonel. The man had obviously suffered violent trauma to the head but I am neither a medical officer, nor did I approach him closely enough to determine what type, or how many separate injuries he received.'

I couldn't believe my ears. If anything I worried more. Steadman certainly wasn't perjuring himself for my benefit: he was crazy but not that crazy. He'd've been a lot happier to see me playing first substitute for Charlie down in the cells, and I couldn't figure why he appeared to be letting me off such a fortuitously offered hook.

'Yet you preferred a separate charge, Charge One, against Colour Sergeant Parrish, alleging premeditated assault solely in respect of the full-face injuries?'

'Parrish has freely admitted to kicking Kondoyiannis.'

'But not to having kicked him with malice aforethought, Major. Parrish admits only to having used reasonable and necessary force to subdue a violent prisoner.'

'In view of the medical officer's later report, I considered that fine difference a matter for the court to decide. He has since given a written opinion that Kondoyiannis's facial injuries had been caused by two or more blows, probably administered subsequent to the laceration. Only then does the question of premeditation arise. I felt it appropriate to list it separately on the charge sheet, confident that you will weigh each count against Colour Sergeant Parrish with forensic scrupulousness, Colonel. That any charge the Board considers unsustainable if brought before court martial will be dropped.'

'And you were, of course, correct in that assumption.' Slake hesitated then, obviously uncomfortable with what he was about to raise. 'We must now turn to the charges concerning those other injuries inflicted on Kondoyiannis's person, Major Steadman: some of them grievous. You are obviously, ah . . . familiar with Colour Sergeant Parrish's statement?'

'Given under caution to Sergeant O'Feely and Corporal Davidson, RMP, in the presence of Captain Blacklock, the Fusiliers adjutant – yes, Colonel, I am.'

'Then you will be aware that, in it, Parrish makes . . .' Slake frowned ferociously, searching for just the right, non-contentious phrase for the record. 'Makes a counter-allegation, Major. Effectively establishing grounds for what, under Scots law, might be described as a defence of incrimination?'

If he'd anticipated dramatic denial, he was doomed to disappointment. Straining to catch the CO's reply, I noticed Timms following closely too. But Steadman merely shrugged. If indifference were an art form, he would have qualified for an Oscar.

'I'm aware of Parrish's claim that it was I – not he – who tortured the prisoner and, during the course of that torture, amputated his finger.'

Well, *that* was certainly grabbing the bull by the horns, Major. Or perhaps more aptly – the Bull by the Bum.

Slake obviously thought so, too, judging by the way his eyebrows climbed aboard the escalator again. 'That is all you have to say, Major?'

'That is all.'

'Your sole response to an extremely grave and, one would think, most disturbing allegation?'

'I've been a military policeman for nearly twenty years. I've lost count of the number of soldiers I have arrested who subsequently proclaimed their innocence. To paraphrase your earlier comment, Colonel Slake: under barrack-room law it is generally described as a defence of fit-up – particularly useful when there's no witness to the crime.'

The Colonel's satisfaction was evident: a perfectly sound counter to an obviously ludicrous smear. One more potentially embarrassing diversion safely navigated without drifting on to the rocks of contention. We were all Redcaps:

we'd all been there as a matter of course. It was down to credibility, the word of a senior military police officer against Charlie's. And so far even the evidence supported Steadman's version. It wasn't hard to judge which way a court martial would swing, if convened.

'Then to recapitulate, Major Steadman. You are prepared to swear under oath that before you left the duty room, you noted no signs of injury to the prisoner other than those you previously described?'

For the very first time, Steadman afforded me a fleeting, almost taunting glance. 'I noted no other injuries, Colonel.'

'Then one happy outcome appears to have surfaced already from this inquiry.' Bull's Bum stared sourly over at me: the concession must have been anathema to him. 'That the character of Staff Sergeant Walker remains untarnished as ever.'

I got the point. Excrement also rises to the surface: it was impossible to miss the sarcastic innuendo, but by then I was too preoccupied to give a monkey's. It hadn't taken long to figure exactly why Untarnished Walker was being allowed to carry on polishing his pristine image.

The Mad Major was playing psychological poker with me again, just as he'd done that night in the Land Rover. Recklessly throwing the gauntlet down, and enjoying every moment of it. Never mind my raising the mountain incident, or even backing Charlie's counter-claim that he himself had amputated Stavros's finger.

Steadman, a hundred times cuter than I, realized he *couldn't* land me in it for having stood by while Charlie gave Stavros a kicking, without giving the lie to his own sworn statement that he, Steadman, had left the duty room immediately after me. No MP, not even one thick as Tosh, would have risked leaving a prisoner alone with another soldier, not even with another Redcap, once he'd been given cause to suspect that individual had already assaulted the detainee.

And then an even nastier consequence began to take shape. Steadman had hung *me* out to dry – he'd placed *me* squarely in the frame as being the only witness who could either corroborate or refute his story. He was offering me Hobson's Choice. Either I confirmed he'd had no reason to suspect that the prisoner would be left at risk in Parrish's custody – or I admitted to having turned a blind eye to Charlie's gratuitous assault while simultaneously booking myself an extended stay in one of Her Majesty's Military Detention and Corrective Centres.

And they welcome disgraced Redcaps in the glasshouse. They even guarantee them extra-special special treatment.

'If I may put a question, Colonel?'

Captain Timms had interrupted my soul-searching reverie. When he spoke, his tone was smooth as the homing run of a barracuda. 'Major Steadman. You said the duty room was left unattended by RMP personnel while you waited outside for Captain Blacklock?'

Steadman stared back, flint-chip icy. 'I did *not* say the duty room was left unattended, Captain. Colour Sergeant Parrish was still there.'

'With respect, I was careful to specify *unattended by RMP personnel*, sir. As Colour Parrish is an infantryman, did you not consider, immediately following a terrorist attack on the camp, that closer control over military police personnel via the facility of the duty room would have been desirable?'

'It would have been desirable, Captain, to have avoided the raid at all. I will only reiterate that I considered Kondoyiannis still to be a Fusiliers' prisoner. You might also bear in mind that a state of uncertainty still existed within the camp area. I judged it more prudent to allow the suspect to remain where he was, rather than risk exposing him to an EOKA attempt at rescue.'

Timms gazed steadily back. 'Or assassination?'

A momentary hesitation, then Steadman opened his mouth to retort but the Colonel hastily leaned forward to insert his authority. 'I believe Major Steadman has already explained his reasons for leaving the duty room to the satisfaction of this Board. The murder of Kondoyiannis while in the care of the Royal Army Medical Corps and outside the camp lines is not within the remit of these proceedings.'

Nice one, Colonel, I thought. Now you've brought the RAMC into the frame of responsibility as well. No more was said about the ambulance hit, but I felt myself warm towards the Adjutant General's young representative.

Pity he was an officer.

After some probing regarding the disposition of 368 Provost Company's other duty personnel prior to the alert, Bull's Bum frowned at his watch. 'We have more interviews to conduct, gentlemen, and time is pressing. Can I take it we have no further questions to put to Major Steadman?'

Timms seemed happy to misunderstand Slake's pointed message. 'I have one, Colonel. With your permission?'

The APM nodded irritable assent. He had all the right answers on the record already, and it was hardly supportive of young Timms to throw a spanner in the provost works. Dammit, the chap *was* a fellow Redcap after all. No one denies that justice must be served, but let's get on with it so's we can shoot the blasted Fusilier soon as possible.

Timms looked contrite. 'My apologies for keeping you from other duties, Major. I would, however, like to return briefly to the matter of the prisoner having suffered the loss of a finger.'

Steadman nodded. Very warily indeed. 'The production before you, Exhibit Bravo. It was retrieved while the man was moved to the ambulance . . . and before you ask, Timms – yes, the medical officer did confirm it to be Kondoyiannis's left middle finger.'

Timms examined the sad human fragment with keen interest, chasing it round the Petri dish with his pencil. 'This one?'

Bull's Bum looked choleric. 'Good grief, man, how many fin . . . !'

Oddly, Timms failed to hear him. 'Setting aside Colour Sergeant Parrish's counter-accusation alleging your own complicity—'

'Major Steadman has already firmly refuted that version, Captain,' Slake snapped warningly. 'At least to the current satisfaction of this Board.'

Always the politician. Always the self-serving reservation.

Always the sting in the tail. Steadman must have picked up on it too, and felt less comfortable as a result.

'Do you have *any* knowledge, sir,' Timms continued doggedly, 'of how the amputation might have come about? What form of implement, for instance, might have been used to such drastic effect?'

'None,' Steadman shrugged, dangerously placid. Like a swimming pond choked with weed. 'I suggest that question would be more fruitfully directed at Colour Sergeant Parrish, Captain.'

'Thank you for your advice, sir. I intend to.'

'Yes, well, I think that covers everything,' Slake interjected hastily before further tiresome friction could arise. 'Which only leaves the Board to thank you, Eric, for—'

'With respect, sir,' Timms said levelly. 'I haven't quite finished.'

Steadman was not at all pleased, you could see it in his eyes, in the strained set of his jaw. The APM wasn't hellish delighted either come to that, but there wasn't a lot he could do other than glare at the captain. Not too intimidatingly, though – the Adjutant General might come to hear of it.

'Then finish, Captain!' he grated.

Timms didn't look at all intimidated. Instead he casually extracted a buff MoD folder from his briefcase and held it for the Board to see.

'I have here the pathologist's report on the body of the deceased prisoner, Kondoyiannis . . .'

'Be advised, Timms, that we have already heard the medical evidence,' Bull's Bum growled dangerously. 'This Board does *not* intend to retread old ground.'

'With respect, Colonel, I referred to this as being a pathologist's report. The post-mortem report. So far the Board has only heard evidence from the camp medical officer. That evidence related to the prisoner's condition when still in the duty room, and still alive. This file contains the more recent findings of Major Robert Kemp, RAMC.'

'And who the blazes is Major Robert Kemp, RAMC?'

'A forensic-pathology specialist flown in to BMH Cyprus following the ambulance ambush, to perform a post-mortem

108

on Kondoyiannis. He did so at the direct request of the Army Surgeon General's office.'

Slake's expression revealed a mix of disconcertion, anger – and dawning unease. 'Then why was my office not informed, Captain?'

'Perhaps because informing you at this stage was not considered relevant, Colonel. In fact I would refer you to your own summary of this inquiry's brief.' Timms riffled through his own notes. 'Your precise words were, I believe: *the murder of Kondoyiannis while in the care of the Royal Army Medical Corps is not within the remit of these proceedings*?'

RMP, one: RAMC, one. Military families again. Always guarding their own backs. Always bloody falling out with each other.

'Ohhhh, get *on* with it, man!' Grandpa Redcap fulminated.

'Thank you, sir. Then with regard to the loss of the middle finger of the left hand, Major Kemp states – I quote: *by virtue of the crush injuries adjacent to the point of severance, it is concluded that amputation was caused by the sustained pressure of a heavy, probably metal, object – possibly the steel-capped rim of a boot heel – rather than a sharp incisive blow.*'

Timms stopped reading to meet the Major's frown head-on. 'Would you agree that a steel heel cap could have caused such a wound, Major Steadman?'

The scar was beginning to suffuse: become a violent purple slash. 'I've already suggested you address that question to the man who did it. Colour Sergeant Parrish.'

Timms raised what I suspected was a most carefully contrived eyebrow. 'I'm sorry, sir. I understood Parrish has only been *accused*, so far. Is it not contrary to the presumption of innocence to claim his certain responsibility for the wounding before the Board has heard his version of events?'

That did it. Steadman erupted. I watched open-mouthed, conscious only of a sense of déjà vu.

'You *impertinent* little man! How DARE you lecture me on bloody presumption? If Parrish didn't do it, then who the fuck ARE you implying was responsib—'

109

'Major STEADMAN!'

Timms didn't even flinch: just sat looking at the Major with that politely earnest expression as if seeking the sage advice of a much respected elder. Steadman swallowed, still battling for control as Slake picked his words with great care.

'I'm sure, Major, that Captain Timms intended no implication. I must, however, confess to some curiosity myself as to why he insists on pressing a point which the medical officer may be best qualified to answer. Perhaps you would care to take this Board into your confidence, Captain?'

Timms kept his eyes fixed on Steadman. 'Of course, Colonel. In essence, the RMP scene-of-crime report makes no mention of any weapon being found in the duty room that might have been heavy enough, and sharp enough, to conform with the specification suggested by the pathologist's findings. Certainly no object remotely answering such a description was found to bear traces of blood. In fact, sir, disregarding the expected arterial sprays and spotting common to most serious assaults, and the considerable volume of blood noted in close proximity of the by then unconscious prisoner, the only evidence of blood transfer was found on Colour Sergeant Parrish's rifle butt, and on the toecaps and undersoles of his boots.'

'Well, there you have it, surely?' Bull's Bum seized on the solution with such evident relief that even Steadman, with typical perversity, allowed the faintest suspicion of amusement to light the tense expression. 'It must have been the heel of Parrish's boot, Captain. Standing on one leg, one can apply quite a sustained pressure, y'know.'

He warmed to his theory, even pushed his chair back to wave his legs in the air: Colonel Blimp riding an imaginary bicycle. 'Field boots do indeed have a steel insert . . . under here, see? Left foot, right foot – obviously the culprits, eh?'

I glanced urgently at Steadman to check if he was panicking as much as me, but if he was he didn't show it. He seemed to have forgotten his earlier outburst: simply following the Colonel's gymnastics with as keen an interest as the rest of us.

Bull's Bum collapsed, looking pleased with himself while Timms nodded, impressed. 'As you so convincingly demonstrate, Colonel, such a conclusion would appear extremely probable.'

'A racing damn certainty, in my book,' Slake beamed before adding hastily, 'While bearing in mind, of course, Colour Sergeant Parrish's continuing right to the presumption of innocence.'

'. . . but not possible,' Timms added.

Slake's expression converted from self-congratulation to disconcertion. So near yet so far . . . damn, damn, *damn* the blighter's persistence!

'Not possible, you say?'

'Im-possible, sir.'

When Bull's Bum finally came to terms with his frustration, it was with a weary acceptance of the inevitable. 'Can I assume you are about to tell us why not, Captain Timms?'

'Because Colour Sergeant Parrish wasn't *wearing* field boots, sir. On the morning of the attack, he was wearing ammunition boots.'

'*Shit!*' the Colonel exploded in a most un-colonel-like way.

Shit, he's right at that, I thought, in a most self-serving way. I even remembered staring critically at them when Charlie'd hoisted them aboard the table that time with Pedal and Jas-whatever. Ammunition boots. Specifically manufactured for the military with compo soles, not metal-studded leather which carries the risk of generating sparks when handling live explosive. Parrish had always favoured them although, technically, they were improper dress for infantry. Claimed they were more comfortable, and gripped better. Either way, the rubberized heel-piece of an ammo boot couldn't guillotine a man's finger. Give it a nasty squeeze maybe, but that's about all.

Bloody *boots* again! Foxie's, Charlie's, Steadman's, O'Feely's . . . shiny boots, dusty boots, blood-stained boots. Always there as the focus of my nightmares.

'So you see, Colonel,' Timms ventured without a flicker of a smile, 'it gets curiouser and curiouser, as Alice said.'

111

Yeah, right, I thought. Except she was in Wonderland when she said it. Then I reflected on the weeks since I'd met Steadman, and decided Timms wasn't too far off the mark. Come to that, Slake was beginning to look less like Colonel Blimp and more like an *Alice* character himself. '*Contrariwise*,' said Tweedledee, '*if it were so, it might be; and if it were so, it would be: but as it isn't, it ain't. That's logic.*'

'I have, however,' young Timms continued, holding out one scrap of consolation, 'ascertained from Major Kemp that detailed forensic analysis of a heel piece might, possibly, lead to the identification of individual characteristics matching those of the amputated finger.'

Slake gathered himself with an effort. 'Then who *was* wearing field boots with steel heel pieces on that morning? Or are you about to produce a list of them as well, Timms?'

'No, sir. Since my arrival this morning I have had neither the opportunity nor the authority to make enquiries within this provost formation. That must be a matter for you to instruct.'

'You have your authority, Captain. Make your recommendation.'

'Firstly, sir, to impound, for forensic examination, the footwear worn by all personnel who entered the duty room both during and immediately following the alert. I include in that category the CMO, his medical and ambulance staff, Captain Blacklock the Fusiliers adjutant and any members of 368 Company later called to attend the incident.'

'You hear, Major Steadman?'

'Yes, sir.'

'Then make it so.'

'. . . As well as the boots worn by Staff Sergeant Walker.' Timms again. He kept more stings in his tail than Bull's Bum. 'And by Major Steadman.'

By then I was desperately trying to remember if I knew any of the disciplinary staffies at the detention barracks and, even more pressingly, if I had anything on them.

'Ah,' the Colonel muttered uncomfortably, while I guessed it wasn't the inclusion of my name on Timms's most-wanted list making him uneasy. Jolly delicate business this: fellow officer and all that. And a Redcap to boot, to, ah . . . coin a phrase?

When Slake did decide how to handle the issue, it was more a command than a request. 'You have no objection, Major? Obviously a question of exclusion from the list of suspects in your own interest, and useful in view of your previously stated concerns.'

For a moment, Timms continued to observe Steadman with the certainty of one who knew the trap was sprung, but the CO simply returned his stare with icy equanimity. I waited for him to erupt again, wishing with sick expectation that I was anywhere but where I was. Even being back up the mountain alone with Foxie would have been infinitely preferable to this nerve-racking wait for a lunatic's mental disintegration.

I should have realized, of course: the Major didn't do predictable. All he actually did was to switch his gaze back to Slake, the scar crinkling in regretful mockery.

'No objection Colonel: but difficult to arrange in practice. My duties later that morning required me to attend the burned-out cookhouse. The debris was still smouldering in places. My boots . . .?'

Steadman looked really embarrassed.

'Returned to the QM stores yesterday, Colonel. For destruction and replacement.'

Nine

Brasses and whistle-chain sparkling: belt and gaiters whiter than fresh snow. Smartly up to the desk as if attending the Queen's Birthday Parade. Heels smashing together – *Hattennnnn*-SHUN! . . . ! *Hup* . . . two, three! *Down* . . . two, thuree! I saluted with such energy that my right arm nearly popped out of its socket then stared unblinkingly at the regulation spot three inches above the APM's head, elbows thrust rigidly into my sides, thumbs extended arrow-straight down the seams of razor-creased BD trousers.

The stage was set. Walker presenting his most impressive Backbone of the British Army image for inspection.

Bull's Bum inspected. And wasn't impressed. After top-to-toeing me, he simply sniffed: managing to imply that even the need to speak my name was causing him severe distress.

'Staff Sergeant Walker,' he advised the Board distastefully.

'SAH!'

The Colonel winced. 'Dammit, Walker, be reminded you're not drilling an intake at Inkerman Barracks. Please contain your replies to a volume appropriate to normal conversation.'

'SAH!' I yelled again, before my brain caught up with my mouth. Only Timms's intervention saved me from the further Wrath of Blimp.

'With your permission, Colonel?' he offered helpfully.

'Grrrruff!' the Colonel retorted.

Timms took that as a yes. 'Good afternoon, Staff. You may stand easy.'

'Sir,' I whispered.

'Speak UP, man!' the Colonel snapped.

'According to your statement, you were present in the duty room on two occasions. Before, and shortly after, the prisoner was allegedly assaulted?'

'Yessir.'

'Major Steadman has already told the Board he asked you to go in search of the Fusiliers adjutant. You would agree that was the case?'

If screamin' *Get OUT!* was asking, then, yeah – he asked me.

'Yessir.'

'And how long did it take you to find Captain Blacklock and return?'

''Bout three-quarters of an hour, sir.'

'So what time would that have been? Say, when you got back to the duty room with the Adjutant?'

'Approximately 0630 hours, sir. I didn't leave till around quarter-to.'

He nodded and looked pensive. 'So it follows you're unable to offer any evidence regarding the events that occurred in the duty room during that crucial period?'

'No, sir.'

At least this time I could tell the truth without landing myself, or anyone else, in it. My self-indulgent virtuosity wasn't to be permitted to last long.

'You are aware that Colour Sergeant Parrish freely admits to kicking Kondoyiannis in the face?'

'I am, sir.'

'*Twice?*'

Pay-back time, Charlie: after this you're on your own. I kept my voice level. 'Wasn't counting, sir. The duty room had been targeted by SMG fire. I was concentrating on trying to avoid tripping over debris while moving forward to help restrain a violently agitated prisoner.'

'Very well,' Timms acknowledged, straight-faced. 'Colour Sergeant Parrish further concedes he may have unwittingly applied the butt of his rifle to the area of the detainee's midriff. Did you, perhaps, witness that occurrence, Staff Sergeant – or were you still engaged in tripping over?'

'As I said, sir: it all happened too fast to be specific.'

'Damn fortunate there aren't stairs in the duty room, what?' Slake broke in caustically. 'Otherwise the chap could have tripped on *them*, too, without Walker noticing.'

It was a malicious implication. Falling down stairs is a well-documented phenomenon unique to constabulary premises and, particularly, military guard rooms. Lots of times I'd seen bolshie squaddies seriously hurt falling down stairs: even in guard rooms that didn't have any. But as I've said previously, this was only the first count against Charlie. Few, other than Steadman, would have considered the charge even worth pursuing, in light of the then prevailing situation.

Timms turned enquiringly to the Colonel, but either Bull's Bum was content to leave it to him, or he simply couldn't bring himself to speak to me. Timms gave a barely perceptible shrug, and continued. 'In your own words, Staff Sergeant Walker, would you describe precisely what you saw, and heard, prior to and immediately following your arrival back at the duty room?'

My back was beginning to ache. It had never been right since Foxie had flown with me on the mountain. Even standing easy was standing hard, aggravated by the strain of being under scrutiny. 'It is in my statement, sir.'

The Captain jerked his chin encouragingly. 'If you would indulge the Board, Staff?'

I gave up trying to avoid the question, and forced my mind to drift back to the moment when I finally tracked down the smoke-blackened Fusiliers adjutant, Captain Blacklock.

I'd eventually found him grimly inspecting the bullet-pocked arms store. I remembered trying to avoid looking too closely at a shredded body huddled close against the still-unbreached doorway where the explosion of a grenade had hurled it. The corpse had clambered out of its bunk earlier, sleep-dulled and resentful: just another bloody National Service squaddie detailed to just another interminable guard duty. Now it belonged to a twenty-four-hours of fame, page-nine national hero.

On the way back across the camp we'd passed a second all-too-familiar mound under a grey bloodstained blanket. I hoped the young conscript's mum and dad would be able to draw at least some sad comfort from knowing their boy – now hidden under the prickly wool anonymity of his dual-purpose shroud with throat slashed, mouth gaping fish-like and tortured lungs surfeited with clotting blood – had done his duty for Queen and Country.

Someone had been overly casual in paying their battle-field respects. The eighteen-, never to be nineteen-years-old Fusilier's boots still protruded from under: toecaps rose-tinted by the rising sun. Bloody *boots* again! They really had got to me. We were an army of boots. Boots on parade: boots splintering NAAFI dance floors: boots deployed in bars as drink-fuelled weapons: boots being bulled over and over an' over again till they shone like black bones . . . and boots inverted pathetically under gore-soaked blankets. The kid's hadn't been polished as glass-smooth as Foxie's, though. I didn't needed to lift the blanket edge to tell Charlie Parrish's sentry hadn't been a Redcap.

When we did arrive at the duty room, Steadman was waiting outside for us just as he'd claimed: pacing im-patiently on the low veranda. According to Captain Blacklock's statement he'd appeared perfectly composed, even irritated. I'd seen him in a different light – but then, *I'd* known what to look for. I'd seen the madman mad. If you had cause to view the soul of the Major, you looked beyond the scar-tortured expression: you interrogated his eyes. I did, and my heart sank for Charlie. They were lustre-less, calculating: every bit as dispassionate as when he'd gazed upon the dead child.

His reprimand, harsh across the closing gap, made no concession to our having stopped by various cadavers. 'About time, Captain. You've damn near obliged me to disregard my better judgement and take charge of your own regiment's prisoner myself.'

Blacklock had even conceded a muttered, 'Sorry, sir,' albeit seething with resentment. But immunity from unjustifiable criticism has never been a pre-condition of military service.

Steadman had rehearsed the next part of his alibi well, if that was the way it was. He'd stepped aside to allow

Blacklock and me to mount the veranda before following, thus ensuring we approached the open door of the duty room first.

He didn't have to choreograph our next move – because we didn't make one. We both stopped dead!

Charlie was down on one knee, bending over the obscenity that had earlier been a terrorist called Stavros. It was spread-eagled, starfish-like, on its back. He was struggling to lever the thing into the recovery position before it suffocated on its own blood.

Blacklock choked, *'Jesus!'* then, no doubt to his later chagrin, retched involuntarily at sight of the bubbling red mask that didn't have any recognizable eyes or nose, and barely a hole for a mouth.

Only after he'd completed his task, and probably saved – well, temporarily saved – Kondoyiannis's life, did Charlie look up at us with a look of terrible anger.

'Did Colour Sergeant Parrish say anything at that point?'

Timms's voice, flat and pressing, extracted a memory rather forgotten. I must have stared at him blankly, because he had to repeat the question. 'What did Colour Sergeant Parrish actually say to you, Staff?

I blinked and looked hesitantly at the Colonel. 'Permission to check with my AB466, sir? Just to make sure.'

Slake nodded shortly, still not speaking, so I reached into my breast pocket and pulled out the notebook. I'd taken extra care to record Charlie's first words verbatim 'cause I thought, at the time, they would maybe help him. I couldn't even begin to indicate the horror and revulsion betrayed in his voice, so I just cleared my throat and read flatly from the page.

'Colour Sar'nt Parrish shouted, er . . . "For Christ's sake, you'd better call the medics. That crazy bastard Redcap has beaten this man to a pulp!"'

I swallowed nervously and looked anxiously to see how my evidence was received. Timms was glancing covertly sideways at the Colonel, probably for much the same reason, but Bull's Bum betrayed only well-honed scepticism. I had no illusions. The CO had made his pitch to the gallery earlier. Without corroborating witnesses, it would be Charlie's word against his, and Parrish's counter-claim would be consigned to the filing cabinet holding the protestations of innocence of nearly every soldier in the glasshouse. Slake was a pro, and pro's become justifiably cynical: including me.

'What happened next, Staff Sergeant?'

I didn't need to refer to my notes. It was seared into my memory. 'Major Steadman said, "My God!" A moment later he added, "Staff Sergeant Walker, you will place that soldier under close arrest. The charges to include serious assault and causing grievous bodily harm to a prisoner in his care."'

'Did Colour Sergeant Parrish make any response after Major Steadman had issued that order?'

'Yes, sir.'

'What response?'

'He told the CO to go and . . .' I hesitated then: was I helping Charlie, or helping to destroy him? 'Go an' fuck hisself, sir. He said it was him, the Major, I should be arresting.'

'Did Parrish give any reason for that, on the face of it, extraordinary claim?'

'Yessir. He said he himself had only just stepped back inside the duty room before we arrived. Was quite emphatic about it, sir, as I believe Captain Blacklock will confirm. Insisted that, within minutes of my own earlier departure, Major Steadman had ordered him – Parrish – to also leave and wait outside on the veranda.'

Colonel Slake couldn't contain his frustration any longer: even to the extent of abandoning his resolve not to speak to me directly. 'Dammit, Walker, didn't we just hear you claim that Major *Steadman* had been waiting outside on the veranda when you and Blacklock arrived? Or do you now wish to retract that statement?'

'Yessi . . . *No*, sir! It was definitely the CO who'd been standing outside the duty room at that point.'

'Then explain PROPERLY, man!'

He was being deliberately obtuse: I knew that, and he knew I knew it. He'd already read Charlie's statement – he

119

was as familiar with Parrish's version of events as I was. With the benefit of hindsight, I should've stuffed the Afrika Korps that time at Tobruk, and given Bull's Bum the bloody whisky. But we all back the wrong horse sometimes, and I'd placed my bet on Slake not surviving the war to hound me in the peace: confident in those desert days that even if the Germans didn't shoot him one of us, his own Redcaps, was bound to.

'Yessir. Sorry, sir . . .' I'd have preferred to stick red-hot needles in my eyes rather than concede that apology, but Slake would've only have come up with far worse. Taking a deep breath, I dived in at the deep end.

'Colour Sarn't Parrish alleged, and continued to allege repeatedly, sir, that Major Steadman had only come out to the veranda a matter of two or three minutes before we'd turned up. That the Major had looked shaken and anxious when he did appear, and that his first words were . . . not verbatim, sir, but to the effect that there'd been an accident in the duty room. He had then ordered Colour Sergeant Parrish to go inside and resume guarding the prisoner until help arrived.'

'So for the avoidance of doubt, Walker, you still state quite definitely that Major *Steadman* was the soldier standing outside the duty room? And that Colour Sergeant Parrish, when you first saw him, was inside, bending over the injured man?'

Perhaps foolishly, I let my eyes stray from the vanishing point until they met Slake's head-on. I didn't know what had gone on inside that room for certain, no more than he did, but I did know Charlie Parrish. And I certainly knew . . . I'd seen what atrocities Steadman was capable of committing. If Charlie swore it was the scar-faced Major who'd further beaten the helpless Kondoyiannis, then that was good enough for me.

I replied frankly. A bad idea in the army. 'Yes, sir. But that doesn't necessarily mean . . .'

The Assistant Provost Marshal rose ominously from his chair. Even Timms flinched when the blast finally completed its passage from the soles of the Colonel's brown boots to

120

the open air. 'By GOD, man – do you think I require a *staff* sergeant to prompt me in finding the truth behind this assault? Do you, eh . . . *do* you? You are not here to draw conclusions, Walker: nor are you here to give an opinion. You appear before this Board as a non-commissioned officer of the Royal Military Police, to give unvarnished evidence of fact – NOT to hawk your own pet theories! Do you UNDERSTAND me, Staff Sergeant?'

It would not be immodest to brag that I didn't flinch like the rest of them. But only because I didn't dare to: flinching isn't listed as procedural behaviour in the book which the APM was engaged in throwing at me. All I did was brace already tortured shoulders. 'Saaaah!' I bawled placatingly while nodding violent assent.

'Then, before you risk further prejudicing Colour Sergeant Parrish's case in the eyes of this Board, Walker: you are dismissed.'

This time it was Timms turn to lever the combatants apart. He was a terrier, I had to give him that.

'If I may be permitted to clarify one further point before Walker falls out, Colonel?'

Bull's Bum waved the back of his hand in sulky assent. Had Timms asked if it was OK to drag me screaming from the room to face a firing squad, he'd have made much the same dismissive gesture. Only more enthusiastically.

Even as Timms turned to me, I knew I wasn't going to like the next bit. When it came, it was indeed the sixty-four-thousand-dollar question: the one I'd been praying no one would think to ask directly.

'Staff Sergeant Walker,' he asked, looking at me very, very straight indeed. 'Do you have *any* knowledge whatsoever of how the prisoner, Kondoyiannis, came to lose the middle finger of his left hand?'

So there it was: I'd been given no option but to face up to Steadman's bizarre challenge: the culmination of a disturbed man's compulsion to gamble by placing his own self-destruct button in the hands of his enemies. In retrospect, the signposts that had brought me to this point had all been there.

His casual disregard for the high-level threat from EOKA snipers on the mountain. His executing the child in circumstances which would have led to his immediate arrest had I turned up with even one more soldier, a second pair of eyes, to corroborate that the initial crime scene did not reflect the carefully contrived tableau that met O'Feely's patrol later. And now, his most reckless gamble of all – his mutilating the Cypriot's hand in front of Charlie Parrish and myself: two potentially credible witnesses . . . and then manipulating each of us into the position of having to confirm, or deny, the other's story.

He must have known he would suffer even more than I, because if I chose to tell the truth and went down for it, I'd have nothing more to lose by giving evidence against him for murder. But what the hell – tilt at the devil yet again, Major, because you're mad as a hatter under all that sub-zero perfection. Risk all on whether Staff Walker has the guts to prove himself a constable of principle, or a corrupt Redcap prepared to lie under oath to save his own skin. He'd given me a straight choice. Either I walked away, image untarnished, as Bull's Bum had already sourly conceded – or admitted I'd been there too, when the Cypriot lost his digit.

Come to that, Steadman had offered *Parrish* a choice, too. Charlie did have the option of refusing to leave the prisoner when the Major ordered him to wait outside. He'd known well enough what Steadman intended – let's face it, had probably been only too happy to turn a blind eye at first, feeling as he did about the killing of his young soldier. But once dragged into playing the Mad Major's game, you were damned if you did, and damned if you didn't. Refusing to carry out the order would've put him in jail even faster. The classic Nuremberg quandary.

Yet I still hesitated. Was there *no* way I could help my best mate who'd once saved my life? I didn't have much time. Slake's baleful stare had already focused expectantly on me: Blimp counting down for blast-off number two . . . *Think*, Walker, THINK . . . ! The mist cleared a little as I began to realize that, whichever route I chose, Charlie was still going to do time. The only issue at stake was who had committed the other atrocities, the ones that had occurred in my proven absence, and on the evidence to date, Charlie was odds-on favourite to carry the can for that one.

Oh, the army would give him a fair hearing, for all my cynicism. Beneath all the bluster, Bull's Bum was perceptive. He had his reservations regarding Steadman's complicity – Timms certainly did – but suspicions aren't facts, and every single fact pointed to Charlie Parrish being the Torquemada of the Duty Room. Thanks to the chaos that ensued immediately following the EOKA raid, not one man in the camp had been traced who might have been able to identify which soldier had been waiting on the veranda during the crucial time frame. Even my own statement, corroborated by that of the Fusiliers adjutant, Blacklock, describing how we'd ipso facto caught Parrish in the act, supported the probability of his guilt.

So either way, Charlie was headed for the deep six of detention – and I neither felt the need, nor had the guts, to drown with him. Not even for the somewhat dubious Pyrrhic victory of dragging Steadman down with me.

I braced myself. Looked Timms straight in the eye.

'No, sir,' I said, so clearly that even Slake would find no fault. 'I have no idea as to how the prisoner came to lose his finger . . . *Saaaah!*'

I was right about the torture of Kondoyiannis having threatened to become as much a political as a military hot potato. They didn't throw the book at Charlie as hard as they might have done. The question of how the Cypriot actually had mislaid his finger was never properly resolved, although I suspect the mercy shown by the court was more because they wanted to avoid giving Parrish grounds to appeal against an overly severe sentence. In other words, prevent him from making too many waves from his cell.

They needn't have worried. Charlie, being Charlie, went before his court martial and hardly said a word. I heard it said that even his defending officer had been fit to charge him with dumb insolence by the time it was over. They

123

sentenced him to six months' detention, and reduction to the ranks. Not too bad, considering.

Except that Charlie would rather have been given a death sentence.

I was posted from 368 Provost Company, Cyprus, soon after that. I'm not saying Slake had anything to do with it, but have you any concept of what it's like in the Borneo jungle? Steadman didn't come out of it smelling of roses, either. He went double-quick, too. The Persian Gulf, I heard. That outburst of his at the inquiry finished his career as far as ever making half-colonel went, of course – that, allied with the question still left hanging over Stavros's amputation. I also suspect that Captain Timms fixed him good anyway, when he reported back to the Adjutant General's Office. I always said he was a bloody good officer, young Timms.

So now you know the story of Foxie, the proudest soldier I've ever served with. And the child on the mountain: the little boy who never grew up. And the poor bloody tortured Stavros Kondoyiannis who, after all, had only been a patriot fighting for what he believed in. And of Charlie Parrish, victim of a war hero turned sour.

Oh, talking of Steadman – I did run into him once more even though I'd tried to avoid him. It was just before I left Cyprus when he drew me to one side and spoke quietly, almost conversationally, affording every regard for the courtesies of rank.

He hadn't said much, come to that.

Just . . . 'Walker: you may remember I made you a promise once? I want you to know before you go, Staff Sergeant – I fully intend to carry it out. No matter where you serve, I shall find, and destroy you!'

I was glad I had the image to front for me.

It stopped me blanching until after he'd turned away.

GERMANY, 1967

Ten

Ten years later I was still ruggedly handsome: still driven by the Walker image: still my own worst enemy – and *still* a bloody staff sergeant.

Well, my own worst enemy apart from a half-remembered Redcap major called something-or-other Steadman, that was, and – more currently threatening – the two sick-scared and consequently dangerous Royal Artillery gunners holed up in the house at the end of the long drive, where we'd cornered them after seven weeks of searching.

For the tenth time that night I hauled out my Browning – they'd finally issued me with an automatic to replace my old First World War pattern revolver – and checked the magazine. I had a nasty premonition I might well need it. So far those two squaddies had loosed off at anything that moved. It was still as uncomfortable to wear as the Webley and Scott. So much so, this was the first time I'd even carried a side arm, apart from on manoeuvres and formal duties, since I'd been posted to the British Army of the Rhine three months ago. Personally I remained a sub-machine-gun man myself: you get a lot more output for your trigger squeeze, and you don't have to stay hero-calm when taking aim. Apart from my always having been a lousy marksman, shaking with fear generally proved a positive advantage in helping me hosepipe the target. But the way I saw it, if I *had* to shoot somebody, I was as well making the most efficient job I could. The other guy would have exactly the same idea in his head.

A rogue bullet spanged off the wall above our heads and the German police inspector and myself competed in a keen game of 'see who can squash himself flattest' on the wet

Teutonic pavement. I saw the CO watching us with sardonic amusement from his vantage point behind the stone statue flanking the entrance to the big house, and grinned back sourly as he settled his shoulders more comfortably between the impressively sculptured breasts of the sandstone Fräulein. Not surprising she wore a bored expression like that, I gloomed. She'd probably been straining to hold that bloody flower-trough aloft since before the Kaiser's day.

Incongruously, the statue caused me to think fleetingly of Charlie Parrish. Or not so much of my old mate, as the two scrubbers I'd treated us to that night out in Famagusta, before it all went pear-shaped for Charlie . . . Jasmine and – Pedal, was it? Their awesome breasts had been almost identical to those of the statuesque Fräulein although now, ten years on, the memory of them stirred much the same level of passion in my loins as those of the stony-faced German bird.

Charlie – and Steadman, my Mad Major . . . I'd had several commanding officers since then. Sometimes they went before me, other times I'd been the one posted to another unit and another CO. The army isn't a career for blokes who need permanent friends, but then again, you don't make permanent enemies either. Or not many. Me, I've always been more of an enemy-collector rather than a dewy mist in people's eyes when I've moved on.

All the same, this new CO was about the best I'd ever served under, and that's a compliment to any officer, coming from me. He was an up-and-coming soldier, too: destined for high rank before they discarded him. Hair grey-flecked now, and distinguished-looking, he was also a bloody good copper. It was generally rumoured that the elusive red lieutenant colonel tabs, and an APM's appointment, were round the corner any day.

His name was Timms, by the way. He'd served a spell in Cyprus, too. Since his arrival in BAOR he'd never mentioned the Kondoyiannis affair. Not once.

Christ, I was miserable. Rain dripped steadily from the back of my cap cover to snake insidiously inside the collar of my RMP mac, gradually converting the neck of my shirt to a hairy, khaki-black pulp. I'd begun to shiver uncontrollably in the biting wind while my eyes ached with the constant strain of peering through the gloom. The old house had gone silent again, and I wondered how the girl was, and if she was still alive. I didn't think they would have killed her, or not yet anyway. At the moment she was too useful as a hostage.

They'd probably raped her quite often, though. They were a couple of real vicious nutters, those two: bad soldiers however charitably you viewed their records. Unusual, that. Most of the real headcases went with the ending of National Service and nowadays we're a pretty tough crowd of professionals, in it for a career and not just a job. Even McCafferty and Irvine had been average Royal Artillery gunner privates before they'd got together. OK, maybe a bit bolshie, right enough, but not exceptionally so. Not until the two of them had run right off the rails for no apparent reason we could discover, other than self-gratification.

They're always the worst, the ones who take a sudden turn. Once they realize they've landed themselves right in it, they get scared. Then they'll panic: do anything out of sheer fear and perverted bravado. I once had a hysterical young lance corporal try to slash me with a Stanley blade when forced to apprehend him in front of his platoon mates. A fatherly reprimand had resulted in his spitting a torrent of filth at me for checking him. That had then escalated into refusing to obey a lawful command, to resisting arrest, to attempted assault with an intention to disfigure. His original offence . . .? The top button of his battledress blouse had been undone. I suppose he'd felt he had some kind of image to live up to, as well.

Anyway, Gunners McCafferty and Irvine had been out on the periodic NATO manoeuvres along with every other squaddie in BAOR. Unfortunately their manoeuvring took them past a pretty sixteen-year-old Hanoverian blonde called Herta Weber. It had been a hot day, and Fräulein Herta had been showing all of Herta to the sun at the time.

It may have begun as horseplay, but by the time Herta began screaming, it was too late. Grandad Weber found her naked corpse strapped face-down along a fallen tree trunk, hands and ankles bound together beneath it by webbing belts. He'd also found the British Army bayonet that protruded from within her.

Fortunately for Weber the Elder, he hadn't found her killers. 84769888 Gunner McCafferty J, and 95723341 Gunner Irvine P, along with two Lee-Enfield rifles, one bayonet and some sixty rounds of .303-calibre live ammunition, had gone AWOL.

They couldn't have been entirely stupid, though. They'd been on the run in a foreign country for over six weeks, and travelled nearly eighty miles into our Brigade area, without either the SIB or the German police catching up, which suggested one of them, at least, was a very smart operator. We knew McCafferty had formed an alliance with a Hamburg prostitute he'd then used to pimp around his buddies as a profitable sideline, but she wasn't saying anything: not even after we'd shown her photographs of the late Helga displaying McCafferty's love token. But she'd helped them, all right. With money, if nothing else. She must have done. So maybe she was a sadist, too.

Then just as we thought the trail had gone cold, the call had come in to the local Polizeiwache. Women's screams had been heard emanating from number 41, Kirchofstrasse.

I screwed my eyes to peer at the glowing dial of my watch. Nearly 0230. That made it over half an hour since they'd propelled the hostage's mother through the front door with blood all over her face, to convey their ultimatum. Clear the area within five minutes, they'd demanded, or Fräulein Schliemann gets the same as the Weber girl. And they still had that other bayonet left.

Pulling out a sodden pack of Capstan, I thumbed one free before recalling my situation and pushing it back in disgust. The idiots had been loosing a random shot every few minutes as a warning, like the one that had hit the wall a few moments ago. A military policeman has a binding duty to try and avoid aggravating a suspect and thereby risk increasing the seriousness of the charges against him. Far as I was concerned,

Staff Sergeant Walker had an even more binding duty to look after himself. Lighting a match in pitch darkness when the other bloke has a gun contravenes both rules of conduct. Not that a couple of holes through me would have aggravated things more than they were already . . . apart from for me, of course.

That aside, we couldn't risk letting McCafferty and Irvine know we were still out here anyway because, technically, we weren't. As soon as the traumatized Frau Schliemann had sobbed out her message, Timms and the local Polizeikommissar ordered a hasty withdrawal: whereupon the RMP Rovers and white Kraut Volkswagens pulled out with an impressive display of flashing blue lights and revving engines, while Herr Inspector, the Major and myself – me reluctantly coerced into volunteering as usual by the never-bloody-learn Walker image – remained in ambush.

The snag was, so far the targets hadn't come out to be ambushed.

The Polizeikommissar nudged my arm and pressed a stick of gum into my hand. I smiled wryly, champing gratefully on the spearmint-flavoured wad. Obviously Herr Inspector had stood obbo like this before, denied the opportunity for a smoke. He was an elderly man, heavy-built with nicotine-stained fingers. It was hard to avoid speculating on how his war had gone. Had he, for instance, been driven to chewing gum as a substitute during *his* tenderfoot time as a cop during the Nazi years: waiting patiently for Wehrmacht or Luftwaffe deserters, maybe even the odd runaway Jew, to break cover?

For some inexplicable reason, brooding on other people's wars led me to thinking about Steadman for the first time in months. I'd long ceased feeling unsettled by the memory of our bizarre confrontation in that Limassol alleyway. Ten years is a long time to bear a grudge, and it seemed safe to assume even madmen lose focus on their madness through time. Not that it mattered either way. I'd never meet him again. My army service was nearly up and I'd be on civvie street in a matter of weeks. Curious, how memories fade. Apart from that livid scar, I could hardly recall what Steadman looked like, yet I still remembered the cat on the wall that night as clear as if it were yesterday. That EOKA cat?

Charlie Parrish, though . . . now Charlie was different. I still felt guilty every time I thought about Charlie, which was often. He'd served his time without a murmur, or not openly at least, though I knew he was all churned up inside. Then he'd been RTU'd – returned to unit – as a Fusiliers' private, and a Fusilier he'd stayed. I'd only met him once since, in Hong Kong about two years ago, but hadn't said much to him. I couldn't, really. Not when he was being helped into a holding cell by two Redcap beat men, stinking drunk and covered in vomit. It seemed Charlie was a bad soldier, now.

I shifted unhappily, causing another runnel of rainwater to cascade inside my collar. I had a discomfiting premonition I'd be meeting up with Charlie again shortly: discomfiting because it would probably be in my professional capacity. The Fusiliers had arrived to begin their routine BAOR tour three days ago, and Fusilier Parrish's battalion were barracked less than two miles out of town. Please, Charlie, I thought miserably. I've done enough to you, mate. Don't give me trouble that'll make me put you inside again.

O'Feely wouldn't have been soft like that, but Sergeant O'Feely was dead. The irrepressible whoremaster's number came up stamped on a Russian AK47 round in Aden's Crater district. The customized dum-dum had taken him in the crotch, I heard, and I was glad it killed him outright. O'Feely wouldn't have enjoyed a half-life minus most of his brains.

Corporal Davidson was still in the Corps, but he'd deservedly been promoted to the most important rank of all. He was a staff sergeant too, now: currently holding down a cushy number as PSI to some Territorial outfit back in the UK.

Oh, and Lance Corporal Tosh? I'd run across him, so to speak, while jay-walking on Manchester's Deansgate about three years back. This bloody flash Jaguar braked hard, tooted at me and, when I looked inside, there was Tosh beaming all over his fleshy, stupid face. Did I just say ten years was a long time to bear a grudge? Well, when I first recognized him, I'd decided seven wasn't. But he'd changed: I had to give him that.

Stupid . . .? He'd become a property developer by then, and employed over three hundred men: pretty impressive for a reluctant conscript who hadn't even remembered to load his gun before embarking on a manhunt. He'd insisted on taking me to his place for dinner that night. Big luxury flat, a huge German shepherd that slobbered me with affection, and a pretty wife. They couldn't have been more hospitable. I felt most uncomfortable after that, thinking back on the way O'Feely and I had treated former Provost Lance Corporal Tosh under the shadow of Foxie's spitted corpse. It was a chastening reversal: me looking guilty instead of him . . .

An urgent elbow in my side shattered the reverie. Swallowing my wad of gum in a nervous spasm, I saw Timms's rain-flecked face frowning at me through the gloom. The CO held up a cautious finger, and gestured at the house.

Our targets were on the move at last.

They were smart enough not to exit through the front door, albeit not smart enough to realize the British Army, to say nothing of the local constabulary, wouldn't simply scarper and let them walk free, hostage or not. But then, they didn't have a lot of choice, and it could equally be argued that killing a pretty girl on a summer's day isn't exactly sensible, either. Or anyone on any kind of day, for that matter.

Unfortunately for them, the ground-floor window they'd selected to escape through, the only one affording minimal cover from bushes, was on the same side of the driveway as us. We could still keep tabs on every move they made

A rifle barrel came out first, then a leg, then a shock of cropped red hair followed by the rest of 84769888 Gunner McCafferty J. Cautiously he eased himself down to the flower border under the window then swivelled, weapon presented, in a searching sweep of the area. This kid wasn't taking more chances than he had to. For time number eleven I reached inside my waterproof for the butt of the Browning, feeling little tentacles of fear tighten round my gut. Then shoved the pistol back in its holster, and spat resentfully. Being a

British Army Redcap has its satisfactions. It undoubtedly has disadvantages, too. Being scrupulously sporting is one of them.

Unlike the Yanks, we don't tend to shoot first then answer questions at the inquest. The mere fact that a wanted man is armed doesn't give us licence to engage him with lethal force: not till he's had a square go at us beforehand . . . all that *Gentlemen of the French Guard: fire first* stuff at the Battle of Fontenoy? Bad precedent. On *that* day General Lord Charles bloody Hay wouldn't exactly have been voted most popular field commander of 1745 by his redcoat infantry. Right at this moment I envied the US Army's MPs. The Snowdrops, the GIs call them. Have you ever seen a Yankee Provost patrol on town duties? Usually mob-handed in fours complete with Omo-white steel helmets, Colt .45s, and those long, snowy nightsticks they just need to flick once to break a man's wrist. Then compare our RMP beat men: out there in pairs if you're lucky, protected by a soft scarlet-covered SD cap and armed with a tiny wooden truncheon – a tiny, highly *polished* wooden truncheon, mind you – that can still land you in dead trouble should you even draw it from your side pocket, never mind actually use it. Not unless you have damn good reason to – like, 'The suspect hit me three times with the axe first, sah . . . !' Nor do we carry side arms, by the way. Not as a rule. Not unless we're on active service, or in a crisis like tonight.

McCafferty signalled up at the window and the girl hostage, Sabine Schliemann, came out next. Disturbingly long legs faintly reflected the glow of the street lamps as she was pushed over the sill. When McCafferty hauled her roughly down beside him, I could tell from the awkward way she fell that her hands were bound behind her. There she just knelt, head hanging listlessly, while the other nutter, Irvine, slipped out clutching rifle number two.

They were both wearing civvies which, presumably, had once belonged to old Schliemann. He hadn't been in the house when they broke in, which made the situation a bit easier, though I don't suppose he would have agreed. Seemingly he'd died the previous year. The girl had a leather coat belted tightly around a slim waist and it didn't look as though she'd much on under it. Frau Schliemann said our bold absentees had kept Sabine in a first-floor bedroom since they'd taken over, the day before yesterday. They'd visited her a lot too, in between terrorizing the old lady and absorbing the late Herr Schliemann's schnapps.

I thought: *Ohhhh, fuck it!* and grimly unholstered my shiny new gun one final time. It would be a pleasure and a privilege to carry the can for topping those two truly evil bastards. Fumbling inside my RP coat to ensure the pistol lanyard round my neck wouldn't get snarled, I placed my mouth against the Major's ear to whisper. He listened, then nodded reluctantly: he didn't have much choice. The two gunners and the dazed Sabine had begun to close on us, heading for the drive exit, and would pass our ambush point in a couple of minutes. The way the smaller soldier, Irvine, had his weapon rammed between her shoulder blades meant a frontal challenge was out. The only solution to try and ensure the hostage's safety was the one Walker's image had figured out.

I was glad it was the image, and not the actual me, that thought this one up. It was reckless to the point of being self-endangering, and as you may have gathered, I don't do self-endangering. The real Walker never volunteers on principle: not since the day when, as a boy soldier, my section instructor had casually asked the billet if anyone knew anything about eyes. 'A bit, Corporal,' I'd lied, not because I knew sod-all about anything, but because I'd been an egotistical little prick even in those days, and constantly sought approval. 'Then get doublin' over to the fuckin' cook-house, Walker,' he'd shot straight back, 'an' dig 'em out of the three ton o' spuds they got waiting for you.'

The Inspector helped me slip from my sodden coat and I felt the rain beating on the tailored shoulders of my walking-out dress as I eased stiffly down to my hands and knees. Gripping the Browning nervously, I began crawling ever so gingerly on an interception course with the three figures now moving warily, backs against the house wall, towards us. Being acutely conscious that a man on all fours

135

isn't in the best position to react instantly, I hesitated long enough to slip my cap off so's the badge wouldn't reflect the street lights, then distastefully smeared a couple of handfuls of gluey earth over my face. Only later did it occur to me that my white-blancoed webbing straps must've shown up more bloody clearly than an autobahn accident-warning sign.

I tensed, virtually stopped breathing as they side-shuffled slowly past, so close I could distinguish tangled black strands of hair plastered unheeded across the once pretty features of the hostage. For a moment that vision of a brutalized Madonna seemed to hang, almost ethereal in quality, against the teardrop night sky, then they were gone and moving down the drive to where Timms and my spearmint-scented Polizeikommissar waited beneath the statuesque breasts of the sculpted stone flower girl.

I forced myself to delay a further moment: let them move that bit closer to the ambush point. I wished I didn't have to. I'd begun to tremble, and silently cursed the inner Frankenstein that compelled me to such recklessness.

Then they'd reached the pre-agreed place: it was now or never. I *had* to act!

Springing to my feet, I sucked my gut in – and mustered the loudest parade-ground bellow heard since Stentor was a lad.

'*HATT*ennnnn . . . SHUN!'

Christ knows what kind of fright it must've given them, but it scared the *shit* out've me! In that terrifying moment, I sincerely believed I was about to save them the trouble of shooting me. Gaily-coloured streamers flashed and popped before my eyes as my blood pressure shot up to a hundred and something over whatever; the lanyard I'd rearranged so meticulously managed to tangle itself around the trigger guard of the Browning anyway, while I even forgot to dive for cover in a desperate fight to drag more oxygen into fast-collapsing lungs.

The girl's already strung-out nervous system imploded in sympathy. She let out a piercing shriek while both soldiers lost precious milliseconds in snapping to attention. It was

136

another of those automatic reflexes I was telling you about. Most people who've served in the military will briefly react with much the same conditioned response: halt momentarily in their tracks, feet together, shoulders stiffening . . .

The only flaw in my theory was that one of our target head-bangers hadn't absorbed basic training assiduously enough to be so conveniently conditioned. McCafferty – well, I *think* it was Gunner McCafferty – recovered quick enough to about-turn, present his weapon, and squeeze off one round just before Major Timms shouldered him low behind the knees in a classic flying tackle.

The bullet nicked the lobe of my right ear. Travelling at over two thousand feet per second, the pressure wave seared a livid trail across my cheek as it passed. The shock of it alone was enough to slam me back against the house wall. I had one brief vision of what O'Feely must have suffered, taking the same thing in the crotch, before retching convulsively down the front of my best walking-out jacket.

A moment later, Major Timms died.

I still don't know exactly how it happened. I don't think anyone did, least of all the two stunned artillerymen. All I recall was floundering impotently in the black mud while registering a pain-blurred image of the girl sagging helplessly between two separate tangles of struggling men. Simultaneously the black Polizie Dobermanns, previously mute, were released by their handlers to race, fangs bared, snarling and barking ferociously, from the entrance to the driveway. Close behind the dogs, pounding boots under bobbing flashlights heralded the return of the Redcaps from the clutch of vehicles parked just around the corner. Right on cue, the accelerating roar of engines, the screech of tortured brakes and a blaze of headlamps smeared the scene in white glare to illuminate Herr Inspector Spearmint kneeling above Irvine, pinning the lad's shoulders down: smashing his fists into the already unconscious soldier's face with a savagery that made me seriously re-evalute my guess at how he'd spent his war.

So how did Timms die . . .?

137

Well, it seemed Gunner McCafferty, granted the manic strength of the terrified, had managed to wrench himself free and boot the Major full in the face before taking off again. Timms had gone down but, being the terrier he'd already shown himself to be during Charlie's inquiry, had struggled back up again to hurl himself full length in an attempt to grab the sobbing escapee's ankles.

. . . Until, all of a sudden, Timms was whimpering horribly and plucking at the bayonet that had entered his left eye, and which now projected from behind his right ear.

Thankfully he didn't survive as long as Foxie did. It was only an eternity of seconds before the CO's brain haemorrhaged, and his still-clawing hands slipped from the haft of the bayonet: slowly relaxing into the mud. The girl took up the lament and stood there shrieking and shrieking and nobody did anything to stop her 'cause we were all too numbed with the horror of it. Even Gunner McCafferty had frozen briefly, ashen-faced in the glare of the headlights, as it began to dawn on him that, having downed a Redcap, he would have been better off killing himself.

I suppose the bayonet must have fallen there, lodged vertically in a fold in the ground, and Major Timms had dived right onto it when he went for the escaping man. It didn't matter anyway, not working out precisely how it had happened, because the Major was dead, the seemingly indestructible had been destroyed, and right away I knew that something had died in me, too.

The Dobermanns took McCafferty before he'd time to turn and run again, pulling him down sobbing with fear. Then he began shrieking too, much longer than the Major, as the hounds savaged the bridge of his nose and tore his upper lip away while I yelled hysterically, 'Leave 'em to fuckin' KILL the bastard!' and cursed the German dog handlers as they tried to haul the beasts off.

And all the while Herr Inspector, roaring berserk, continued to pound at the jellied features of 95723341 Gunner Irvine P, and the girl's coat had flapped open to expose her violated nudity as she screamed and screamed and screa . . .!

. . . And Foxie, and the stick-thin mountain child, and

138

Sergeant O'Feely and the tortured Stavros all grinned macabrely down at me for the first time in many years as I clamped trembling hands over my ears and buried my face in the trampled wet grass.

Eleven

The following day I'd found myself alone in the duty room, completing Royal Military Police Report Form AF2100, in which I described, in terse officialese, the manner by which Major Timms had died in the execution of his duty as a provost officer.

I further stated how Irvine had resisted arrest: how he'd fought like a lunatic, and why, in my opinion, it had been unavoidable that, during the course of his apprehension by a German Inspector of Police, 95723341 Gunner Irvine P, Royal Artillery, did sustain facial injuries serious enough to cause endangerment to his life.

I also confirmed that the Polizie dog-handlers had displayed every initiative in regaining control of the dogs, although, I regretted to report, not before said animals had uncharacteristically savaged the once brutally handsome features of 84769888 Gunner McCafferty J, RA. Mind you, I did try to end on a more positive note by stating that an assiduous search of the area shortly thereafter did recover three (3) masticated pieces of human flesh: two (2) strips of scalp with hair attached, and the remains of what was believed to be one (1) human nose: all said parts being immediately placed in a suitable container and urgently . . .? I crossed out 'urgently', which hadn't been quite true . . . and *eventually* delivered by the hand of 77519430 Sergeant Harris A, RMP, to the Senior Medical Officer, Plastic Surgery Department, BMH 14, BAOR.

Actions taken immediately following the incident . . .? That's where I had cause to scratch my head. Can you charge two subsequently waggy-tailed and thoroughly unrepentant Dobermann Pinscher dogs that can only understand German,

140

with: *That you did use excessive force in the apprehension, arrest and subsequent devouring of the suspect*? Then formally caution them that *Anything you bark will be taken down in writing, and may be given in evidence . . .*?

Lighting a Capstan Full Strength, I shoved my chair back from the desk and tentatively fingered the scrap of sticking plaster standing in for the lower half of my right earlobe. It hurt. I'm good at coping with other people's pain, unmoved by the sight of other people's blood, but I get precious when it comes to my own.

The door banged open behind me and Thomas entered, whistling. I swivelled irritably. 'Haven't you got nothin' better to do, Corporal, than come charging in here like a sixteen-stone bloody canary?'

He looked guilty for a minute and that reminded me of Tosh again, except that Thomas was a good soldier, and a professional. 'Just looking for that Section 43, Staff. The one you said you would definitely have completed two days ago?'

I sniffed. 'Yeah, well we've had more immediate concerns since then, or had you forgotten?'

'Major Timms?' Thomas went quiet for a moment, then said hopefully, 'We could get a decent enough CO again, though.'

'They don't come better than Timms, lad,' I retorted, viciously erasing the Capstan. 'The Major was one of the best officers I've served under. Him and Captain Jackson both, come to that.'

Jackson was 2 I/C of the company and a sound bloke as well. I couldn't help but smile sourly to myself. Maybe officers were getting better in general now, or was it me mellowing in my dotage? I'd seen many changes, even a few for the better, since first being told to *Getcherbloody'aircut!* by four different corporal instructors in between each of three visits to the regimental barber on the same afternoon.

The door opened again. Thomas snapped briefly to attention as Jackson entered with the timing of an actor on cue while I levered half-out of my seat, but he signalled

141

casually for me to save energy. I thought he looked tired too, and recalled he'd taken the news of the Major's death hard. But that was yesterday, and this was the army, and we didn't betray emotion, and Thomas was already walking around whistling, and Timms would be replaced. *The Major is dead. Long live the Major.*

Captain Jackson sat on the corner of my desk, picked up the AF2100 and scanned it expressionlessly. 'Epitaph to a good soldier, eh, Staff?' was all he said.

'A gentleman, sir. A proper gentleman.'

He let the paper float to the desk. We both watched it fall. Dead leaves land like that when the tree discards them: gently, and without fuss. Then the Captain stood and tugged at his belt. 'Came in to say I've had a call from Brigade. The new CO will be arriving at the station at 2120. Can you arrange for a driver to pick him up, Staff. Come to that, he'll probably fancy a bit of something to nibble when he gets here.'

Like I said: the Major's dead. Long live the Major.

'I'll detail Lance Corporal Wetherly to take the Husky. Sergeant Devlin can lay on a cold supper in the officers' mess for you.' I made a note in the duty book. 'Will you be going down with Wetherly to meet the train yourself, sir?'

Jackson smiled. 'You suggesting I blitz the local biergartens while Major Steadman arrives, Staff?'

I grinned back. 'No, sir.' I even laughed a bit.

Before it hit me.

The import of what he'd just said.

I sat, numb at first, while the creepy-crawlies I believed I'd left in Cyprus vaulted a ten-year, two-thousand-and-twenty-eight-mile span to catch up right between my shoulder blades. I must have paled perceptibly because Jackson frowned.

'You OK, Staff?'

Even the image was hard put to adopt a reassuring smile. 'Yeah . . . Yessir.'

Jackson looked uncertainly at me for a moment before moving to the door, then hesitated. It seemed Bull's Bum hadn't cornered the market in perception.

142

'You don't happen to know the new CO, Staff?'

I became acutely conscious of Corporal Thomas staring hard at the back of my neck, ears flapping. 'Served with him, sir. Cyprus. Fifty-seven.'

'Bog-standard three-pipper in those days, was he?' The 2 I/C indicated the captain's insignia on his shoulder with admirable self-deprecation. 'He'll have grown up by now.'

I didn't return the smile. 'He was a major, sir.'

Jackson betrayed a flush of embarrassment as he glanced uncomfortably over to the intently listening Thomas. The whole company would know about it before the new boss even got off the train, and staying a major for ten-plus years was hardly a recommendation for any officer. But the irony of the new CO's appointment was made no less exquisite by it. Steadman's prospects of attaining high rank had been irretrievably damaged by that tirade triggered, initially, by young Timms. Now Timms had been erased from the plot, and Steadman was replacing him.

Like I said: the Major is dead. Long live the Mad Major.

Jackson cleared his throat, and muttered something about nipping over to the QM store. I was left staring at the AF2100 and reflecting bitterly on Sod's law. Why *does* it decree that, soon as you reckon you've got it made, something always comes along to bloody spoil it?

Corporal Thomas must have burned with curiosity for a good three minutes until he couldn't stand it a moment longer. 'So what's the SP on the new CO, Sta—'

I chopped him off brutally. 'Jus' shut up and get your fuckin' finger out on that paperwork, Thomas!'

He looked as if he might answer back, then thought better of it, lowered his head and began writing furiously. He couldn't help betraying the crimson flush of resentment that coloured the back of his bull neck. It wasn't his fault, so I added quietly, 'Watch yourself with the new CO, lad. He can be a bit . . .'

I couldn't say more: you just don't in the services. But he knew the score: appreciated it was the nearest thing he'd get to an apology.

'Right then,' I said, forcing a briskness I most certainly didn't feel. 'Got the patrol rosters there? Over here with 'em, Corporal Thomas – *hon* the double, lad!'

We were looking through the duty lists when the door slammed open yet again. This time a pair of boots, field pattern, size twelve, smashed to attention while a throaty voice bawled, 'One prisoner for committal, Staff Sergeant!'

Thomas didn't lift his head. Just gritted a tightly controlled, 'It's Flint, in't it? Tell me it isn't Flint, Staff.'

I counted slowly to ten. OK, so Steadman was currently the worst news I'd had by a long shot, since being posted to BAOR, but not the only bad news. It seemed Germany was set for an encore: that all my long-forgotten nightmares had been posted here along with me. Take Acting Lance Corporal Flint, for instance. I cherished the black conviction that Flint had been squeezed from the same mould as my former Lance Corporal Tosh before the recruiters realized what they had done, and decided to destroy it.

Did I say we were all professional soldiers now? I take it back. Every time I saw Flint, I felt I was glowering at a re-incarnated National Service Tosh. Like now, for instance: spotty-faced and flushed-cheeked, with an eighth-inch bristle of hair crowning his personal, stomach-protruding interpretation of the attention posture: boots like boats moored at precisely forty-five degrees from each other; all conspiring to make him look more like an art-nouveau toilet brush with a hat on than a military copper.

'All right, all right: I'm not in bloody Poland, Flint,' I gritted. 'What's the charge?'

Flint drew breath, then hurriedly deflated when he saw the glint in my eye. 'Drunk and disorderly, Staff Sergeant.'

'Who is?'

Flint gestured to the vacant space beside him. 'Him, Staff Sergeant.'

I looked in vain for the alleged prisoner whom, it appeared, Flint had forgotten to march into the room with him. I made a mental note to check *his* ammo pouches next time we went on manouvres. Flint probably kept his condoms in the same pocket as his mum's photo, too.

'Not him, surely?' I queried reasonably. 'The Invisible Man?'

'*Shit!*' Flint muttered, mortified.

'Fuckin' banana,' Thomson defined.

'Go and re-arrest him,' I advised wearily. 'If he happens to have waited around for you, that is.'

Had we been closeted in a concrete bunker with blast-proof doors, we'd still have heard the bellow from the corridor. They should've got Flint, not me, to yell at our two wannabe escapees last night. It should certainly have been Flint getting shot instead of me – ideally about eighteen inches lower, and slightly to the left . . . I would have helped haul the dogs off McCafferty myself as a thank-you gesture.

'Prisoner . . . . Prisoner hatten-SHUN! Prisoner will move to the front: *by* the left . . . Kweek MASH! Left, right, lef' right, lef' right . . . Prisonnnnner – 'ALT!'

I uncovered my ears cautiously, in case he had anything to add when I wasn't expecting it, then let them focus on the private soldier who stood to attention before the desk, eyes fixed on the mandatory infinity above my head. He'd fallen foul of the military police before. I could tell from the way the well-practised blank expression erased all individuality from the drawn face.

Then the prisoner's gaze flickered down and met mine, and I went all cold and prickly inside.

While Fusilier Charles Parrish allowed the faintest glimmer of a smile to crease the corners of his mouth.

It had to happen. First Steadman, stepping into a dead man's shoes. And now, Charlie – about to step into one of my cells. The vicious circle was complete. We were back together again, the reunion of the Unholy Trinity.

For a moment I just sat and weighed him up, and felt sad. He looked different to the Charlie of ten years ago. Older of course, but more than that: the brightness had gone from his eyes and the uniform didn't appear to fit so snug as before. He seemed even smaller too, though Parrish had never been what you'd call a body builder: more a public-bar gymnast. I couldn't help but reflect uncomfortably on how wrong he looked without the three tapes surmounted by a crown on his arm.

The protective blank expression shuttered down again, and the empty stare refocused on the wall behind. When he reported, it was as an automaton.

'71532291 Fusilier Parrish C, Lancashire Fusiliers, Staff Sar'n't.'

'Stand at ease, Fusilier,' I said, then looked at Flint. 'Has he been cautioned, Corporal?'

'Yes, Staff,' Flint advised, then about-turned to leave the office.

Corporal Thomas said blankly. 'Where the fuck's *he* going?'

'Where the fuck are you goin'?' I called.

'By the book, Staff Sergeant,' Flint explained, hesitating.

'And what does the book say, lad?' I asked ominously.

Flint regained his confidence. Bad mistake number two. 'Until the prisoner is confined in the cells, the patrol should remain outside the guard room, Staff.'

'And *why* does it say that?'

'To avoid any possibility of the prisoner bein' incited to strike the arresting NCO, thus aggravating his or her original offence, Staff.'

'Tell me, Flint,' I asked, always tolerant of the views of acting lance corporals. 'Does this soldier look incited? Does he give the impression he's going to run berserk and strike you?'

'Er . . . no, Staff Sergeant.'

I frowned at Charlie. 'And are you planning to run amok, Fusilier?'

Charlie smiled a little then, making sure Flint couldn't see it. 'No, Staff. On my oath, Staff.'

I nodded solemnly, 'I'm relieved to hear it, Fusilier Parrish: very relieved indeed. You'd be a terrible man to have to restrain by force, what with there only bein' three of us Redcaps in here.'

I suddenly remembered about Major Timms and, even worse, Steadman, and lost all taste for banter. Instead I fixed Flint with a baleful eye. He anticipated what was coming

146

and his neck telescoped into his collar like a turtle confronted by a tsunami.

'Lissen, Flint. When you parrot the book to me, you make bloody sure you read it proper. First off, you do NOT leave your prisoner waiting outside to catch a bus, while *you* come in! Second, you do *not* barge into my duty room like a sar'nt bloody major on speed – and third, whatever the book says, you use discretion. This is RMP territory and I shall decide how to process the alleged offender, not you: so *don't* bloody turn about without my leave, and DON'T confuse bullshit with lack of respect for the prisoner!'

OK, so I shouldn't have hauled off at Flint in front of Charlie, I knew that. Corporal Thomson knew it too, although, from the way he was trying to smother a joyous grin, sympathy for the down-trodden wasn't his over-riding emotion. But I needed the therapy: I needed to be a bastard to somebody right then, and this was the army, and I carried the rank, and Tosh . . . sorry – *Flint!* . . . *had* kind of volunteered to be taken down a peg or two for his sometimes barely concealed air of superiority.

. . . And honestly, I *wasn't* jealous of Tosh having made all that money while I only had my army pension to look forward to. I really *didn't* resent his having been a useless, thick-as-mince thorn in my side for most of his National Service only to go out and land on his feet with a far-too-pretty wife and a bloody great Jag and a flash city pad an' a . . .!

I forced myself to get a grip. The Mad Major's imminent reappearance on the plot wasn't Tosh's – *Flint's* – fault, either.

'Look, Corporal,' I growled, conceding just a hint of paternalism, 'if this was another unit's guard room and not – repeat, *not* – my nice friendly office, then you *will* go by the book. You will remain outside and request the sentry to call the guard commander. You will then hand your prisoner over to that guard commander and you will not enter until the accused is confined in a cell. Then, and only then, will you enter the guardroom – upon invitation, mind? You will promptly fill in the Handing Over Committal Receipt form . . .'

I chose to disregard Thomas's raising reverential eyes to

the ceiling and crossing himself. '. . . Army Form number eight six zero zero niner: one copy of which you will retain . . . do I make myself CLEAR, Lance Corporal Flint?'

'Yesstaff!' I could see the guilty look in Flint's – Tosh's? – *Flint's* eyes, and that spiteful victory afforded me the first twinge of pleasure I'd felt all morning.

'Good. Then make your report. What's Fusilier Parrish done to warrant his arrest on a charge of D and D before bloody lunchtime?'

'He was swimming, Staff Sergeant.'

'Swimming?'

'Swimming, Staff.'

I knew it was going to be one of those days. Didn't I *say* it was goin . . .?

'Is that illegal?' Thomas asked of the wall.

'It is when it's in the fountain at the bottom of Harbenstrasse, Corporal.'

I levered myself erect and paced a critical circuit round Charlie. 'He's not wet?'

Flint looked uneasy. 'That's, like, the second count in the charge, Staff. Fusilier Paris—'

'Parri*sh* . . . *ish* with an ess haitch!' Charlie corrected with a touch of asperity that showed how easy inciting a prisoner can be. 'Same as in pi*sh*.'

'Sorry: I thought he was just slurring his speech. Bein' drunk an' that,' Flint explained, pushed on the defensive.

'The point is,' I growled, anxious to define the problem, 'are you claiming that Fusilier Parrish's *not* being wet is a contravention of Queen's Regulations, Flint?'

'No, Staff: I'm saying he's not wet 'cause he was, well . . . swimming in the nuddy.'

'The nud . . . You mean he'd no clothes on?'

'None, Staff.'

'None at *all*?'

'Not-a-bloody-stitch-Staff.'

Tears began to squeeze from the corner of Thomas's eyes and he kind of slumped in his chair. I frowned at him absently. 'Two mugs o' tea and a wedge. On the double, Corporal . . . No clothes on, you say?'

148

Flint shook his bristle head firmly, conceding not one further inch. 'Not even underpants. *And* exhibiting himself in a public locus, like I said.'

I couldn't let it go on. It was becoming more vaudeville than serious accusation against a member of Her Majesty's Armed Forces. Anyway, I still felt bitter at seeing Charlie Parrish stood there in front of me, because it wasn't like he'd been a bad soldier all his life. Charlie had been a hero – still was, in my eyes – and there'd been a time before he met Steadman when he should have demanded respect, indeed veneration, from a still-wet-behind-the-ears Redcap like young Flint.

I looked to Charlie appealingly, but he wasn't having any either. He could dig his heels in, too. Parrish had written the book when it came to awkward. He seemed happy to play Laurel to Flint's Hardy.

'Got anything to say for yourself, Fusilier Parrish as in pish?'

'Only that I just happened to be walking down the street, Staff Sar'nt: sort of reflectin' on how I hadn't had a drink for the past four days . . .'

'Jeeeezus *Christ*!' Flint said.

Charlie disregarded the scepticism implicit in Flint's response. 'Until, just as I passed by, I thought I heard a young girl screamin', "Help, 'elp," from that fountain . . .'

'English, was she?' I asked.

Parrish magnanimously disregarded the sarcasm. 'Well, I mean, what else could I do . . . '

'But jump in and save her?' Flint concluded distantly.

'You learn fast, Corporal,' I conceded. 'I'll give you that.'

Flint glared accusingly at Charlie, encouraged. 'You still didn't have no clothes on, did you?'

'Course I didn't.' Charlie looked mystified, then saw what Flint was driving at. 'Surely, Lance Corporal, you wasn't thinking I would be a party to the wilful destruction of . . .'

'Army property?' I anticipated, resigning myself to the inevitable.

'. . . Army property. Exac'ly that, Staff Sergeant,' Parrish the Virtuous endorsed.

149

I walked back to the desk and sat down, hoping Flint would surrender of his own volition, but he wasn't beaten yet. 'The prisoner used abusive language as well, Staff. In answer to the charge, the prisoner became insolent and called me a . . .'

I raised a resigned eyebrow and rested my chin on my hands while Flint, after a bit of fumbling in his breast pocket, produced his notebook to refresh his memory. '. . . The prisoner did refer to me as bein' a "fucking doormat", Staff Sergeant.'

While I was gloomily pondering that it was a pity to have to arrest a man just because he told the truth, Charlie still rebounded like he'd done at Dunkirk: even more so having since accumulated a lifetime's experience of dodging the column.

'Yeah, well, that can only be down to another misunderstanding on the part of the Lance Corporal. What I actually said, Staff Sergeant, was that if he thought I was drunk, then 'is faculties were *dormant*.'

Definitely time to call a halt.

Before the custard-pie act came on.

I couldn't let Charlie off the hook entirely. I owed it to Lance Corporal Flint – he'd been right to lift Parrish, and Charlie knew that too.

'Make out a report for forwarding to Fusilier Parrish's Commanding Officer – and Flint? *Don't* push the insolence bit too hard. Off you go then, lad.'

Going through the door, our crime fighter almost collided with the returning Thomas. The Corporal did a snappy tango to save the two mugs of tea and wedges of cake on the tray he was carrying, then shoved his head back into the corridor and bawled 'FOETUS!' after the departing Flint.

He planted the tray carefully on my desk, licking his lips in anticipation. 'Char an' wedge as ordered, Staff.'

I lifted my boots onto the desk and settled comfortably. Thomas was about to pick up the second mug when I stopped him. 'We haven't time to lay about drinkin' tea all day, Thomas. Where's the duty wagon?'

'Gone over to Brigade, Staff.'

'Right. Get on to M/T section and draw a Rover. Then nip back here and take Fusilier Parrish back to his own guard room. Turn him out on the street, he'll only get himself re-arrested.'

Thomas looked at the clock, pointedly aggrieved – it was nearly lunchtime – then read my expression and decided protest would not advance his career prospects. Unfair maybe, but a long-overdue word with Charlie came first, especially that morning.

But of course Charlie, being Charlie, didn't help either. Even when there was no one else in the duty room, my best mate still remained stiffly at ease, staring fixedly at the bloody wall.

I pushed one mug towards him and said, 'Oh, siddown for Christ's sake.'

Hauling out the Capstans, I threw one across the desk and lit up as he sat, still not saying a word. I started to feel uncomfortable, just sitting there with him silently poking at his tea with the spoon. I blew an elongated ring of fluffy smoke and tried to stab it with the cigarette, then looked thoughtfully at Parrish.

'You're a stupid bastard, Charlie.'

He didn't look up. 'You should know, Staff Sergeant.'

I got needled at that. 'Don't come the bloody barrow with me, Charlie Parrish. You want to keep acting like a comic-opera soldier, go ahead. But don't expect me to pull your neck from under when the chopper falls.'

He did lift his head at that, and the hard eyes stared in mine. 'Like you done in Limassol, for instance?'

'Limassol, crap!'

He shrugged, and went back to poking the spoon again while sort of smiling cynically to himself. I waved a hand in frustration. 'Look, you got a bad deal in Cyprus, mate. Shit happens. You got dragged in by Steadman and the circumstances got out of hand ... circumstances, Charlie. Nothin' I could say or do would have changed them.'

The tea slopped in the tray as he stood angrily to lean over the desk. I could smell the drink on his breath as he shoved his set face against mine.

'See here, *mate*?' He slapped his sleeve viciously. 'Your so-called fuckin' circumstances stripped three tapes and a crown off this arm. Your fuckin' *circumstances* lost me seventeen years of previous exemplary conduct . . .'

I did a double-take at that. Exemplary? Charlie *Parrish*?

'. . . and the chance to make somethin' out of this stinking bloody army. From colour to squaddie in one slick Redcap bastard carve-up – and you say, "Jus' one of those things, Charlie boy."'

I really saw red then. Maybe it was the culmination of ten years of guilt compounded by ten years of my own resentment. He'd not exactly been the Good Samaritan with the Cypriot himself. We were both standing by then, shaking with collective rage, and I thought Charlie was going to hit me so I started yelling at him and banging on the desk in all the slopped tea.

'Yeah, we're all Redcap bastards in provost. That's why I stuck my neck right on the block to cover up the way you rifle-butted the guy when all he'd done was spat at you. That's why Major Timms . . . Royal Military *Police* Major bloody Timms, Parrish! – put Steadman through the grill on your behalf till he went off his bloody head . . . all so's we could frame you for somethin' which every single scrap of evidence went to prove that you bloody did anyway! I warned you, Charlie. I warned you to stay well clear of Steadman, but you were too goddam clever, weren't you? You had to act the big, smart tough guy just to show us Redcaps what the fuckin' infantry could do . . . !'

I stopped abruptly and fought for control: nervous in case somebody should come in. Parrish's face was white and strained too, as I spoke clearly and succinctly. 'And *that* is why, mate, this particular Redcap bastard's goin' to need every spark of luck he can scrape up, just to retire from this army with a pension instead of a dishonourable discharge.'

Charlie blinked at me. In that moment, he looked like the old Parrish. He never asked why. He knew he didn't need to. He just said quietly, 'Sorry, mate.'

I gestured gloomily to the chair. 'Forget it.'

We sat down again, and Charlie clicked the spoon against

his teeth as he watched me thoughtfully, waiting. I knew I looked terrible but I couldn't even draw on the image right then: not that I had to with Charlie Parrish. We both sipped our tea, not saying anything for a moment, then I dropped my bombshell. 'He's coming, Charlie.'

'Who?'

'Steadman. As our new CO.'

I didn't quite know what reaction to expect, but I certainly hadn't anticipated what I got. Charlie didn't so much as flicker an eyelid. Just reached out and ever so deliberately stubbed his butt out in the tin lid.

'When?'

'Tonight.'

It was an anticlimax in a way. For a long moment we just sat and sipped the stewed cookhouse tea, and I guess both our minds were far away. Ten years away. Finally Charlie put his empty mug back on the tray and, as he did so, I could see the muscles working at the side of his jaw: betraying the passion he felt.

'When he does, I'll swing for the bastard,' he said flatly, and I knew right away that he meant it.

'No you won't, mate,' I said anxiously, trying to keep it light. 'Not for the next twenty-three days anyway, till I get my gold watch and a flight back to Blighty. After that you can plant a land mine under his bunk, and the best of bloody British.'

Charlie shook his head slowly, and I realized he wasn't really listening. I think, in fact, Charlie Parrish had gone a bit mad himself over ten years: maybe even a lot mad. The tension fomenting inside him was almost tangible. 'I swear, Bill, I'm goin' to top the bast—'

The door swung open. Thomas stuck his head round; frowned a bit when he saw us both seated, then jerked his chin at Parrish. 'On your feet, Cinderella: the golden coach awaits.'

Charlie's beret slipped out of his shoulder strap as he rose, and landed in the tea slops. He grinned at me, wrung it out, and shoved it back again. I wished it hadn't happened. It reminded me too much of the good times.

I called to him as he walked to the door. He turned and I saw he was still smiling. 'Remember, Charlie – no vendetta: not till I'm gone.'

The smile grew hard. He went through the motion of pulling the pin from an imaginary grenade and lobbing it back into the room, then made a noise like an explosion.

'Brown bread, Staff Sergeant,' he said. 'You'll not know whether to scrape 'im up, or paint the bastard over.'

I sat staring after him with the tentacles of fear closing ever tighter in my guts.

Foxie on his tree spit; the ragged child with a high-power Browning round below his eye; the unfortunate, tormented Stavros? They must have been laughing pretty hard just then. Wherever they slept.

Twelve

That night the sergeants' mess was busier than usual: generally there weren't enough of us staying in barracks to make up a poker school, not at peace-time establishment. It was obvious most of the nosy bastards had only hung back in the hope of seeing what the new CO was like. I leaned against the chipped servery and smiled cynically at the back of Sergeant Harris's bull neck through the distorting bottom of my drained beer glass. They'd bloody find out soon enough – listening in on my court martial once Steadman figured out how to fit me up for one.

Or funeral. If he really had stayed mad as a hatter and opted for his proposed alternative.

On his knees, wedged into the little cupboard optimistically called a bar, Lance Corporal Flint was struggling to bring order to the mass of beer crates and bottles that filled every inch of free space under the counter. Remembering how I'd been a bit hard on him earlier, I forced an appropriately distant smile of friendliness. 'You been working hard today, Flint. Where's our usual bar steward, then?'

A perspiring, bristle-topped head appeared briefly above the counter. 'Corporal Gates? Gone up to Berlin, Staff: escorting a prisoner. Asked me to stand in for 'im.'

I nodded as if interested, and gestured to my empty glass. 'Top up, lad.'

He panted to his feet and reached for a bottle of brown ale while I flicked on the battered radio that stood in the corner. The mess had only filled with the throbbing beat of British Forces Radio Germany for a few seconds before Harris swivelled irritably in his chair and glared at the unfortunate Flint.

'Turn that bloody row off. Noisy git.'

Flint, who'd begun jigging like a man with St Vitus's dance soon as he heard the music, stared at Alf Harris in barely concealed outrage: the frustration of a true connoisseur. 'But it's the *Stones*, Sarge.'

Alf, a dislikable man-mountain I'd never taken to at the best of times, and who would have bullied his grandma given half an excuse, shoved a paw inside his shirt to scratch his chest. 'I don't give a monkey's bum if it's the Rock of Ages, Flint – *switchitOFF!*'

Flint sniffed loudly and switched the radio off. That minor insolence made for the Acting Lance Corporal's Bad Mistake number three for the day. But Tosh – *Flint!* – had been getting a bit stroppy for a while now, and senior NCOs collectively have ways to pre-empt the spread of such potentially dangerous democracy. I couldn't help but hold my breath as a flush rose ominously above Harris's collar.

'You want to stare disaster in the eye, Billy Bunter, you jus' sniff like that again.'

Flint sniffed again even louder, then, realizing he'd gone too far, converted it to a spluttering cough. Harris looked hard at him for a moment before permitting his neanderthal features to soften to an uncharacteristic expression of concern.

'That's a terrible affliction you're sufferin' from, lad.' He turned solicitously to the room. 'Ain't it a terrible affliction the Lance Corporal's got? The sniffin' and coughin' an' that?'

Everybody nodded worriedly while Flint grinned uncertainly. CQMS Guy shook his head and looked sad. 'Shocking, Alf. And him such a healthy young feller otherwise.'

'Needs treatment, I say. Lots of fresh air,' Sergeant Lewis suggested helpfully.

Harris brightened. 'Long walks – that's it, Sid!'

Flint's brows came together in a frown of anxiety as he worked out the course the conversation was shaping. He looked at me appealingly but I buried my face in my glass as the CQMS blew his nose loudly before wiping away an alcoholic tear. 'In my experience, a bit of extra beat walking generally helps clear the lungs of sniffin' at sergeants. Or even a spot of bracing point duty: ideally on a nice, windy-cold junction.'

The worried Flint tried desperately to stem the flow of helpful advice. 'Sorry, Sarge. I mean, I was only . . .'

'Dandruff,' diagnosed Sergeant Devlin portentously.

Alf frowned. 'What's that you say, Andy?'

'Dandruff, Alf. In his lungs.'

Harris slapped the table in relief. 'By God, but you're right, Sarn't Devlin. It's his long hair rubbin' against his knees when he bends that's doin' it. Scraping the dandruff off.'

They all nodded solemn consensus while the despairing Flint ran a bemused hand over his shaven pate. The CQMS still had the sad look, making his normally lugubrious face look even more funereal as he scrutinized the amateur steward. 'Not much like a copper, is he? I mean, not really?'

Harris had got a bit chokker with the game by then, though, and reverted to his usual homely gorilla-glower. 'Not much like a bloody barman, come to that. A platoon of empties on the table and not a pint being pulled . . . Listen, Flint, in this mess we don't bloody tell you when we wants to *start* drinking – we tells you when we wants to bloody STOP!'

Hurriedly Flint grabbed a glass and started to draw a pint, nodding and pumping furiously at the same time. Alf got up and, sauntering over, shoved his red face close to the Corporal's. 'And first thing tomorrow – getcherbloody 'aircut!'

Then, after all that, he leaned across the bar with a triumphant three-tape glare of superiority – and switched the radio ON again!

Just before the door opened, Sergeant Parker came in and walked straight over to the bar only to shove *his* beefy, sweating face close up to Flint's, and yell, 'Switch that fuckin' row OFF!'

And Flint's eyes filled with furtive tears of misery.

It was time to come to the unfortunate corporal's aid. I looked at my watch, which said one minute to eight: nearly zero hour for the Ritual.

'Right, lad. Know what you have to do for twenty hundred, do you?'

He sniffed, but ever so cautiously this time, and only because he needed to. 'Gates told me, Staff.'

Bringing out two glasses, Flint polished them with tongue-protruding concentration then held them, critically professional, up to the light. Placing them carefully on the bar top he poured a generous measure of Islay malt into one and, producing a bottle of Tartan Special with a flourish, emptied it all foaming into the other. Then, tugging nervously at his borrowed white mess steward's jacket, he stepped back from the bar and snapped to rigid attention. Like I said, he could be a quick learner when he wanted.

With everybody watching by then, I squatted and, squinting along the level of the counter, placed the two glasses exactly dead centre and in line.

Alf Harris began to intone sonorously, 'Five . . . four . . . three . . . two . . .'

On cue to the millisecond, the mess door swung wide and I stepped smartly aside. He stood in the doorway momentarily, hands behind his back, pace stick tucked under his arm, and I couldn't help feeling as I always did when I saw him – that I was proud and grateful to be a soldier in an army that could produce men of the calibre of Regimental Sergeant Major James Halliday, Corps of Royal Military Police.

Put simply, he was the greatest, most terrifying, and yet the most humble man I had ever known.

His origins were in the Scottish Highlands, from out of the legends and misty hillsides that have spawned some of the world's greatest fighting men. His bearing was awesome: his features surmounting a Goliath frame might have been hewn from Aberdeen granite, but his voice? Ah, his voice was the most riveting thing of all. It embodied the softness of a heather hillside and the music of a sparkling salmon river, yet throbbed with the muted power of a hydro-electric generator. It was a voice with magic in it, which could be turned at will as an instrument to hypnotize and delight, or as a weapon to flail the courage out of any man alive.

158

He stood there quietly, looking around the room, and you could sense his presence radiate through the mess. Then he removed the gleaming pace stick from beneath his arm and placed it carefully along the top of the coat rack beside the door and, above that, laid his webbing belt: a belt so white you felt that God Himself had permitted the white dust of an angel's wings to settle upon it.

The service cap with the near-vertical slashed peak was lifted from his head and tucked in above the crook of his elbow, whereupon, duly prepared for this most sacred moment of the day, he strode majestically to the bar, and the scarcely daring to breathe Lance Corporal Flint. I took a respectful pace back and, though I'd observed the ritual countless times before, watched in silent fascination.

The great, fearsome sand-coloured moustache twitched as Halliday halted in front of the bar. A hand like a slab of venison reached to close with infinite gentleness around the whisky glass. Her Majesty the Queen smiled regally down upon him from the issue frame behind the bar as he came to attention before her, arm bearing the glass bent stiffly at the elbow, and I swear a glance of mutual respect passed between them as the glass was raised in homage.

'Your good health, Ma'am!' said the RSM before draining the gill of Highland dew with the reverence of a bishop taking communion.

The big glass came next. He took one step to the left and drew himself to his full imperial height before the gold-painted plywood RMP crest that hung, slightly below Her Majesty, out of deference. The ale, too, was raised in salute.

'The Corps!' he whispered. Then the whole pint vanished into the moustache-bridged maw and the RSM wiped his hand across his mouth, managing to do even that with enormous dignity. Marching back to the door he hung his cap precisely below the gleaming belt buckles, upon the hook that no other dared occupy, then returned to the bar a man refreshed, rubbing his hands briskly while nodding friendly acknowledgment to the sergeants.

'A very good evening to you, gentlemen,' he greeted in that soft lilt of his.

'Sir!' they all chorussed – smartly at that, 'cause they knew he didn't really mean they were gentlemen, not unless they called him *sir*.

He nodded to me too, as he came over, 'And a good evening yourself, Staff Sergeant Walker.'

I raised my glass. 'And to you, Sergeant Major Halliday.'

I didn't need to call him *sir* all the time, 'cause I was an old sweat as well and I think he respected me just a bit for that. Or maybe it was only the image he approved of, never having seen the real me cowering behind it.

Observing Flint still standing to attention stiff as a board, he smiled a kindly smile at the boy and waved a hand. 'Relax, laddie, relax. I'm not wantin' ye on parade at this time o' night.'

The straining Flint sagged with relief as the RSM continued, 'Mind you, Corporal, it's not a bad thing for you young soldiers to be on hand when a wee bit of tradition is being observed. Now, I mind when I was a bright laddie like you . . .'

The crowd at the sergeants' table looked knowingly at each other and grinned furtively. I heard Harris whisper throatily, 'Servin' wi' the Colours . . .'

'Servin' wi' the Colours in Her Majesty's Royal Highland Regiment, the Black Watch,' continued Mister Halliday with lofty disregard. 'Now thon is a regiment fair steeped in tradition, laddie. Proud Scots, braw soldiers and fighters every one. If they couldnae fight the Germans, then they fought the Argylls . . . and if the Argylls wasnae handy, then they fought one another.'

I held up two fingers to Flint, who double-smartly poured the spirit with a pink tongue peeping from the corner of his mouth. Pushing one to the RSM, I raised my own.

'To the Black Watch, Mr Halliday.'

'I'm grateful to ye, Mr Walker. The Black Watch – *Slai'nth a Mhor*!'

The malt whisky felt warm and cosy inside me and I thought what a lot of good ideas the Scots had produced. Except for porridge and kilts . . . and bagpipes, according to Foxie. Our amateur steward had obviously taken Harris's instructions to heart, 'cause he refilled the glasses soon as they hit the bar empty. Halliday, well launched on his favourite thesis by now, turned paternally back to Flint.

'What was I saying? Ach, yes: I mind a wee battle in Minden just down the road there, a few years back. Now that was the Black Watch tradition, Corporal: carried down from father to son. Fighting the Germans just as their fathers had done before them at Vimy Ridge and the Somme . . .'

The RSM stopped and considered for a moment. 'Mind you, seeing there wasnae a war on at the time, we military policemen had to suppress them a wee bit, but, och, bonnie men, Corporal. All of them bonnie fighting men.'

Halliday turned to the mess in general and I waited in happy anticipation as the fearsome eye locked on to the suddenly uneasy Alf Harris. 'That is a fine gift of mimicry you have, Sergeant Harris. It's near as good as my hearing, I do believe.'

Harris's bull neck went the colour of beetroot, while everyone else in the room smiled inanely and found sudden cause to critically study the ceiling.

Halliday nodded thoughtfully. 'Aye. Should they ever have need of an imitation Highlandman to say "Serving wi' the Colours" on the BBC, then you must ask for an audition: you being *such* a funny man.'

I thought young Flint was going to collapse in ecstasy, judging by the delighted look on his face, then the other sergeants were roaring at Alf's discomfiture and Mr Halliday and I winked at each other over our glasses, while the unhappy Harris shrank by three sizes to look less like a gorilla and more like a toad after the steamroller had passed.

'And now, Staff Sergeant Walker, might I trouble you for a wee word in your ear?'

'For as long as you wish, Sarn't Major.'

'I thank you.' The RSM glanced pointedly at the anxiously hovering Flint. 'But seeing it's not just rabbits that have long ears, we may be as well to find a quiet table in the corner. You'll hae a dram to take with ye, man?'

We carried our drinks to a table well away from the mob. I was curious, but neither of us said anything till the drinks

161

were well down. The RSM obviously had something on his mind and that made me uneasy: I didn't need more problems, not sitting there with one eye already cocked at the door, just waiting for that scarred, sardonic face to appear. I doubted Steadman would be aware that I was here in Germany: it seemed unlikely, with him having been posted at such short notice, and I couldn't help speculating on the Major's re-action when he first recognized me. Would he be less mad, equally mad, or madder? Would he see me as a half-recalled irritation effectively time-barred from posing any threat to what remained of his own career, or as a promise yet to be fulfilled? A turkey trussed by the constraints of rank, inviting slaughter.

In the latter event, all he'd need to do in my three remaining weeks would be to precipitate the early arrival of Christmas.

Finally the RSM stirred. 'You'll be a wee bit apprehensive about your impending retirement, Mr Walker?'

'It can't come soon enough,' I retorted with feeling, brooding on how it wasn't the retiring that worried me so much as getting the chance to.

Halliday raised an eyebrow. 'No regrets? Thirty years of a man's life coming to a close? It must afford some room for doubt about the future.'

I shrugged, 'Maybe. But me, I've had enough.'

Then, as the wise eyes probed deep into mine, I found myself hard put to maintain the image any longer. All the anxiety triggered by the day's events came welling to the surface: particularly when I remembered Charlie's parting threat before following Corporal Thomas from the duty room.

'The army, it's like a . . . a bloody octopus. Things you thought were over and done come reaching out like tentacles to take hold and drag you back to the past.' I shook my head bitterly. 'No thanks, Mr Halliday. Give me my brolly and bowler hat: I'll take my chance in civvy street.'

The moustache bristled. In criticizing the army, I was trespassing on hallowed ground. 'You never used to think like that, man.'

'Circumstances change, Sar'nt Major.'

Halliday frowned for a long moment then, but I wasn't

162

letting the image slip any further. Eventually he lifted an imperious hand and Flint scuttled over with two more malts. The RSM raised his glass.

'To brollies and bowler hats, then,' he said quietly.

I lifted mine. 'I'll drink to that.'

We drank, then sat lost in thought again while the RSM toyed absently with his glass. Even before Steadman's arrival, the evening was hardly turning out to be a social tour de force. Finally he did break the silence.

'I have been a regimental sergeant major for over seven years now.'

'You've done well, Mr Halliday. No one can deny that.'

'Och, but I have been fortunate too, Staff Sergeant Walker. Very fortunate indeed.'

'You're a good soldier and a good copper. You've deserved it.' I didn't need to ingratiate myself any longer. I meant it sincerely.

He ran his finger round the rim of his glass. I could hear it sing. 'I've had something else, too. Something more than that.'

'Such as?'

'Good commanding officers, Staff. Bonnie men, most of them . . .' He held my gaze, and I felt the spell of his personality enfolding me. He spoke very softly, 'They were never men to place you in the position of having to be disloyal, if you see what I mean?'

I grunted cynically, still not quite understanding what he was driving at. The finger stopped its circling movement abruptly. 'Have you had good commanding officers, Staff Sergeant Walker?'

I shrugged, retorted a bit nastily, 'I'm not a regimental sergeant major, am I?'

He didn't take offence. 'True. Yet you, too, are a good soldier and a good policeman.'

'Maybe I jus' been unlucky,' I muttered, avoiding his eye.

'Aye, that could explain it, I suppose. Luck is an elusive thing indeed.'

The RSM fell silent then, while I assumed the subject had run its course. So when he slipped the next question in, I

163

was caught off guard. 'Could it be possible that you are not welcoming the arrival of our new commanding officer?'

I couldn't help but direct a wry grin at the crafty old dog: the way he was pretending to come the innocent. That casual query of his wasn't inspiration, it was perspiration. He'd already done his homework, talked to his peers within the Corps, was as familiar with the proceedings that had taken place in Limassol ten years ago as I was. In particular he would have paid close heed to the doubts Timms had raised about Steadman's part in the Kondoyiannis affair, never fully resolved by Charlie Parrish's court martial.

But then, didn't I just say he was a good policeman?

'I gather you've been chatting with Captain Jackson, Mr Halliday,' I said, still trying to keep it light.

He didn't answer. He didn't have to, not the way he just sat there with those perceptive grey eyes boring right into me. I shifted uncomfortably, but it was no use: I couldn't simply evade the question.

'OK, the Captain's obviously told you I served under Steadman in Cyprus. Truth is, I didn't get on too well with him – but twenty-three days from now he can be the biggest bastard in BAOR if he chooses, and no skin off my nose.'

I could see he wasn't fooled, not one bit. When the imperial head shook from side to side in disbelief, I realized I was cornered. There was only one way out, and that was to take refuge behind the protective mantle of military formality. I rose and snapped to attention, conscious of the crowd at Harris's table turning to stare curiously.

The whisky unsteadied me, but my voice was still tightly controlled. 'With your permission, sir, I would prefer not to discuss the matter any further.'

'You do *not* have my permission,' the tongue lashed me with an almost physical violence. 'Sit *down*, Staff Sergeant!'

As I stiffly reseated myself, all heads in the mess shot assiduously to the eyes-down-and-study-yer-beer-glass position: everybody making like they hadn't heard a thing. But there's an establishment, a rigid code, among sergeants too. When Halliday leaned across the table towards me, his voice

164

had once again become as gentle as that of a shepherd coaxing a recalcitrant lamb.

'Och, Staff: you have my word it's no' the regimental sergeant major that's askin' ye. After thirty years wi' the colours a man's entitled to speak his mind wi'out prejudice.' The eyes crinkled a bit at the corners then. 'But only upon invitation, mind you?'

I frowned at him dubiously, trying to still the maelstrom of anxiety in my mind. I'd never opened my heart to any man in three decades. Not fully, apart from to Charlie Parrish. He lifted his chin encouragingly. 'Right now it's Jeemy Halliday you're speaking to. Out wi' it, man.'

The image finally lost a battle. But the real Walker didn't care. He wasn't going to need it for much longer, anyway.

'Another drink first, Jeemy Halliday?' I said.

The venison-slab hand came down on the table like a stamping press. 'You're a bonnie thinker, Billy Walker.'

Two more glasses of the real stuff appeared as if out of thin air and Halliday nodded, '*Slai'nth a Mhor!*'

'That'll be right,' I agreed, never having understood what the Gaelic meant but drinking deeply nevertheless, while beginning to feel a bit easier as my blood-alcohol content mounted steadily.

And then I told him all about Foxie, and the murdered child, and the terrorist, Stavros – and Charlie. I didn't hide anything: not even the fact that I'd withheld the whole truth at Bull's Bum's inquiry. He didn't say a word: just sat and nodded occasionally as I let the true story of what had happened in another country ten years before gush out. The only time he showed any reaction was when I described the Major's madness, what Steadman was really like, and I could see it was a hard thing for him to take, being the army man he was.

Even when I'd finished, he still didn't say anything until Flint had resupplied us with duty-free dream mixture. Halliday held the amber glass to the light and looked through it critically.

'To the eternal damnation of bad field officers, Mr Walker.' His tone couldn't have been more bitter had he discovered his dad with a whore.

As we drank I detected an awestruck voice from the other tables. 'Staff's fair stackin' it way tonight.'

Someone else commented, 'RSM's not exac'ly falling behind.'

Then Alf Harris growled, 'So what the hell are we waitin' for?' and Flint sighed as he started another spell of violent font-pulling in the little sweat box of a bar.

'I believe you because I must, Staff Sergeant Walker,' the RSM said looking grave. 'And I am awfy worried for the future.'

I glanced at the clock as I heard the duty Husky draw up outside the door. Steadman's train had been due twenty minutes ago.

'You, Regimental Sergeant Major Halliday,' I answered, 'are not the only one.'

Thirteen

I gazed at a white-clawed hand reaching from the tangled wreckage and noted with stomach-churning apprehension how the gold signet ring had been crushed and elongated violently enough to puff and distort one already-stiffening finger.

The engraved initials RJ captured the glare from the Rover's headlights and, somewhat inconsequentially, I found myself speculating on what sort of a bloke RJ was. The only certainty was that, less than ten minutes before, he'd been a British soldier travelling on the camp evening-pass bus heading, no doubt with the testosterone-driven optimism of youth, for the dubious delights promised by the town's biergartens and satellite Fräuleins.

Until twelve tons of juggernauting steel bridge section on a jacknifing low-loader had scythed the bus body from its chassis while compacting seats, alloy panels, razor-edged shards of glass and an estimated twenty-one pleasure-seeking troops into a funereal omelette.

Lowering my head I tried to squeeze further into the compressed tunnel between the now-inverted floor section and what I think had formed the rear of the driver's position. Someone had begun to groan weakly within the mess, and I could detect the steady gush of liquid, presumably from ruptured fuel tanks. I hoped no silly bastard would decide to light up, though I suspected it was diesel and not petrol by the cloying, sickly smell that filtered through the shambles. There was a smell of something else, which didn't help my already-knotted stomach.

Registering the approaching scream of an emergency siren, I closed my eyes momentarily in relief. Thank God the professional rescue squads were on the way.

* * *

167

We'd actually seen it happen, Alf Harris and me. We'd been following the khaki-painted military bus on our way to check the patrolmen in the town centre, when the huge Mercedes tractor-trailer coming towards us began to skid on the wet autobahn. The sixty-foot-long castellated bridge section had started to broadside slowly but implacably across the central reservation between the north and south carriageways. As Alf snarled 'Fuckin' HELL!' and desperately stood on his brakes I'd registered great ridged tyres tearing soft earth into flying clods, then everything was screeching metal and tortured glass bursting out of compressing window frames, and an indelible image of a fluttering, flashy tie still encircling the neck of a headless corpse: rolling and tumbling and finally smearing into paste below the breaking-up bus chassis.

I was out of the quarter-tonner and running before Harris had killed the ignition. Before me, my lengthening shadow bobbed and flailed in the beam of the Rover's headlights while a little voice within kept screaming, 'What the hell are you *doin'*, Walker – what're you hoping to achieve on your own . . .?' but the image had insisted I did something before the shock set in and I froze with the horror of it.

Then splinters of Triplex were crackling under my feet; the road was becoming shiny with blood and oil and vomit until, eventually, I reached the eviscerated carcass of the forty-seater Leyland. While I hesitated briefly, trying to decide where to start, a little Opel drew up and a tall woman in a fur coat got out and stood, sobbing convulsively, beside me.

I swung furiously and roared, 'Shut *up*, for fuck's sake. I'm tryin' to hear if anyone's still alive!'

She turned a shocked face to me that was all black-running mascara and bloodless lips, but she couldn't speak. Not that it mattered 'cause I didn't sprechen sie Deutsch anyway and she was hardly in a state to do anything useful . . . then Sergeant Harris came pounding up, skidded on a patch of diesel, went down into the broken glass and blood: scrambled back up shakily sucking at a ripped palm, and gazed at the wreckage.

'Jesus!' he blurted, dead shattered.

All of a sudden someone came stumbling and whimpering round the back of the bus and we looked and it was a young bloke with tight trousers and a Harris tweed sports jacket. He held his hands cupped to his face, but otherwise seemed OK. It was only when Alf gently sat him down in the mess and eased his hands away, we saw that his left eye had been gouged from its socket to dangle like a dead squid down his cheek.

I started to swear: uttering such a string of obscenities that the blonde woman turned her eyes up and fainted flat out, though it might have been that the state of the young soldier had precipitated her reaction as well. Alf bent and swept the lad up in his gorilla arms and carried him over to the verge, then took off back to the Rover for the field dressings – for all the bloody use they were going to be in that charnel house.

I listened to him calling for assistance over the vehicle's radio while the bloody image continued to demand action. I couldn't put it off any longer. Biting my lip, I tentatively eased down on my hands and knees, and forced myself to crawl in under the collapsed alloy roof section. I registered a brief flash of nylon frillies and silk stockings below the hem of the still-prone blonde's fur coat and, somewhat inappropriately in the circumstances, couldn't help reflecting on what nice legs she had, even despite the fear of what I would unquestionably find awaiting me in that grotesquely compacted tomb.

Then I'd wriggled inside, an ungainly, panting worm, and come across the hand of someone initialled RJ.

Jay . . .? Rick Jay? Eric Jay . . .? Eric *K* . . .? Eric K *Steadman* . . .? Hardly the moment to play word-association. I started feeling memory-sick as well as environment-sick. A bead of sweat trickled down my nose. Cold sweat . . . fear sweat? Either way it tickled. Angrily shaking my head, I felt the warm splash of it on the back of my wrist . . . I'd finished up sweating that night a week ago, too.

The night the Major had arrived to take up his new posting.

When we'd heard the Husky door slam outside the mess, my drinking companion had raised a warning finger. 'Do

169

nothing for now, Billy Walker. Like the three wise monkeys, you must hear all, see all . . .'

'And say bugger all,' I finished bitterly.

Regimental Sergeant Major Halliday afforded a fleeting smile. 'You will find I am right, man.'

Then Captain Jackson had stuck his head round the door to request permission to enter the sergeants' mess, which is the way of the services. Said the CO was anxious to meet his new senior ranks before bedding in to his quarters. He'd glanced at me a little uncertainly then. 'He'll be surprised to see you, Staff. It's a long way from Cyprus.'

I hadn't smiled back: just nodded. Not far enough away, Jackson, I'd thought uneasily. Not by a long chalk.

Steadman swept briskly past Jackson to enter the dingy little room. Immediately I saw that his once-matinee-idol features still betrayed an arrogance made all the more magnetic by the scar, and couldn't help but feel a surge of resentment at how he'd managed to remain much the same. While he didn't appear to look a day older, I'd spent *my* first few post-Cyprus years worrying myself into an early grave – or more specifically, half-anticipating that the Mad Major might just keep his promise and arrange one for me. Nor did he seem a whit less confident.

But then, why should he think any differently? He'd been given every reason to believe he was fireproof. I'd blown my opportunity to elicit the confession that could have brought him to book for the ragged-trousered goatherd's murder. Charlie Parrish had gone down for the duty-room assault . . . and they never *did* resolve the ambulance whodunnit outside the camp gates, having failed to trace the EOKA marksman presumed to have terminated Nine Fingers Kondoyiannis to stop him talking. Call me a cynic, but I still maintained that setting Acting Lance Corporal Tosh up to provide an alibi proving he'd been on camp during the critical period would, to a Machievellian crazy like Steadman, have been like shooting a particularly dense fish in a barrel.

Or a child. Trapped, terrified, in a rocky cleft.

*　*　*

170

But that was then, and this was now. Halliday, *his* regimental image positively exuding Highland charm, had stepped forward to pump the Major's hand with uncompromised hospitality. 'I am very pleased to meet you, sir. You'll hae a dram while you're here?'

It was evident that Steadman hadn't immediately become aware of my presence, me glooming in the corner like a spectre at the feast while the great Scot introduced him to the other members of the mess.

'The company's no' very select, ye'll understand, sir,' he'd apologized with a mischievous glance around, particularly at Alf Harris. Despite that less-than-wholehearted endorsement, the un-insulted company had gathered before their new boss wearing beerily ingratiating grins. Enjoy his brief indulgence, lads, I thought bitterly, because tomorrow you'll see a different face to the monster.

While they were shaking hands, the RSM seized my arm with the grip of a man well used to leading errant soldiers into penal servitude, and virtually dragged me over to the Major.

'And last but not least, Staff Sar'nt Walker, sir,' the sleekit old bugger said with one eye cocked warningly at me. 'Who has, I understand, already had the pleasure of serving under you?'

Before the introduction had time to register, Steadman had turned with the senior-officer-tolerant smile still on his face and hand extended, but I didn't make any move to take it. Jeemy Halliday or no, I was damned if I was going to. The very prospect stuck in my gullet. Instead I came stiffly, *very* stiffly, to attention.

Recognition evidently came as a shock to him – so he obviously hadn't been forewarned I was in Germany. Uncertainly the proffered hand dropped to clench knuckle-white by his side, while Jackson's already-apprehensive smile faded to deepening discomfort: not understanding, but hardly reassured by my determinedly unsociable response. He cleared his throat diffidently. 'I believe Staff Walker was with you in 368 Provost, Cyprus, sir.'

I registered Alf Harris's brows beetling curiously as

171

Steadman collected himself enough to gaze coldly at me, evidently not feeling the slightest compulsion to make a second abortive attempt at shaking hands.

'Indeed he was, Captain.'

Even despite having supped a few myself, I could smell the drink on his breath. It seemed our new CO had unwisely resorted to the German railways buffet car to provided fortification against the rigors of travel. That wouldn't have happened ten years ago, suggesting at least one crack in the facade had set in since Slake's inquiry put the buffers to his career. Principle established, I decided to play safe. Following Charlie Parrish's example of earlier that day, I fixed my eyes rigidly in the remote middle distance: the refuge of the militarily disadvantaged.

'*Sir!*' I snapped tightly.

I hadn't stepped out of line although, within the limits of informality normally considered acceptable when officers enter other ranks' messes, my boot-stamping response might just have been interpreted as over-zealousness. But then, had I allowed myself to display even a flicker of the contempt I felt for the man, I'd have swung too far in the other direction. Either way, it was a fair bet I'd be damned if I did, and damned if I didn't.

Steadman could – *should* – have let it go, for that matter. Certainly no one else would have thought twice about Walker over-doing the bullshit image: they were used to it. But he obviously didn't intend to allow me one inch of latitude.

'At least you have the grace to appear less democratically minded than you were some years ago, Staff Sergeant,' he said, while the purple scar crinkled in all-too acutely recollected mockery. All it needed to transport me back a full decade was a Land Rover, a terrorist cat on a wall and an FN high-power Browning pistol grinding into my temple.

'Sir,' I snapped again, determinedly objective.

'Malt whisky, sir?' RSM Halliday interjected, smooth as the offered distillation itself. 'Or maybe ye'd prefer something softer?'

But Steadman hadn't finished. Either the drink or the suddenly revitalized hatred in him, pushed him from arrogance to recklessness. 'If memory serves, Sarn't Major: before they kicked Walker out of Cyprus I had cause to reprimand him for dumb insolence.'

There fell a disbelieving hush. He was right out of order, confronting me like that in what was, effectively, my home and off-duty refuge. The mess knew it, Captain Jackson knew it – and from his granite-hard expression the RSM certainly knew it. But regimental sergeant majors also know they have to play the long game with indiscreet officers: particularly officers with tongues loosened by drink. It's why they became regimental sergeant majors.

Jackson tried desperately to cover. 'Sir, perhaps you would care to—'

Steadman's arm raised vertically from the elbow in a peremptory, halting gesture. Not unlike the Nazi salute, it struck me, which was a real bloody irony considering how he'd become the monster he was.

'Not *now*, John! Staff Sergeant Walker was an unreliable NCO during his Cyprus tour. I'm damned if I'll give the impression of being pleased to find him serving under me again.'

That was when I felt the sweat break out. I couldn't respond 'cause I didn't know how to – how do you when the maddest of the mad is in command of the asylum? All I could think of was to concentrate on controlling my resentment while letting the Major's clearly undiminished hatred wash over me for another twenty-three days. Just say nothing that could exacerbate the situation further . . . If the RSM's bloody monkeys can do it, Walker, I kept repeating to myself over and over again, then so can you.

But Jackson was of sterner stuff: not prepared to be browbeaten when defending his men. Just like Timms. Or maybe that signalled weakness in Steadman's disturbed imaginings.

'Your quarters are ready, Major, if you—'

'That's ENOUGH, Captain!' Steadman rounded on him. 'I will not have my officers interrupt when I'm talking.'

'No, sir,' Jackson gritted, having gone as far as he dared.

The scar bobbed the barest acknowledgement before turning back on me. 'As I said, Walker, you were difficult

173

to the point of being insubordinate in Cyprus. Or has your attitude to authority changed somewhat since then?'

Over the Major's shoulder I saw the RSM's brow wrinkle in ferocious warning but I couldn't ignore the challenge. I was damned if I was going to. The message had been passed loud and clear: he was still disturbed: still out to get me. The man was as dangerous, as unpredictable now, as he'd ever been – *and* as compulsively self-destructive, once triggered. This exhibition would do more to undermine his authority in the eyes of those he would depend on than anything a bolshie NCO might do.

I felt the nervous tic pulling at my mouth again. 'I'd say my attitude has changed at that, sir.'

The surprise was evident, almost as great as his satisfaction. He even smiled tightly. 'I'm glad to hear it.'

'Yeah,' I growled, thinking what the hell – you're on a hiding to nothing anyway, Walker. 'My memory, and my previous intention, have just become a bloody sight more acute!'

Behind him, Halliday's craggy face screwed into an expression of weary resignation. I even heard him mutter, 'Och, man, man: you're a bonnie fighter – but an awful bluidy fool.'

Alf Harris was the only one to act. He frowned warningly at the by-then utterly gob-smacked sergeants before turning to the bar and the spellbound Lance Corporal Flint.

'Keep your ears same as yer mouth, Billy Bunter – bloody *shut*!' he snarled before reaching to snap the radio back on so's Flint couldn't hear anything but BFR anyway.

Meanwhile Steadman continued to gaze at me calculatingly, the scar turning an ever-deeper purple then, biting his lip, he pivoted. 'Sarn't Major Halliday?'

Halliday crashed his heels together, though we could all see he didn't like it, not with it being his mess. In here, the only person who could command him to attention willingly was Her Majesty.

'SAH!' he responded, stiff as his own pace stick.

'You heard Walker's impertinence, Mr Halliday. Now you might better appreciate my concern at finding such an unsatisfactory senior NCO serving with the company.'

'Bloody *hell*,' someone muttered from the back of the room while young Jackson's expression became a picture of outraged disbelief. Halliday, on the other hand, remained steadfastly unruffled. Ominously so.

'With respect, sir, I am surprised to hear you say that. Unsatisfactory is hardly a criticism borne out by Staff Walker's army recor—'

'I don't give a DAMN about his record, Sar'nt Major!' The implied reprimand cut him rudely short. It was the biggest mistake any officer could make. 'I'm telling you that this man's actions in Cyprus bordered on conduct prejudicial to good order and discipline.'

There was, to coin a phrase, 'a stunned silence'. I felt sick with embarrassment as every eye in the mess swivelled to see how I was taking it. Sergeant Harris looked pretty put out himself, for that matter, and I sympathized. Alf was nearly as old a soldier as the RSM and me, and a lot like O'Feely had been when it came to rebellious. He could see trouble looming as clearly as anyone.

Jackson, too, looked ready to explode with mortification and, just for a fleeting moment, I clung to a reassuring vision of another young captain standing up to Steadman a long time ago – then I recalled the scream issuing from under Timms's bayonet-pierced eye, and lost faith in the power of good over evil.

'Sir, I must remind you that we're guests in the sergeants' mess.'

Steadman turned on him viciously. 'By *God* but you're as insolent as he is, Jackson. You and Walker should get together. You'd be happy as a couple of gays at a pyjama party!'

Well, that was the ba' burst, as they say in the land of Halliday's birth. I'd go so far as to say that everybody stopped breathing for a full minute while the unfortunate Jackson's face went white as a fresh-blancoed belt. Even Steadman paled perceptibly, realizing he'd gone too far. His hand fluttered nervously to caress the scar, but nobody came to his aid, not even RSM Halliday, who simply stood there with the most fearsome look I have ever seen in a man's eyes.

175

Even when the tension continued to mount until it became tangible as the smoke-thickened air itself, nobody moved.

I closed my eyes, trying to fight off the nausea that was rising in me.

Then suddenly, out of all the heavyweight action men in the mess, Acting Lance Corporal Flint came to the rescue.

His ear went down, close to the radio, listening intently. Then, crossing himself while raising his eyes to the ceiling with an expression of abandoned resignation – he spun the volume control to full blast!

. . . Whereupon the BBC's closing national anthem blared into the mess with the impact of a regimental band marching through a convent.

Flint swallowed apprehensively. He had to yell to even make himself heard. 'Sorry, sir. Er . . . slip of the hand, sir.'

I saw the RSM smile the faintest suspicion of a smile then he jabbed Harris sharply with an elbow before yet again snapping to attention. Alf and the rest of the sergeants conformed like military automatons which was, all said and done, precisely what they were. The coordinated stamp of Redcap-glossy boots caused the glasses to rattle behind the bar.

I didn't need to: I was already there before them, but I did spare Flint an appreciative glance. I didn't begrudge him that small concession: I could afford to let the image slip just that once, couldn't I? Especially when, last but not least, Captain Jackson frowned around with a bewildered expression then bemusedly came to attention as well.

The Major was beaten this time, and he knew it. But then, maybe he was relieved: he must have seen the hole he was digging ever deeper for himself. Either way, Flint's 'accident' had defused the tension, and drawn the sting from his attack on me. He was left with no option but to stare impotently at the ring of stolid faces who were, after all, merely conforming to the protocol laid down in Queen's Regulations. Steadman didn't even hesitate: just slapped his leg angrily with his swagger stick, then whirled on his heel and stalked out.

I did wonder – what with them all being military policemen and constrained to remain uninfluenced by external pressures and everything – whether anyone might feel duty-bound to charge their new CO with conduct prejudicial to good order and discipline: him walking out on Her Majesty like that. But I didn't think anyone would. There are easier ways to commit suicide in the army.

I couldn't shake off the feeling that jabbing your commanding officer in the guts with a sub-machine gun was one of them.

The anthem came to an end, leaving only the loud hiss of static filling the mess. As one man we turned to gaze silently at the guilt-ridden Lance Corporal Flint. He waved a tentatively apologetic hand. 'Forces Radio was goin' off air, sir. Didn't realize the switch needed to be turned, like, *anti-clockwise* . . . sir.'

Captain Jackson was the first to smile tightly, though he could hardly be seen to approve. 'Then I wouldn't recommend you ever put in for a transfer to Royal Signals, Flint.'

He turned to the RSM and me. 'I can't say how sorry I am, Mr Halliday. And you, too, Staff. For our regrettable intrusion into your mess.'

Halliday let him off the hook, particularly with him being the gentleman he was. 'Don't you worry yourself at all, sir. We all realize the commanding officer has been under a strain, what wi' his sudden posting and everything.'

Jackson hesitated, frowned, seemed about to say more, then changed his mind. As soon as the door closed behind him, everyone let their breath out with a rush. Especially me. Harris's throaty voice came over, tinged with a respect that made me feel a bit more up to the image. 'You and the Major must've been real mates in Cyprus, Staff. The affection 'e shows for you: it's heart-warming. Straight out of one of them romance magazines, it is.'

'And you get fuckin' knotted too, Alf Harris,' I said pleasantly.

Halliday looked at him pointedly. 'Good *night*, Sergeant Harris. I am sure you must be anxious to get to your bed now the bar is closed, to help you think up some more funny jokes for tomorrow.'

Alf went beetroot as he got the message. They shuffled out casting sad, wistful glances at the bar. Then Harris stuck his head round the door again and glared at Flint on the principle of big fleas and little fleas. 'And you're *still* a big, fat, stupid bastard,' he gritted vindictively before he finally disappeared.

Mr Halliday and I walked to the door and put our belts and caps on while the ruffled Flint pulled the shutters down before cupping his chin morosely in his hands. We could just hear him muttering to himself. 'In the recruitin' office they says to me: you'll be *somebody* in the army, lad. And so I am . . . I'm a big, fat, stupid bastard!'

He came wearily to attention as the RSM about-turned majestically to fix him with a ferocious eye. 'Nothing official, laddie, but a wee reprimand is called for. Don't ever do anything like that again. You will never get to be Provost Marshal by taking the kind of chance you just did.'

Flint closed his eyes. 'No, Sar'nt Major.'

The RSM nodded sagely, then flourished his gleaming pace stick. 'Mind you,' he said solemnly, 'you could finish up being even more highly thought of. As a regimental sergeant major.'

Out in the corridor we grinned at each other as Flint's plaintive protest carried bitterly through the closed door. 'An' I'm NOT fat, Sergeant bloody Harris: I'm jus' sort of . . . of well-built, like!'

Which was when something poked me sharply in the back-side, and I yelled with fright as the projecting white fingers swam into focus again. Screwing awkwardly round under the jagged steel, I found myself staring back at Alf Harris, who'd crawled in behind me.

'Need a hand?'

I jerked my head back towards RJ.

'I've fuckin' GOT one, Harris!' the image snarled, but only 'cause Alf's unexpected prod had scared me shitless. 'Now get the hell out of here and make sure no one rocks the boat while I'm under it.'

'Your mad mate's arrived, by the way,' he whispered, eyeing what little we could see of RJ.

178

'Who – Charlie?' I asked in surprise, still not quite back to the present.

'Not unless his name's Charlie Steadman and he's a major,' he muttered a bit uncomfortably, then hurriedly did the sensible thing and wriggled full astern.

I bit my lip and lay for a moment listening to the guttural commands of the Teutonic rescue machinery as it moved into top gear. With a spluttering of superheated carbons, the white glare of portable arc lamps abruptly scythed through the wreckage to highlight the montage now seemingly entombing me: black-jagged silhouettes of twisted metal ripped into jigsaw pieces by the impact with, here and there, softer shapes that were equally still. I remember thinking of the admin they would entail: hoping they'd all been wearing ID discs and carried their AFB2603 cards so's we'd know who the pieces belonged to.

Effectively it was a worm's-eye view of disaster I was being favoured by, my field of vision restricted more or less to ground level by the overhang of wreckage. Over to the right I could make out the long underbodies of low-slung white Mercedes ambulances moving slowly into parking position to await cargoes yet to be extricated from around me. Swivelling fractionally, I found myself confronted by a knee-high jungle of boots – jack boots, wellington boots, firemen's leather, British Army field pattern and just plain medico-white rubber . . . why *was* it, I brooded morosely, that every time Steadman appeared on the scene he seemed to generate images of boots? The Cobbler of Death, he was: the Pied bloody Piper of footwear.

The wheels of a fire appliance churned slowly past, blue-flashing warning light injecting sporadic colour to the sizzling glare of the arcs. I couldn't help but notice the way the ring on RJ's bleached middle finger alternated in tone with each revolution of the strobe. It was behaving like a baffled chameleon, the way it changed constantly from a bright gold flash to a greenish, sparkling copper. That was something else Steadman seemed to conjure by his presence – the fingers of dead men.

White gaiters immediately identified the next two pairs of

179

boots that stepped into view below the interlaced wreckage. Like book ends, they were: spoon-boned surfaces reflecting the flickering reds, whites and blues of the emergency beacons. Definitely Redcap boots, I concluded. Very British. They had to be, with such patriotic highlights.

It fell quiet momentarily: enough to recognize the low voices of the CO and Alf Harris. I could hear just enough to gather that signs of life had been detected only within the after end of the bus, and they were debating the Firemaster's decision to use a mobile crane to lift the roof off the Leyland's mangled carcass at the risk of compressing other, more severely damaged areas – including, presumably, the fore part under which I'd crawled. I heard Steadman order Harris to go and supervise setting up the RMP incident post, and Alf's anxious response.

'Remember Staff Walker's down there, sir,' was precisely what he said.

'Not for much bloody LONGER, Harris!' I'd shouted, panicked by the mere mention of compression.

Although maybe they *didn't* hear me, on reflection. Not over the throaty roar generated by the turbo-charged diesel of the crane as it suddenly began to manoeuvre into position.

I'd begun to withdraw even before I heard the clang of the hook seeking purchase in the wreckage above. Then I reflected angrily on how I'd prevaricated while achieving precisely nothing for the past several minutes, and that RJ was still waiting patiently for succour.

I didn't relish delaying. I'd attended too many RTAs, didn't really need to confirm that life was extinct – but for his sake, for my own peace of mind, I had to make one positive attempt to ensure that Private, or Corporal, maybe even Sergeant *R*-something *J*-something was indeed beyond help before the crane disturbed the wreckage. Steadman had been made aware that I was in here, so it was safe enough: they wouldn't lift the jagged mess until I was clear. Tentatively stretching to my fullest extent beyond a distorted spar that separated us, I just managed to reach the hand.

180

It was surprising how easily it moved. Till then I'd assumed he was trapped irrecoverably. I still couldn't make out the rest of the casualty, every top surface was arc-dazzling reflective: what voids existed below lay in impenetrable black shadow, as did the rest of RJ. I pulled experimentally at the projecting fingers. They followed quite easily – hell, maybe he wasn't trapped at all: maybe there *was* still hope . . .? By worming forward an extra inch I managed to take a firmer grip of the wrist, feeling awkwardly for a pulse . . . nothing my cold-numbed fingertips could detect. Suddenly my cruelly-extended shoulder muscles rebelled, contracted in an agonizing spasm. I drew back involuntarily, cursing with the shock of it – whereupon RJ's fingers, then his wrist, then his forearm eased out of the tangled mess.

. . . and that was all.

There was a tattoo on the forearm: some sort of snake entwined around a dagger I think, although I confess to having found myself more hypnotized by the effect the blue and orange strobes had on the tendrils of drawn sinew trailing from the stump of the severed elbow. Then my face went down into something indescribable: the wreck spun crazily, I decided *Sod the fuckin' image, Walker*, and vomited with the horror of it all.

Not for very long, certainly. A harsh command in German suggested I'd little time left for such self-indulgence. Especially when the mutter of the crane's diesel increased to a throbbing roar, the hook dragged and screeled across metal, then lodged firmly with a resounding *clang*!

. . . And the whole bloody top-hamper above me began to vibrate as the cable took the strain.

Fourteen

I'd begun with an outraged bellow of protest, and finished on a scream. Understandable really: no reflection on the image at all. Not considering I'd just started to die, and rather horribly at that.

The folded-back section of Leyland coach roof I'd crawled under must have weighed well over a ton. OK, so I exaggerate slightly: maybe just *under* a ton depending on how much of the rest of the coach, and how many of its former passengers, remained attached to it. Either way the actual weight was likely to prove academic so far as I was concerned because drag *that* across me, even ignoring the razor-edges protruding from its underside, and Staff Sergeant Walker, RMP, would be posing for the post-incident photographer as, to borrow Parrish's imaginatively-phrased rhyming slang, brown bread.

Ready sliced.

I desisted from conjecturing further on the likely pathology of my impending post-mortem when the mass of tangled alloy – until that point, a greatly appreciated umbrella which had helped shield me from the discomfort of the sleet falling steadily on the world outwith mine – suddenly jerked, creaked loudly in metallic protest . . . then started to MOVE.

Worse – it began to drag the rest of the hooked-up wreckage with it.

Even WORSE, for Chrissakes – the longitudinally stressed wreckage immediately began to conform to the laws of physics, and close *around* me: what little void space I'd started with beginning to elongate and, at the same time, draw inwards. Even before I'd exhausted my capacity to keep yelling, I found myself trapped within a razor-edged, already remorselessly diminishing, cocoon . . .!

They can be bizarre, the sort of things you think about during your last moments. And I'd experienced quite a few in my undistinguished military career, what with Dunkirk and the *Princess Louise* going down, and Tobruk just after I'd told Bull's Bum the Afrika Korps had blown up his whisky: and the time I'd been chased across the parade square by a full clip of EOKA SMG rounds, and my low-altitude ground-to-air experience with Foxie as a prelude to my head-to-Browning muzzle confrontation with the Mad Major.

This time I found myself philosophizing on what a soft touch the modern army is. How tolerant we Redcaps are of those nurtured lambs who stray from the paths of red, white and blue righteousness in defiance of Queen's Regulations. On what it must've felt to be a recalcitrant yeoman-squaddie in the William of Cassingham's founding days of the Provost Corps. *Lost 'is issue quiver of arrows, has 'e, Tipstaff Corporal ...? Pikestaff filthy an' 'ardly sharp enough to pierce a throat, you say ... ? Top button of 'is ruff undone, wus it ...? Bang 'im in the Iron Maiden for thirty seconds – all them inward-facing spikes: they oughter do it!*

It was about then that my situation became *really* fraught. One downwards-projecting remnant of the Iron Maiden – no, wrong century: the Leyland *omnibus*! – hooked neatly under the back of my webbing belt and instantly I felt myself moving too ... being drawn helplessly towards those scalpel-honed alloy shards that concealed the rest of RJ someone or other.

I got angry then. Or more petulant, really: getting uncer-moniously hauled along like that. Sod this for a game of bloody soldiers, I reflected furiously. If anything can go wrong, it bloody *will* for bloody WALKER ...! Another couple of feet and I would disintegrate into tattered, bloody streamers destined to be scraped into a body bag and labelled *Probably Staff Walker RMP* unless, of course, my B2603 in its little plastic case escaped the mincer, and they could omit the probably.

Forcing my hands beneath my belly, I squirmed on my side while scrabbling frantically to release the burnished brass buckle securing the tautly stretched belt. Visualizing the way *that* was being mutilated made me even more pissed off. All those hours wasted: all that effort spent stripping the brasses from it, then soaking its unyielding canvas in buckets of bleach so's the RMP-white blanco would take better . . .

An alloy sliver carved past my cheek, the pain made more excruciating by the sting of sweat. I hardly noticed, pre-occupied as I was with attempting to disengage the belthook while the sides of my British Leyland-built Iron Maiden continued to elongate and close around me . . .

The temptation to give up was proving ever more enticing: to simply seek refuge within the billows of unconsciousness already threatening to overwhelm me. But I knew if I gave way to such fleeting impulse, that I was finished – that Staff Sar'nt WW and rank-unknown RJ would join together to form a bloodied anagram of death they'd never be able to decipher back at Brigade.

With a last terror-induced spasm, my numbed fingers managed to release the buckle. Instantly the clamp round my waist eased and I curled into a foetal huddle, sobbing with fear as the mangled alloy sheet above me continued to bump and screel and tear its way over and past.

. . . Then blinding light sizzled down on me from the jib of the giant crane, and somebody uttered a guttural shout, and a whistle began to blow frantically to halt operations.

Slowly I became aware of the blessed discomfort of sleet falling to mingle soothingly with blood from my slashed cheek. 'Probably lost the *rest* of your bloody ear as well,' I gloomed morosely: still wandering in the twilight of terror.

Then I sensed the Iron Maiden jolt again while, at the same time the white flare of the arcs became masked by an intervening object. Screwing eyes tight shut, I panicked some more – no, a *lot* more! – before realizing it was only the wreckage subsiding fractionally beneath the weight of a man.

When I dared open them again to frown into the blinding haze, I decided for a moment I was brown brea . . . *dead* after all, and that it was an angel hovering above: the way the steadily falling sleet captured and diffused the glare so's it looked just like a halo surmounting that ethereal apparition.

It wasn't, of course. It was anything but.

It was Major Steadman. Grinning tightly down at me.

'You murderin' *bastard*!' I croaked, coming straight to the point.

He raised a mildly reproving eyebrow. 'You've forgotten something.'

'WHAT?'

'The *sir*.'

A German paramedic came running over carrying an ambulance bag and I yelled, 'Fuck OFF an' kill someone else!'

The crews were moving in now: more and more casualties being extricated from the after end of the crushed coach. Playing to the audience, Steadman bent solicitously. 'Remember we're guests in this country, Walker. Don't disregard the pleasantries.'

Furiously I pushed the Judas hand away and clambered to my feet unaided. 'You bloody knew I was under there, Steadman. I heard Alf Harris tell you.'

'Did he?' He shrugged unconcernedly. 'Or is that another of your spite-influenced assumptions?'

'He told you, all right.' I spat to clear the stale sickness. 'Which means there'll be two witnesses at the next court martial, Major. *Not* just my word against yours.'

His hand betrayed the first sign of unease at that, lifting to trace the scar in that all-too-familiar gesture I'd long learned to interpret as insecurity. I grinned in dishevelled triumph. He'd gambled on being fireproof once too often. OK, so it could only lead to a charge of criminal negligence: attempted murder at best if they could prove intent, but I'd settle for either. Me and Charlie, we'd drink a toast the day they banged him up. This time Walker was in command and he didn't need a Sten.

'I say again – *two* witnesses, Steadman,' I gloated. 'For the prosecution.'

'Alleging what: that you got the impression he'd warned

185

me? Hardly a cast-iron case, Walker. My best advice is to forget taking it further.'

I shook my head emphatically. 'No way, Major. I could've died down there. This goes right to the APM's office.'

It did worry me a little: how mildly he was taking it. It seemed the ten-year-old crack in the facade was deeper than I thought: especially when he spread his hands in resignation.

'All right,' he conceded wearily. 'What, exactly, *did* Sergeant Harris say?'

The trap was baited. All I needed to do was set it, and I even had correct procedure on my side. Fumbling in a crumpled breast pocket I rescued my AB466 with its battered stump of pencil. 'I'll note it down for you, Major. So's neither of us forget.'

Still a tad hysterical, I licked the pencil lead out of habit, opened the notebook, and recorded my memory of the conversation between Steadman and Harris of what must only have been a few minutes before. I didn't embellish it: I didn't need to. Just recounted how Alf had warned the CO I was still beneath the wreck, as best I could recollect hearing from within my self-elected tomb.

OK, so maybe I did resolve to cheat a *little* by refreshing Harris's memory at the first opportunity. And obviously I didn't expect Steadman to hold his hands up, admit, 'It's a fair cop, Guv,' and go straight to jail. But I couldn't resist offering the book to him, baiting him for a change.

'Care to initial the entry, Major? Confirm it was made immediately following the event?' I invited sarcastically, really putting the boot in hard.

I assumed he'd walk: disregard such a clumsy invitation to incriminate himself. To my surprise he took it from me and scanned the page, frowning.

'You're certain these were Harris's precise words, Walker?'

I nodded emphatically, then wished I hadn't because doing so made my battered head feel as if it was going to fall off my shoulders. 'Enough to swear to them in court.'

He tilted it to catch the light. 'Sergeant Harris, RMP, informed our Commanding Officer, Major Steadman: quote

– Remember Staff Walker is down there, sir – unquote. You're quite sure of that, Staff Sergeant?'

'Quote – *Yeah!* Unquote – *Sir!*'

He smiled a little at the blatant insolence; a suddenly-most-tolerant lunatic. It seemed ten years had left him madder than I'd thought.

Even madder that *that*, it seemed. When he initialled my entry with a flourish.

I confess to disappointment. I'd expected more resistance to his being asked to endorse what was, effectively, his own admission of guilt. Yet all he did was hand the book back without expression.

'You're showing excessive zeal: you know that don't you? The APM's office won't like it. Not only do you have a weak case in law: they'll consider you're being damned hard on a fellow Redcap in even attempting to pursue it.'

'You argued that line before, Steadman,' I retorted impatiently, desperate to get away and lie down somewhere. 'The difference being it's no longer your word against mine.'

'Assuming you're referring to the accusation you made in Cyprus,' the melting sleet highlighted the scar, making it seem as if freshly administered under the glare, 'the difference is considerably greater than that.'

'True. There's no dead child involved, we're not in a back alley this time – and you can't shoot me even if you were carrying.' I hastily qualified that rejoinder: no point in tempting providence. 'Well, not with these spotlights on us, anyway.'

This time when he spread his hands it was unquestionably an acceptance of defeat. Worryingly so. 'Very well, Walker. Make it an issue as you feel strongly, but be warned there are precedents in military history that will go against you.'

I blinked uncertainly. The one thing I could never accuse him of being was predictable. 'Precedents?'

'Balaclava,' he supplemented.

'*Balaclava?*'

'The Light Brigade, Walker. Into the Valley of the Shadow of Death—'

'I *know* what the Light Brigade did. Got themselves mostly killed to provide inspiration for a bloody poem,' I interrupted sourly. 'What's that got to do with me getting squashed?'

'Lord Cardigan gave the order to charge the Russian guns partly on the basis of a misunderstanding, Walker. No disciplinary action was later taken against those the War Office believed to be responsible for the troopers' deaths. This allegation of yours could prove to be an equally difficult case to establish ... the issuing of inadequate or misleading intelligence regarding the dispositions of personnel at any given time?'

A Nasty Thought insinuated itself in my already traumatized mind: made all the more unsettling when, suddenly, he didn't look so much like a beaten man as a cat that's stolen the cream.

'Meaning?' I growled uneasily.

'Meaning you might wish to analyse your contemporary statement, Staff Sergeant. The one entered in your own AB466 and verified as such by your commanding officer. I quote from memory – Sergeant Harris said, *Remember Staff Walker is down there, sir* – unquote.'

'So?'

'So any Board of Inquiry will first seek to establish the precise context in which Sergeant Harris's warning was given ... or if, indeed, it *was* intended as a warning.'

I saw what he was driving at then, and began to wish I hadn't bothered unhooking my bloody belt. When he continued it was smooth as a striking snake.

'Fortunately I also took the precaution of recording my conversation with Sergeant Harris, Walker. The one we had immediately prior to him giving what you allege was a warning of your being under the wreckage?'

He produced his own AB466 from an immaculately creased pocket and held it to me mockingly. 'Would you care to initial it – or shall I paraphrase?'

He didn't need to.

I'd already turned in bitter defeat, and begun to clamber unsteadily down from the compressed tangle that he'd planned should form my coffin.

* * *

188

The Major had just ordered Harris – Alf *himself* would be forced to confirm he'd just been ordered – to go and supervise the setting-up of the RMP incident post. *That* was what had triggered Harris's response. 'Remember Staff Walker's down there, sir,' he'd called as he left.

A warning to maintain watching over me to ensure my safety – or an implied protest at being told to leave unneccessarily because I was already down there *at the incident post*? I knew damned well – Steadman had *certainly* known damn well, which scenario Harris had been referring to . . . but when repeated verbatim in the dispassionate, forensic atmosphere of a formal provost inquiry . . . ? If anyone was going to carry the can should I pursue my complaint, it would be Alf Harris. For failing in his duty of care on handover to the CO. For not having been explicit in giving full, and vital, information regarding my actual whereabouts while knowing that failure to do so might lead to my death.

The malice in Steadman's parting caution was clear and chilling. It stayed with me long after I'd stumbled from that gruesome place.

'Do be careful during the next few weeks, Staff Sergeant. You've just seen how easily accidents can happen. One moment of inattention, and you could find yourself retiring from provost in a box.'

Fifteen

Corporal Thomas drove through the centre of town like he'd veered off course from a Formula One circuit. Lamp standards passed in a blur: elderly jay-walkers discovered new reserves of energy. Me, I just kept my eyes tight shut and clung one-handed to the safety bar across the front seats while clamping my scarlet-covered SD cap to my head with the other. In the back of the patrol Rover, young Flint was bouncing up and down on the side-bench seat like a mis-hit ping-pong ball. Each time we powered over a bump in the road, I heard his compo-soled boots crash uncontrollably back to the chipped alloy floor.

Blues and bloody twos in response to a call from a brothel – all I needed on my last working day in the army. I was becoming more despondent by the minute about the way the shift seemed to be heading from bad to worse. Oh, it had dawned well enough: I'd risen with unaccustomed zeal and, despite the assorted sticking plasters that the British Army tends to substitute for GIs' purple hearts, had cheerfully inspected the shaving mirror with an air of self-satisfied well-being. This was it: me and the image both were about to become redundant. Walker had run the gauntlet of thirty years' service and was going out tomorrow at cock-crow.

I'd hesitated then. Thought maybe I shouldn't dismiss the image too precipitately? Maybe I was going to need it a bit longer. Truth was, the prospect of becoming plain Mr Walker, cast adrift to sink or swim in a sea of civilian anonymity, scared me more than I cared to admit. For three decades Queen's Regulations had been my bible: the Rod and Staff that had comforted me. The army had, for all its sometimes-

190

brutal patriarchy, fed, clothed, housed and directed my every action – well, *nearly* my every actio—

Shit . . .! Thomas threw the Rover into a bend that would've tested the suckers of an octopus, never mind the tarmac-adhesive qualities of Dunlop treads. I swear a vision of Foxie flashed before me then: dangling from his tree up there with a cadaverous welcoming grin like he was sayin', 'See you shortly – *very* shortly, Staff,' as I fought the lateral G-forces intent on shooting me sideways out of the Rover like a fly landed on a centrifuge.

'At least slow down to a HUNDRED miles a bloody hour, Thomas!' I snarled.

'It's a cracking knocking-shop, Staff,' he turned from the wheel to grin, as if that explained everything. 'Some of the Fräuleins are worth a bit of wellie. Accordin' to hearsay, of course.'

'Watch the fuckin' ROAD!' I screamed back.

I shouldn't even have *been* there. I wouldn't have been if, perhaps predictably, the CO hadn't done all he could to ensure I didn't have a nice last day. OK, I'd known Steadman had long determined I'd be listed on this morning's patrol-duty rota, but I'd thought I fixed that. Sergeant Harris had offered to stand in for me, which went to show what an accommodating bloke Alf really was under that gorilla-cuddly anti-social exterior. Mind you, before I asked, although purely for insurance purposes, I'd casually let him see Steadman's initialled entry in my AB466, recording the regrettable lack of clarity contained in his warning on the night of the bus RTA.

Then RSM Halliday had come into breakfast and told me, with a glint of diappointment in his eyes, that Steadman had also cancelled my passing-out party scheduled by the mess committee for that evening – and I do mean passing out in the alcoholic sense of the word. Not only that, but the malicious bastard – my description, not Halliday's, who, being a regimental sergeant major and intending to remain one, stuck inflexibly to the wise-monkey philosophy when it came to criticizing officers – had also refused to approve Harris substituting for my duty spell: presumably a last display of bloody-minded frustration at realizing his favourite fly-elect was about to escape the web for ever.

I'd brightened only marginally after Halliday had pointed out that, providing I stayed sober until midnight, and went strictly by the book – then I'd technically become a civilian guest, and the committee could hardly order the bar to be shut in my face until I'd fallen on it.

'And anyway, it's Tuesday, man,' the sergeant major had concluded, airily confident. 'You'll not be likely to have any incidents to interrupt your dozing in the duty-room chair for the day. Ninety per cent of BAOR's skint by Sunday morning. I mean, who's going tae gie the Redcaps trouble on a Tuesday, eh?'

I did succumb to a nasty thought called Charlie Parrish, but only momentarily. Because of course, seeing the RSM himself had decreed it, the answer could only be 'no'.

. . . Apart from the anonymous British soldier who had, seemingly, been unaware of such authoritative constraints placed by Jeemy Halliday on his diary of things to do for the week.

The one reported dead in a bordello bed, in company with a drink-paralysed Teutonic whore.

We hurtled down the last hundred yards of litter-strewn back street like a ground-to-ground missile. When Thomas braked to a rubber-acrid stop, Lance Corporal Flint didn't. Instead he kept going, decelerating only with a final crash of heels and a squeal of oaths on hitting the back of the front bench seat. I cut the blues-and-twos switch then fell gratefully out of the Rover in front of a uniformed German cop about ready to take cover behind the issue-boots-battered front door of the establishment. The indentations alone provided evidence enough to suggest no money-back guarantee of client satisfaction was offered with every purchase.

Either that, or no one had told the British Army the war ended twenty-two years ago.

'In there, mate?' Thomas queried. The young cop hurriedly stood aside: perhaps worried we might go back for a tank if he didn't. Piling into the house of ill repute we found another plainclothes officer, presumably the scenes-of-crime photographer, already unloading his Leica at the foot of the stairs. He scrutinized our red caps, RMP duty armbands, snowy webbing and super-gloss size elevens with an expertise that proved he was no mean detective.

'Waffenpolizei?'

'No, the Red Army fuckin' ballet troupe,' I grumbled disregarding, out of sheer childish pique, the Major's insistence on the international pleasantries.

Maybe he had a Steadman as his boss, too, because he just smiled bleakly while jerking a thumb at the stairs. At the top we were confronted by a corridor full of scantily dressed scrubbers all talking at once. Latvian, Polish, Ukrainian or whatever – a regular United Nations love-fest. And before 0900 on a Tuesday *morning* . . .? Either the day shift coming on, or the back shift coming off. In a manner of speaking.

I elbowed Flint in the stomach, embarrassed, on the British Army's behalf, by the way he was ogling. 'Get 'em back in their rooms and no touchy-feely. *Now!*'

The stench of booze and sickness struck us with almost physical impact when we went through the next door. Corporal Thomas stopped dead to fumble for a hankie but, drawing hard on the image I continued, outwardly unmoved, to join the elderly German sergeant standing equally stolidly by the bed. He looked at me, offered a part-understanding, part-fatalistic shrug, then lit a cigarette from the butt of his previous one. No chewing gum this time, or maybe it was to combat the atmosphere.

But like me, he'd an image to keep up. It didn't necessarily get easier with repetition. Sometimes it was the only way old hands like us could cope.

It hadn't been a surfeit of testosterone-generated ecstasy that had killed the young soldier. The bulging eyes and blue-contorted lips told me all I needed to know. I'd seen it all before, especially in the Singapore and Hong Kong garrisons where the National Service conscripts had sometimes resorted to experimenting with opium to alleviate their regimented misery. Out there, unless the Chinese drug master dumped the body in a handy monsoon ditch first, we'd be called to the poppy dens to find them laid out neat in their jungle green, with necks arched over those hollowed wooden blocks the opium smokers use as pillows. And I'd seen too many mottled faces and protruding tongues emulating this poor bloody kid's to harbour any doubt that the cause of death was similar. He'd merely substituted raw schnapps and lager for Tiger beer and poppy bliss.

He'd got paralytic drunk, managed to make it as far as collapsing backwards on the bed, then passed out cold: ultimately drowning in his own vomit 'cause the girl he was with was too far gone herself to bloody notice she was trying to earn a Deutschmark from a dead man.

Nobody had bothered to help her, not even to cover her nakedness. She couldn't have been very old, not more than seventeen or eighteen. Lying motionless as she was, the only way to tell she wasn't dead as well was when the red-varnished mouth sagged to emit a stentorian snore of alcohol-laden breath.

She'd have been quite pretty in other circumstances, though I did note several ugly contusions low down on the gravity-flattened belly. That made me wonder bleakly if she'd ever entertained a client called Eric, but then, there weren't any bruises on the painted face, and she still retained all her fingers.

'The happy snaps man downstairs finished, has he?' I asked.

The sergeant nodded. 'And the *doktor* has gone to call for the ambulance. Just now he lets her sleep it off, *ja*?'

Maybe. But he hadn't even placed her in the recovery position before he left. 'You sure he was a *doktor*?' I growled, tugging a corner of the stained blanket to cover the girl's still-carelessly splayed thighs. How they treated their own was outwith my jurisdiction, but I figured enough was enough for young Flint. He'd already be well topped-up on ecstatic, ordering naked ladies around in the corridor.

'We can move her to another room, Feldwebel. Allow you to complete your business?' the sergeant offered.

194

. . . And my final duty as a Redcap, I thought, brightening. Thomson perked up too: overcame his revulsion enough to volunteer helpfully, 'I'll take the leg end, Staff.'

'No, you bloody won't,' I retorted. 'Rank has its privileges, and he outranks you.'

It didn't need three of us to lift her off the bed. She was so stoned she hardly sagged in the middle: just stayed rigid as a levitated magician's assistant. After they'd shuffled out with her I stood a moment, looking carefully round the foetid room for anything untoward that might need preserving as evidence, but there didn't seem to be – apart from a dead British soldier with tousled black hair and, presumably, a mum and dad somewhere who'd shortly be crying a lot. The Poliziei SOCO might or might not bother with forensics when, or if, he arrived. Our own Provost SIB had automatically been notified when the call came in, so there wasn't a lot more to do.

A BD blouse with lance-jack's tapes lay on the floor. I could tell he'd been proud of having earned them, the way the chevrons had been neatly picked out with white blanco. The shoulder flashes and divisional insignia told me he was – *had* been – Royal Corps of Transport. I didn't relish handling the soiled identity disc around the boy's neck and, anyway, there was no one else in the room to put on the impassive act for, so I confined myself to rummaging through the deceased's pockets in search of his ID card.

A comb, ball-point pen, a wad of crumpled Deutschmarks thick enough to suggest either the RSM had been unduly cynical about the state of BAOR's mid-week finances or this lad earned a second income stream as many did: usually by passing vehicle spares over the wire back at the depot. There was the inevitable army-issue condom, intercourse, soldiers for the use of, but obviously disregarded in the excitement of killing himself: three female hair clasps and a tampon which, despite having seen most things in my time, still caused me to raise a mystified eyebrow: and a snapshot of what I took to be his mother, although I'd learned ten years back not to jump to over-hasty conclusions . . . come to that: how *had* Flint – I mean TOSH, this time! – ended up with such a lovely wife considering the pic I'd found of his then-girlfriend that still all-too-vivid morning in the Cyprus mountains?

There were three more dog-eared photos of a generously proportioned frau wearing jackboots, a Nazi armband and not a lot otherwise who, it seemed safe to hazard despite her obvious maturity, definitely wasn't Mum. No more than the athletic younger gentleman courting her was likely to be his dad . . . these I stuck in my own pocket for destruction. I'd always considered a Redcap bears responsibilities over and above those laid down in QRs. They were hardly the personal effects his bereaved next of kin would have viewed with nostalgia.

Corporal Thomas came back in, trying not to inhale too deeply, while I was entering the particulars from the lad's AFB2603 in my notebook. 76580963 Walsh, Stanley, RCT . . . add, RIP. I checked his leave pass: that was in order, too. In fact the only thing Lance Corporal Walsh, RCT, had done wrong had been to drink too long, too unwisely and too well.

I lit a Capstan with hands that shook just a little more than the image would have approved of, then nodded at young Stanley. 'He'll need someone to hold his hand till SIB show up. Where's Flint?'

Thomas shoved his head into the corridor. 'Hey, Don Juan – get in here!'

Flint clomped in, took one look, and went pale as a ghost. I guessed he'd never seen a dead soldier before. Or not one who'd died as hard and pointlessly as 76580963 Walsh had. But every copper has to be blooded some time.

'You stick to lemonade, lad,' I said paternally.

'And don't touch nothin',' Thomas added less paternally. 'Or I'll fuckin' 'ave you!'

I don't know if Flint heard us. The way he was bent over the chipped washbasin as I gratefully closed the door on Walker's Last Case.

. . . Or so I thought.

Blowing an impatient column of smoke across the duty rosters on the desk, I glanced irritably at the clock. Corporal Thomas was still missing. How long did a bloke need to fetch two mugs of tea and a brace of NAAFI bacon sannies? Over half an hour had dragged by since our return from Walsh's death bed, and he'd been gone most of that time. Thomas – not Walsh.

Reluctantly I stretched for an AFB2100 report form and began writing up the lad's epitaph while promising myself darkly that if Thomas didn't get back sharpish, I'd be filling in two – the second one for him.

When he did finally appear, he still wasn't juggling a tray. He just opened the door and stuck his head round looking uneasy.

'Where the hell've you been, Cinderella?' I growled.

'Found a problem, Staff,' he said uncomfortably.

'You'll have two unless you produce a very creative excuse for bein' AWOL,' I grumbled, not even alerted then by what should have been the deafening clamour of warning bells.

'Sorry, Staff, but I . . . Look, I got a prisoner out here.'

He swallowed nervously, hesitated, muttered a resigned, 'Ohhh, *fuck* it!' and came right into the room followed, at a cooperative amble, by a small person. Perhaps I'd missed something, some Army Council Instruction or whatever, because it seemed it had become de rigueur for military policemen to act as guides for, rather than escorts to, the arrested.

'Fusilier Parrish,' Thomas announced wearily.

If somewhat superfluously.

Eyeing him only through parted fingers, my first impression of Charlie was hazy, largely on account of my having buried my face in my hands the instant I heard the name. Hours to go before I gave the Queen back her shilling, and *Parrish* turns up. In other circumstances I'd have been pleased: in the present climate of impending doom, the coincidence worried me. A lot.

Give him his due, he seemed a bit taken aback himself on recognizing me behind the duty desk, though if he was he recovered quick enough. Certainly his response did nothing to reassure me.

'Well, if it isn't Staff Walker,' he greeted amiably – none of that staring stolidly at the vanishing point this time, I noted uneasily. 'My old mate of the Royal Military Carve-ups.'

'Shut it, Parrish!' Thomas beetled in justifiable outrage. 'Don't you come the lippy in here.'

I massaged my face savagely while lowering my hands. That's when I started to feel curious, as well as appre-hensive. He didn't give an impression of being under the influence and, rather more ominously in an illogical kind of way, he'd smartened himself up since the last time provost bade him welcome as Flint's guest. His Fusilier's beret fitted like a glove, not a beer stain to be seen: boots almost shiny as mine: his anklets' blanco and buckles flawless. Even his issue warm looked trim and neat, which is next to impossible with British Army greatcoats, espe-cially for vertically challenged soldiers like Parrish. Usually their hems hang so close to the ground that as they march they sort of glide along like those floaty Cossack girl dancers, seemingly self-propelled on ball bear-ings, rather than boots.

But what unsettled me most was that he looked more like the old Charlie: the old, *hard* Charlie Parrish. OK, so maybe I should have felt pleased for him, but that was far from my initial reaction. Again, and no doubt perversely, I construed it as justification for further unease . . . but *why*? Why *should* seeing my best friend apparently having taken a firm grip on his self-respect afford me such grounds for alarm?

Come to that, why, for Christ's sake, was he here in the first place? Why *had* Corporal Thomas, an eminently sensible NCO, felt he'd had cause to apprehend him?

Then a thought struck me, and it didn't directly concern the seeming rehabilitation of Fusilier Parrish. I re-targeted my scowl at Corporal Thomas. It wasn't too late to pay him back for denying me my last-ever NAAFI bacon sannie.

'How come you picked him up when you was only going to the canteen? That didn't give you reason to go walk-about outside the barracks gates.'

198

Thomas prickled virtuously. 'I didn't, Staff. When I said I'd found a problem, I . . . well, I meant it literally. I came across Parrish *inside* the perimeter fence. Far as I could tell, he'd just climbed over the wire.'

I didn't need to ask, the suddenly wooden look on Charlie's face told me all I needed to know. But I asked anyway: I'd need it for the charge sheet. For 7153229l Fusilier Parrish's next court martial.

'Exactly *where* inside the wire?'

Thomas didn't know, of course: about Charlie's earlier threat. The specific locus held little significance for him.

'Right behind the officers' mess block, Staff,' he said. 'About halfway along. Under the CO's window?'

The trusting part of my nature, the infinitely lesser part, surrendered unconditionally at that. Deep down I'd already become tight-strung as the wire Charlie had just breached, but I forced myself to keep it a bit jocular, what with Thomas being there and everything.

'I've heard of soldiers breaking out of provost lines before, Fusilier Parrish, but never once in thirty years have I come across anyone tryin' to break *in*. Never realized you was so fond of us.'

'I'm RMP's biggest fan.' His eyes betrayed the merest flicker of irony. 'To who else would I owe my successful career – *Staff* Sergeant?'

I got mad at that. If Charlie wanted it that way, jocular was out. 'Oh, change the bloody record! Jus' cut the smart talk and explain what you were doing inside the perimeter.'

'Hadn't nicked anything, far as I could see, Staff,' Thomson interjected, obviously uncomfortable about the whole affair, what with it being my last day and everything.

'Whaddyou mean – far as you could *see*? Didn't you search him?'

Thomas shuffled uneasily. 'I thought, well, seeing he's a mate of yours, Staff . . .'

I even got up from the desk to give him a proper glare. 'What do I have to do to get it through your thick skull,

Thomas, that a Redcap don't *have* no mates? One more feeble excuse like that and you'll be on report and all . . . search 'im NOW!'

Thomas nodded guiltily then swung on Charlie. Little fleas and bigger fleas again . . . 'Get your greatcoat off, soldier – HON the double!'

Parrish threw me an impassive glance, then shrugged out of the heavy coat. Neatly folding it over the back of a chair he clasped his hands on top of his head in an obviously well-practised gesture. Corporal Thomas began to search him dead carefully. As he patted under the raised arms his eyes met Parrish's. Charlie gave an apologetic sort of smile. 'No hard feelings, son?'

Thomas shrugged. 'You're the prisoner.'

He finished his body search then stood frowning at Charlie, who simply eyed him back coyly: hands still on head, a paragon of disciplined innocence. I was just beginning to wonder if Thomas had learned *anything* from me, when he turned to Parrish's warm, examining it thoughtfully.

Charlie said conversationally, 'Thought you blokes always missed the coat thrown casual over the back of a chair.'

I continued to keep my eyes on Thomas. He was hefting the greatcoat critically, now. 'You been watching too much telly – go on, Corporal: get in them pockets!'

'Mind the mousetrap, son.'

'Shut it, Parrish!' Thomas grated.

He hefted the coat again, then looked at Parrish a bit oddly. Charlie simply continued to stare back deadpan, though I noticed he did jiggle a little uncomfortably, but that could simply have been with the strain of keeping his hands above his head.

That was when Thomas's hand ever so cautiously went into one baggy pocket – and he tensed.

'What is it, lad?' I forced myself to ask quietly.

Thomas's lips were tight as he slowly withdrew whatever he'd found, and held it out to me.

The object was roughly the size and shape of a small pineapple. Its outer casing was even divided into segments like one. Somewhat oddly, it wasn't British in origin: it was

American. But I knew enough to claim with authority that it weighed exactly one-decimal-three pounds.

When primed, it had a four-second fuse.

Even the *thought* of Charlie Parrish prowling around the officers' block with it scared the shit out of me.

Sixteen

A crack in the plaster of the duty-room ceiling had always offended my sense of good order. For weeks I'd intended to get on to public works and get it fixed. Now, all of a sudden, it seemingly held a fascination for Charlie Parrish too. I could tell that by the way he was staring skywards with frowning concentration while whistling tunelessly through his teeth. A cynic might have claimed he was studiously avoiding our somewhat hostile scrutiny, but I gave him the benefit of the doubt.

He wasn't being furtive at all. He was an honest to goodness, what-you-see-is-what-you-get fuckin' lunatic.

Corporal Thomas was the first to react, even while I was still trying to come to terms with the awareness that I wouldn't be going home tomorrow. He shoved his face close to Parrish's and snarled, 'Stop playin' silly buggers, soldier!'

Charlie stopped whistling, lowered his gaze and suddenly caught sight of the US-pattern M2A1 fragmentation grenade in Thomas's hand. 'Now I wonder who planted *that*?' he said.

I just shook my head, and felt sad. 'You silly . . . stupid . . . homicidal *bastard*!'

Charlie looked me straight back in the eye, and said mockingly, 'But then, like you say, Staff Sergeant: a Redcap don't have no mates. Not when it comes to fitting them up?'

It wasn't so much what he said, as the way he said it. The self-serving petulance in his voice. The way ten years of simmering resentment had distanced him so far from his own less than commendable part in the Kondoyiannis affair that he now saw me and Steadman as the sole causes of his downfall. So much so that now my once-best friend lumped *me* together with that murderous psychopath . . .?

Something snapped inside, while the room dissolved in red mist. Charlie Parrish's scornful grin seemed to get bigger and bigger . . . I forgot all the good times we'd been thick as thieves: all the tight spots we'd shared. I forgot how his once-indefatigable humour had given me the strength to survive the terror of Rommel's repeated assaults on the shell-torn sandy hell of Tobruk. I forgot the memory of that same man, pushed to the edge of endurance yet still grinning savage encouragement through a black-pitch film of fuel oil while he doggedly held on to me: hauling me bodily through the water towards the *Princess Irene*'s liferaft: refusing, even as the Stukas returned yet again to strafe our diminishing group of survivors, to do what I was pleading with him to do – release me to slip below the flotsam-strewn waves and sleep for ever and ever.

I most certainly forgot I was a policeman.

My hands were lunging for his throat, thumbs spearing for the carotid arteries . . . then Corporal Thomas's arms locked tight around my waist, dragging me away from the unresisting, still mocking Charlie, while yelling, 'F'r Chrissakes don't DO it, Staff! Not on your last day. He ain't bloody *worth* it!'

I stumbled back breathing heavily. Charlie simply stood there, hands still clasped above his head despite the red pressure bruises blossoming round his neck, and all the time eyeing me with that secretive, knowing smile playing at the corners of his mouth. Had he given even a little, I'd have embraced him for it. I wanted so desperately to say, 'Sorry, mate,' but I couldn't – he didn't intend to let me.

'Not worth it. Right, Staff?' Thomas repeated, tentatively easing his grip. 'You got too much to lose.'

I shrugged away roughly. 'The damage is done already, lad. Steadman's goin' to drag me into this, no matter what. He'll see it as his last chance to—'

I broke off, at that. Thomas's suddenly wary expression told me I was heading where he didn't want to go. Sure, he was aware of my head-to-head with the CO on the night of his arrival – the whole company knew something had happened by next day's breakfast: it had only needed one loose mouth among those who witnessed it – but none of them knew the story behind it. Only Parrish, me and, latterly, the RSM knew that. And I wasn't entirely convinced that Halliday had accepted my version, even then. Certainly he'd never referred to our conversation since.

Either way, Thomas apparently felt strongly about Charlie's placing my future at risk, which took me a bit aback, considering all the times I'd been over-hard on him, albeit for his own good. That realization actually worried me out of all proportion – loyalty instead of fear? It implied the image hadn't done its job properly.

Swinging on Parrish, he snarled, 'Get that fuckin' GRIN off your face, Fusilier! You dropped yourself right in it this time: five to seven in the glasshouse is best guess, pal.'

''*Ow* many years?' Charlie remained stolidly unimpressed. 'Come off it, Corporal. For strayin' into a restricted area without an invite?'

'No – for fuckin' having THAT on you when you did!' Thomas slammed the grenade on the desk with such force that I jumped apprehensively. Munitions have, in my view, always been objects to be treated with the reverence one would accord a baby. You didn't abuse them like you would, say, a Lance Corporal Tosh.

I trundled back around the desk to slump again, glooming at our uncontrite prisoner in exasperation. It didn't seem to matter how we handled it: nothing was getting through the armour-plated carapace that resentment had built around Parrish. I tried again: I owed him that much.

'For Christ's sake, mate: can't you *see* you're in dead trouble, man? The worst trouble you've ever had.'

That did it: finally got through to him this time. Before Thomas could restrain him he'd unclasped his hands and lunged right across the desk, practically spitting venom in my face. '*Trouble* you call it, Staff Sar'nt . . .? I already HAD the worst trouble you Redcaps could lay on me durin' my life – try Cyprus fifty-seven, *mate*! Cyprus, nineteen fifty-bloody-SEVEN.'

He calmed a bit then, but the bitterness was still evident

in the hardness of his eyes: the tight set of his jaw as he turned his ire on Thomas. 'And don't bother threatening me with the glasshouse, Corporal. Don't you ever get to thinking it's the worst thing can happen to a man. I been reduced to the ranks ten years now and every minute of every day since, I've wished to God some kind bloody soldier would come along and shoot *Fusilier* Parrish clean and neat through the head.'

Thomas opened his mouth uncertainly but I frowned and surreptitiously shook my head. Just for that moment, the shell had parted a crack.

'Detention ain't the only punishment for a long-service regular: it's just the first, see?' Charlie finished with a suddenly lost look in his eye. 'I hope you never finds out the hard way, son. By giving 'em reason to strip your pride along with your tapes.'

For a moment none of us said anything, then I swallowed with a bit of difficulty and hooked a chair over with my boot.

'Siddown, Charlie – you too, Thomas. Let's try and sort this bloody shambles best we can.'

When Charlie sat it was almost grudgingly: he was still simmering, still glowering at me like I was the enemy. Only after half a Capstan did the frown ease and he began to grin the old, irrepressible Parrish grin. OK, so time had shown it wasn't entirely indefatigable but still, I hadn't had it turned on me for a very long time, and suddenly the world seemed a better place.

'Sorry, mate,' he said, and there was no hidden inflection this time. 'You too, son. I was out of order.'

Thomas shrugged, uncertain of whether I intended him to be good cop, bad cop or all three wise monkeys together this time round. 'Forget it.'

Forget it . . .? I sat there frowning anxiously at Charlie while knowing we couldn't just forget it. Not everything – not the grenade. Hadn't I just pontificated to young Thomas on how a Redcap doesn't *have* friends when it comes to them breaking the law? And until midnight I was still a military policeman. Thirty years ago I'd sworn an oath and lived my life as best I could by it . . . well, most times. So I had to pursue it. No way could I let Charlie wriggle out've this one with a glib story and a newly resurrected smile.

Apart from which, after all the occasions when I'd wished in vain for a witness to bring the Mad Major to book, this time I had one when I might otherwise have covered for him. Corporal Thomas had arrested Parrish, had also been the one to find the grenade, so turning a blind eye was a non-starter. I simply hoped Charlie wouldn't dig himself even deeper into the mess. It wasn't an entirely selfless prayer. The deeper he dug, the more Steadman could exploit it as an opportunity to bury me with him. Quite how, I didn't yet know. But the mix of circumstantial evidence was already shaping to be lethal, and not only for Fusilier Parrish.

Take a provost field officer – a much-decorated major, say? Add a history of resentment over the conviction of a former infantry NCO whose career had been destroyed on the strength of evidence given by that same RMP major. Bring to that already potentially volatile mix a third soldier, a close lifetime friend of the second: a Redcap staff sergeant who – as already established by a confrontation that took place immediately after the CO's arrival – also harboured grounds for disgruntlement against the major, once again his commanding officer.

Stir with ten years of simmering resentment: inject a whiff of implied conspiracy to grievously injure, or kill . . . throw in an M2A1 fragmentation hand grenade?

'Straight up, Charlie,' I said almost pleadingly. 'Where did you get that?'

He looked the picture of innocence. If I needed proof he was about to lie, I had it.

'Found it, Staff,' he said deadpan.

'You found it,' Thomas repeated, just to confirm he'd heard right.

'Yeah, Corp.'

'*Corporal!*'

'Yes – Corporal.'

206

'Where did you find it?' I interjected hurriedly.

'Lying in the street.'

'Not the only thing bloody lying,' Thomas muttered to no one in particular.

'So what were you doing with it in officer country, then?'

He spread his hands in a mystified gesture. 'What else would I do with lost property? I mean, like – this *is* a sort of police station, yeah?'

'The officers' block isn't.'

'I got lost.'

'So you're claiming you found a US Army grenade simply lying in the street,' Thomas clarified, 'and bein' a responsible soldier, brought it here intending to report it as lost property?'

'Exac'ly what I just said, Corporal.'

'Only you got lost inside the barracks area,' Corporal Thomas leaned forward intently, 'after scaling the *wire* instead of doing what ordinary soldiers would do. Like using the front gate where the guard room is situated? Am I correct, Fusilier Parrish?'

'It's a long way round to the gate, Corporal,' Charlie went all virtuous as he developed his thesis. 'Meaning I'd have been placing women and children at extra risk, wouldn't I – carrying it further than necessary on a public thoroughfare? Remember, that's an old M2A1 frag pattern you got there: could be unstable.'

I eyed the grenade apprehensively at that, and hoped it wasn't. Or not as unstable as Charlie apparently was. OK, so Thomas had already tested it to the verge of destruction, slamming it down like he did but, nevertheless, my last day had proved its determination to go from bad to worse. It was still only late morning and already I had an iffy bomb sittin' less than three feet in front of me.

'Go on, then,' our prisoner encouraged helpfully. 'Get it down on one of them statement forms and I'll sign my name, rank and number to it.'

'Or we could batter you with truncheons then put you in a holding cell, of course. Until you fabricate a better fairy tale,' Corporal Thomas retorted every bit as considerately.

'One a prosecuting counsel won't tear to bloody shreds in two minutes.'

But like Flint, Thomas was a quick learner.

I offered Fusilier Parrish one last lifeline.

'Hold your horses. You haven't been cautioned yet, never mind charged. Now hear me loud and clear. This is you about to enter the Last Chance Saloon, Charlie Parrish. You give me cause to even suspect you intend to swear that black is white, then my notebook and pencil's coming out. Until then, we're still talking informally.'

I looked hard at Thomas. 'I say again: informally, Corporal?'

He gave a little smile. 'No one's said a word yet, Staff. Not till you decide they have.'

He really was shaping to be a bloody good Redcap, Corporal Thomas. Foxie had been a lot like that, not that I could remember much about him after ten years. Except for his boots, of course. At the risk of detracting further from the image, I let him see I was grateful. 'Good lad.'

But time was marching on and I was worried someone might come in before I could get this mess sorted out. Thomas was obviously willing to play along. All we needed now was a bit of cooperation from Parrish and at least we could play the matter down a lot. I didn't even try to disguise the fact I was pleading with him now, to help himself.

'Charlie, I'm still asking you off the record, but it's a one-time-only offer . . . Where – did – you – *get* – that grenade?'

Even before he got up from his chair without being told, I saw the defensive wooden expression shutter down, and knew I'd lost: that we'd moved to opposing sides of the field again, and I was simply another bastard Redcap. The army barrack-room code had beaten me.

'I found it lying on the street, Staff Sar'nt. I identified it as a dangerous munition, so I shoved it in my pocket and came straight here to hand it in. I lost my way within the perimeter area until the Corporal found me . . .'

My hands were shaking, partly in anger, mostly through frustration as I brought out my AB466 and pencil. Parrish didn't bat an eyelid: just came to attention in anticipation while Thomas rose to stand uncomfortably beside him.

I didn't have to keep my voice flat and impersonal. Every emotion I bloody possessed had gone flat.

'Fusilier Charles Parrish. You are charged that, on this date, you did enter a restricted military area without lawful authority and without reasonable explanation. You are further charged that, following your apprehension, you were found to be in possession of an unlawful weapon: namely a live hand grenade.'

His eyes flickered at that, but I couldn't stop now. For the second time in his life, Parrish's bloody-minded recalcitrance had caused him to commit military suicide: all I could do was lead him to the gallows.

Or just conceivably – accompany him.

'I must caution you that anything you say will be taken down in writing, and may be given in evidence. Do you wish to make any reply to the charges, Fusilier Parrish?'

He was looking a bit grey-faced by then, but still stubborn. 'Only that I was walkin' down the road when I found that grena—'

. . . Which marked the precise moment when the dutyroom door yanked open without so much as a by-your-leave knock.

The scar, shadowed below the peak of the officer's cap, was enough to establish that my last day wasn't about to get better.

Thomas and I stamped to attention automatically. Fusilier Parrish on the other hand, who'd already been at rigid attention while I was charging him . . .? He did exactly the opposite – *he* stood easy! In fact, it wasn't so much a stand easy as a provocative slump the moment he registered who'd entered. I willed him to conform, show due respect if only to the rank and not the man, but, being Charlie Parrish, and being finished anyway, he didn't. Stopping short only of actually sitting down and lumping his feet up on the desk, *he* went out of his way to show active disrespect.

Steadman hesitated a moment, framed in the doorway: swagger stick tap-tapping time and metronomically measured time again, at the seam of one razor-creased trouser leg. He completely ignored the Corporal and me, reserving the cold stare for the slouching Parrish. I suspect he recognized him immediately, though he made a good fist of covering it up.

'You *scruffy* little man!' he snapped. 'Return to the attention position immediately.'

Parrish didn't move a muscle: simply countered the stare with an even bleaker one of his own. 'The day I stand to attention for you, Major, is the day they bury you.'

. . . Then, ever so deliberately, Charlie went and shoved his hands in his pockets.

Well . . . young Thomas's previously army-issue blank expression just crumpled in disbelief. Steadman, to give him his due, betrayed no immediate reaction although the scar tightened and the cane did slap-slap a little harder – while me? Three decades of being brain-washed into responding to martial stimuli, of being turned into a military Pavlov's dog, just made me bloody furious with Parrish. Funny, in retrospect, how my fear-hate relationship with the Mad Major had been punctuated by – from my point of view, anyway – a not entirely productive reliance on conditioned reflexes: the running thread that linked us in much the same way as did covert violence and shiny boots . . . on this occasion, my wariness of the man became automatically subsumed by my aggrieved sense of propriety: my outrage reserved entirely for Charlie bloody Parrish.

I stepped close up to the recalcitrant prisoner, resisted an overpowering temptation to punch the little bastard's lights out and, instead, shoved my nose with an inch of his, and bellowed, 'When an officer enters the room, Fusilier – you *will* come to ATTENTION!'

For a tense moment I thought Charlie was going to defy me as well, make a fool of me in front of Thomas, but he didn't and, perversely, I was grateful to him for that. Grudgingly shuffling his boots together, he withdrew his hands from his pockets to dangle the thumbs more or less down the seams of his trousers. I didn't feel mollified: it was a Pyrrhic victory at best. Steadman had me where he wanted. He'd seize the opportunity to tie me, Parrish, Cyprus and the grenade all in two tidy courts martial briefs. He was good at seizing the moment, did tying neat little bundles together very well, but then, he'd had practice. The first time was when he'd gathered fragments of a child's eggshell skull into a pristine white handkerchief on a sun-washed mountainside: the second when manipulating every piece of evidence, both witnessed and circumstantial, to contrive that Charlie, not him, went down for the torture of Stavros Kondoyiannis.

Only then, and for the first time, did the CO acknowledged my presence as senior NCO. Not to have done so immediately on entering the duty room had been an inexcusable slight in itself but, hey – I was happy if that was as bad at it got. Mind you, I wasn't optimistic. Even when he raised the bamboo cane to level it arrogantly at my chest, he gave the impression of wishing he'd got a live round in the breech.

'I wasn't aware that you were in the habit of entertaining your chums in the duty room while on duty, Walker?'

I opened my mouth to put him right, then shut it again sharpish. He'd only entered after I'd charged Charlie. Meaning he didn't have a clue, so far, why Parrish was here . . . I didn't know whether there was advantage to be gained from that, but I wasn't going to shove my head in the lion's mouth voluntarily.

'Come to that, Staff Sergeant,' he continued acidly, 'I could justifiably consider you derelict in your duty by failing to warn me this man is also here in the Rhine Army. A provenly violent soldier, conceivably harbouring grounds for holding an imagined grudge against me?'

'No cause to suspect that's the case, sir,' I lied outrageously: more wooden-faced than Charlie Parrish ever managed.

'No?' He studied me for a moment: I could almost see him calculating what benefit, if any, could be exploited in pursuing that line of attack. The irony was, Charlie Parrish had done the spadework for him – once Steadman clocked the grenade lying on the table, now seemingly big as a fluorescent football in my fevered imagination, he'd be able to put away his calculator and order Thomas to produce the key to the cells, equation solved.

In the meantime he settled for a dismissive shrug. Or I thought he did. I should have known better that Steadman never dismissed any advantage lightly. 'But then, I could hardly expect loyalty, could I, Walker? From an NCO with your history.'

He swayed slightly then, and I frowned, slightly disconcerted, before it registered – *Jesus*, I thought hopelessly, he's been drinking again. The minefield was even more lethal than I'd feared. A mad major sober was a dangerous enough animal to reckon with: the sergeants' mess had already borne witness to the CO's reckless determination to pursue our vendetta when in his cups.

The nervous tic dragged at my mouth, only it wasn't nerves this time: it was bloody outrage at the way Steadman was behaving in front of an other rank, lips loosened by drink or not. When he afforded the still-rigid Thomas a covert glance I could see what was coming and, for the Corporal's sake, tried to forestall it. The lad already looked as if he was praying for the ground to open up and swallow him whole.

'Don't hang around, then – get on over to the MT section on the double, Corporal Thomas,' I growled urgently. 'Check which vehicles are serviceable for tonight's patrols.'

Thomas eyed me gratefully – we were square, now – and broke for the door.

'As you WERE, Corporal!' Steadman snapped.

Thomas returned white-faced to attention, looking to me for support, but I'd pushed it as far as I could in the face of a direct order. Besides, the way Steadman seemed determined to shape events, with me as a friend the lad didn't need an enemy. I studiously avoided his eye.

'I referred to history, Corporal,' Steadman continued curtly while young Thomas looked more and more bewildered: more and more trapped in a scenario he didn't understand. 'You should be aware that Walker holds a long-standing grudge against me on account of the punishment *ex*-Colour Sergeant Parrish received for a certain murderous lapse in Cyprus.'

I opened my mouth to protest, but Charlie beat me to it.

'I feels another murderous lapse comin' on right now, you lyin' rodent,' the ex-colour sergeant broke in mutinously.

It was the only time so far he'd chosen to disrupt the conversation: a bloody first for Fusilier Parrish in any company. It wasn't worth my reprimanding him. Morosely I'd already decided to save banging my head against brick walls till they put me in the holding cells next door. Meanwhile Steadman dismissed the interruption which, to be fair, suggested he wasn't entirely crazy. Ignoring Charlie meant he'd at least got *somethin'* bloody right since he came in.

'You should also know, Corporal, ' he continued venomously, 'that Staff Sergeant Walker actually threatened to kill me once. The man actually placed his Sten against my chest while we—'

'That's *it* – jus' shut your fuckin' MOUTH, Steadman!' I heard myself erupt with headstrong disregard for the consequences. 'Talkin' like that to a young NCO: it's right out of order for any officer. I said you were crazy before, Major. Now I'm bloody CERTAIN of it!'

Even Charlie Parrish looked stunned – OK, thoroughly approving, but still stunned – while Corporal Thomas's cheeks drained whiter than his belt. They both recognized I'd just committed verbal suicide by any yardstick, no matter what the provocation. I knew it better than either of 'em, but what *really* hurt was that I'd fallen for Steadman's inducement to step out of line at literally the eleventh hour of my remaining vulnerable to the penalties of military law. Had my mouth not overtaken my normally innate sense of self-preservation, I'd have seen the trap being laid.

He hadn't been at all reckless by being indiscreet before Corporal Thomas. He'd used the lad's presence to advantage: an independent witness to my gross insubordination. With Machiavellian artifice Steadman had deliberately goaded me to this point of open rebellion. He'd instantly recognized the volatile potential in finding the three of us together for the first time since Cyprus and, by doing so, had meticulously dug the grave for my honourable discharge, liberty and pension.

He hadn't even *needed* Parrish's contribution. That bonus was still to be revealed. True to form, even before Steadman discovered the grenade on the desk, I'd already presented him with a lorry load of infill.

Neither Parrish or Thomas would have noticed, but I did because I'd come up against it before, the last time directed over the muzzle of a high-power Browning. That barely perceptible glint of triumph in my adversary's eyes, the way the scar crinkled in long-awaited satisfaction.

'You will, of course, be cited as a witness, Corporal,' Steadman said predictably. Where he was concerned, I'd developed considerable expertise in being wise after the event. 'When I charge Staff Sergeant Walker with conduct prejudicial to good order and discipline.'

I disregarded my earlier resolution and banged my head once more against the solid wall: more for the masochistic satisfaction than in hope.

'You're drunk, Major. Just go to bed and forget it.'

'Forget it, Walker – *forget* it? But of course, you'd like tha—'

The CO stopped short abruptly. I didn't need to track his line of sight down to the desk behind me.

I already knew it was all over.

When Steadman said, 'Where in God's name did *that* come from?'

Nobody responded. The silence in the duty room hung oppressive as a shroud awaiting the hangman's labours. The CO looked hard at each of us in turn, the scar slowly deepening in intensity. Thomas was obviously scared stiff, while Charlie just watched equably. I think I hated him more even than the Major at that moment, for having dragged me into the psychotic's web only hours before I was free of it for ever.

Steadman's cane smashed across the desk like a rifle shot. Me, I jumped higher than the grenade. Why did *everybody* seem determined to challenge Parrish's theory that the bloody thing could be unstable?

'I put a question and, by God, I'll have an answer!' He

swung on the unfortunate Thomas. 'I'll ask once more, Corporal. Where did that grenade come from?'

Cute as a barrowload of monkeys, he was: putting the screws on the one man who still had a career left to look forward to. Yet, for whatever reason, young Thomas didn't reply straight away. He simply stood there looking white and sick, and appealing to *me* of all people. But there's a sort of barrack-room code, even among Redcaps.

I returned his gaze guiltily. He shouldn't be dragged helplessly into this monstrous manipulation of justice. The corporal wouldn't have been ten years old when all this started. About the same age as a small, ragged-trousered goatherd when he was executed on a whim by a British officer. I couldn't leave him to be hung out to dry. I stepped smartly forward, braced my shoulders back, and stuck my chin out.

Right out. For bloody Charlie too.

'Lost property . . . Sah!'

The Major raised a genuinely disconcerted eyebrow. I wasn't sure whether his surprise was caused by the explanation, or at my having accorded him the pleasantry of rank. 'Lost property, Walker – a grenade? Come on, man: now tell the truth?'

The duty room reverted to silent service routine again: non-cooperation appeared to be proving the watchword for the day. I occupied my time by glowering at our dogmatic prisoner, who'd bloody invented the technique. Congratulations, Parrish as in pish, I reflected bitterly. You've finally landed me in it deep as you.

Steadman's lips tightened. The cane slapped once, twice in barely controlled irritation, then he brushed angrily past me and reached for the PMBX.

Whichever Signals squaddie was manning the base exchange must've been snatching a fly zizz 'cause he took a good half-minute to answer. When he did, he received both barrels. 'Steadman here – YES, the Provost CO, you idle bloody soldier! Inform Captain Jackson that his attendance is required at the RMP duty room immediately. And get RSM Halliday over here on the double . . . *What*? How the HELL should I know . . .? Either track 'em down damn quick, man, or find yourself on report.'

When the phone slammed back in its cradle, it was with a plastic crash and a jangle of agitated bells. It wasn't the only thing agitated. As his hand continued to rest on it momentarily, the stress-white knuckles revealed Steadman's mounting inner tension before, almost as if recognizing that brief betrayal, he abruptly relaxed. But the crack in the facade had shown itself yet again.

He smiled a thin smile. 'I told you I'd keep that promise, Walker.'

I abandoned straining at the attention position. I couldn't bring myself to slouch like Charlie, I'd been a Redcap too long, but if I was going down, I might as well go comfortable. And anyway, that was when I recalled that old military axiom from way back. *The best means of defence is attack* – one of those options that hadn't actually worked on the Mad Major that night of the EOKA cat, when he'd been waving his Browning at me? But this was different. As on the day of the coach crash, he didn't have a gun, there were witnesses this time . . . and I'd run out of alternatives.

See, the way I saw it, his calculated provocation had got under *my* skin, whereas I was reasonably sane – well, other than having chosen Parrish for a friend, anyway. But Steadman . . . a disturbed man already under pressure?

'Your promise, Major? Don't you mean the threat you made after killing that kid on the mountain?' I goaded. 'Or was that another of Parrish's murderous lapses? The fact he wasn't even *in* Cyprus at the time shouldn't stop you still giving evidence against him. No more than did his not being in the room while you tortured a terrorist suspect prior to fitting *him* up for the crime.'

Corporal Thomas's mouth fell open and he looked about to faint any minute. The disciplined cocoon the army had built around him had begun to split apart with breakneck speed. The emerging larva must, to him, have presented a nightmare alternative. The lad simply couldn't keep up with a world where majors bared their innermost secrets to corporals, private soldiers wandered, seemingly aimlessly, carrying live munitions like they were cabbages and, especially, where NCOs accused senior officers of torture, perjury and child murder.

Drop his defences? In your dreams, Walker. Blow his top like *I'd* been needled enough and stupid enough to do . . .? I don't reckon Steadman even heard me. Certainly he ignored my cunning plan as if I'd never spoken. He simply homed in on the most vulnerable target as before, turning to Corporal Thomas only, this time, regarding him with a most avuncular eye.

'Corporal,' he said silkily, 'it would count to your credit were we to resolve this ludicrous situation before Captain Jackson and the RSM arrive. Time for the truth now . . . how did that grenade find its way into this duty room?'

I knew it was all over bar the shouting. Probably quite a lot of shouting, mostly by abusive staff sergeants in the military detention block . . . but no youngster could be expected to stand up to the power conferred by the major's crowns on Steadman's shoulders, not when he was a trained soldier, no matter how strong a sense of loyalty he felt towards me. Sensing victory in the air the moment Thomas started to shake perceptibly, the hand rose to trace the scar.

It froze halfway.

'I brought it in,' Charlie said flatly.

Young Thomas subsided in relief while, for my part, I eyed Charlie Parrish with a modicum of renewed respect. At least he didn't propose to drag a good corporal down with him, even if Thomas was still a hated Redcap in Fusilier Parrish's eyes.

Steadman blinked at that: seemingly astonished. But of course, he'd initially assumed Charlie's presence in the duty room to be a social visit – one that had fortuitously provided him with the ammunition to provoke me and my self-destructive mouth into rank insubordination. So maybe he was genuinely mystified by Charlie's sudden co-operation. I know I was.

'Why, Parrish? What did you intend to do with a grenade?' Did he *really* have to ask? Or was his mind so distanced from emotion that he couldn't recognize a fellow psychopath when he met one?

Once having embraced the values of truth and veracity, Charlie seemed happy to continue conversing frankly. 'I wus plannin' to shove it up your—'

I interrupted urgently, 'Don't be a bigger bloody fool than you are. Keep your mouth shut, man.'

Which advice, coming from me, was hardly based on sound example. Charlie obviously agreed 'cause he just kept on talking, though he probably would've done anyway.

'Stuff it, Bill: this crazy bastard's goin' to see you inside if it's the last thing he does.'

He walked deliberately to stand in front of Steadman, looking hard. 'And if I have anythin' to do with it, it will be at that.'

I watched tensely as the two men stood toe to toe, glowering at each other. It was like viewing some Popeye cartoon film, with the big villain towering over the little pugnacious sailorman character. Then Steadman's lip curled. 'Feeling another of those murderous lapses of yours coming on – *Private*?'

I should've seen it coming. Charlie went white as a sheet then and, before Thomas or I could move, grabbed Steadman's jacket so's it was all bunched up in his hand. When he replied it was with a hiss so low and vicious I could barely hear.

'I brought that grenade in, Steadman, 'cause I planned to spread you over your billet like margarine across a slab o' bread – *Fuck* Pig!'

I started to move forward then because I knew Parrish wasn't big enough or smart enough to tackle a tough, experienced Redcap like the major. I also knew he'd stuck his neck out too far by grabbing Steadman's jacket like that. It was an assault, and Steadman was drunk enough, and vindictive enough, to take advantage of it though he'd already achieved what he'd set out to do. Entitled to defend yourself with minimum force, the book says. It doesn't describe what comprises minimum force.

I had a memory of a berserk German Polizeikommissar

pounding at the already pulverized features of a certain Gunner Irvine, not too long ago. In my report I'd described *that* arrest as having been made using minimum force.

Either way, I was too slow: a condition aggravated by a chronic lack of sympathy.

Parrish folded, sobbing in agony as the Major's knee took him in the crotch, then one gleaming toecap caught him under the ribcage and he went over backwards with a crash that made me wince. Steadman drew his boot back, hesitated, then, ever so deliberately, kicked him again in the kidneys. That second kick, aimed with premeditated malice at a prisoner already well subdued, was the one that breached the fine line between reasonable and excessive force. Give 'im another, I thought optimistically, and a defence of having been provoked into insubordination by an unstable officer could well merit some consideration.

A runnel of blood on the floor showed where Charlie's scalp had split open and it got me bloody angry, 'cause he should never have fallen for a chestnut like that in the first place. Maybe I should have warned him that Steadman had been a squaddie himself once, so's he could have been a bit more careful.

Steadman stood above the retching Parrish and I hoped, for a moment, he was going to boot him again, but he didn't. He'd gone too far already, before witnesses. He must have realized that himself, because he fought to regain control of the situation. Simply stepped back and looked icily over at the gobsmacked Thomas.

'See this soldier is made to clean up his own mess before you place him in cells, Corporal.'

OK, so I confess to disappointment at Steadman's managing to confine himself to one extra kick. If he'd gone that bit further and *really* hurt Charlie, even whacked him a few times with the swagger stick, it would have helped a lot.

Nonetheless I sensed grounds for optimism, albeit of the clutching-at-straws variety. I might still be able to negotiate some compromise involving a Mexican stand-off – Steadman to keep mum about my conduct predjudicial, in return for me and the corporal turning a blind eye to the excessive zeal he'd exhibited in subduing Parrish . . .? Thomas would almost certainly be up for it – his expression of revulsion suggested Steadman was on his own: that the lad wouldn't help one bit more than he had to. And Charlie would bear his scars bravely soon as he came out of hospital or I'd see he collected a few more. After all, the incorrigible little turd *had* been asking for it since he'd turned up with the grenade, mate or no ma—?

Shit – I'd overlooked the *grenade*! No way was the Major, for all his unpredictability, going to disregard the grenade.

Which marked the moment when a peremptory rap on the door heralded the arrival of that most committed of truth-seekers, Regimental Sergeant Major James Halliday, a military policeman from cap cover to the burnished soles of his boots. An incorruptible man who showed neither fear nor favour.

Especially, I anticipated morosely, to provost staff sergeants foolish enough to become over-friendly with nasty wee infantry sodgers apprehended while unlawfully secreting hand grenades aboot their unsavoury persons.

Seventeen

The moment the RSM caught sight of Parrish, by then dazedly attempting to lever himself to hands and knees, his priority was clear. Concern for the condition of the injured took precedence.

'You'll not allow all yon blood and sick to stain into the floor, Staff Sergeant?' he ascertained anxiously before turning to salute the CO. 'Good morning, sir. You sent for me?'

'And you've taken your time to respond, Mr Halliday,' Steadman snapped ill-humouredly, 'I want this private soldier committed immediately. I will frame the charges later.'

For all his professional equanimity, the RSM looked less than pleased. 'Is it not a wee bit unusual to summon the Regimental Sergeant Major to lock up a solitary private soldier, sir? Surely that is a duty Staff Sergeant Walker is eminently qualified to carry out.'

'We'll address Staff Sergeant Walker's fitness to carry out his duties in due course,' Steadman retorted coldly. 'Meanwhile, please do as I request, Sarn't Major, and place Fusilier Parrish in cells.'

The RSM darted a suddenly wary look at me. 'Did you say Parrish, sir?'

It struck me then that he couldn't have known it was Charlie messing up his floor, having been fortunate enough, until now, never to have set eyes on the little foetus.

Steadman didn't miss the hesitation. 'What difference does it make?'

'No difference at all, sir. But as regimental sergeant major I am loath to go over the head of a senior NCO without even an explanation as to why. I trust you appreciate my point, Major?'

The scar began to pulse. 'What I do appreciate, Mr Halliday, is that you appear bent on laying yourself open to a charge of refusing to obey a lawful command.'

Well, if he'd struck the RSM across the face with his cane he couldn't have offended the great Scot more. What the hell was he *thinking* of, turning everyone against him? He'd already let the mask slip in the sergeants' mess, that first night of his arrival in BAOR. I'd always known him to be a driven and unpredictable man, reckless to the point of self-destruction, but this marked a new level of antagonism. Or was the Major's paranoia finally beginning to overtake his previously ice-cold self-control? Whatever the reason, I couldn't allow the current situation to escalate, not to the point of involving the RSM in direct conflict with an increasingly unstable officer, a confrontation the system would ensure that even he was unlikely to weather.

I stepped forward reluctantly. 'It's my problem, Mr Halliday. I don't wish to see anyone else dragged down by him.'

The great Scot swung on me coldly: the mountain peaks of Caledonia in winter would have looked less bleak. 'I would be obliged, Staff Sergeant Walker, if you will keep SILENT while the commanding officer and myself are in discussion.'

So whatever happened to *Jeemy* Halliday . . .?

'Yessah!' I yelled, and tried to make myself look very small.

'No discussion, Sar'nt Major,' Steadman snapped. 'Following Parrish's detention, Walker is to be relieved of his duties. You will escort him to his quarters where he will remain under open arrest. His return to the UK tomorrow will, of course, be cancelled.'

Jackson appeared in the doorway just as an ominously granite-faced Halliday was drawing to his full imposing height. No wonder the captain had cause to do a double-take – the CO and the RSM evidently head-to-head: young Corporal Thomas frozen to ashen-faced attention in the corner: me attempting to blend in with the furniture . . . and a small fusilier, who apparently belonged to no one, clawing himself weakly to his feet up a blood-smeared wall.

The cane gestured irritably. 'Stop gaping for God's sake, John. Come in and close the bloody door.'

Jackson frowned uncomprehendingly, making a valiant effort to catch up with the rest of us as the RSM addressed Steadman.

'Sir, I have never questioned an order from a superior officer in all the thirty-two years I have served wi' the Colours. The wee soldier I shall jail as you instruct – just as soon as he has been examined by the medical officer. However, I must express my disquiet at being ordered to place Staff Sergeant Walker under arrest without even the courtesy of an explanation from yourself.'

He sealed the formality by stamping to ramrod attention.

'With the greatest respect, sah!'

'I'm glad to note your reservation is made with respect, Sar'nt Major,' Steadman smiled dryly, unpredictable as ever. He slapped his leg sharply with the cane. 'Very well. I am prepared to outline the charges against both men.'

'I am very grateful to ye, sir,' answered the Regimental Sergeant Major.

Without a trace of irony.

I'd have arrested myself by the time Steadman had finished putting the blackest slant to the events in the duty room. While Parrish . . .? I would've let them shoot *him* out of hand without even bothering to convene a second, obviously superfluous court martial. Come to that, having listened to the major outlining the basis of a possible case against me, I'd cheerfully have topped Fusilier Parrish myself. He'd offered us both to my sworn adversary on a plate . . . grounds enough to imply, if not actually establish conspiracy: motive: potential weapon, and opportunity – certainly on Charlie's part, having managed to get himself arrested right under Steadman's bloody window.

Corporal Thomas had betrayed increasing disquiet as he'd learned from the master how circumstantial evidence could be presented as a damning indictment by an accuser skilled in the arts of advocacy. Jackson and the RSM listened grimly and without interruption, although the captain exhibited evident concern at the malice evident in Steadman's delivery. The reaction from the canny Halliday, I wasn't so sure about. The only time he even spared me a glance, and a disapproving one at that, was when Steadman indicated the grenade on the duty desk.

'I'm surprised at you not realizing yon could well be dangerous, Staff Sergeant Walker. Leaving a possibly unstable munition where any Tom, Dick or Harry might disturb it.'

Predictably Steadman had concluded on an arrogant note. 'Any further justification required before you see fit to conform with my orders, Sergeant Major?'

Halliday looked cooperatively placid. 'I've always been an awfy man for going the whole hog, sir.'

Charlie suddenly returned from the land of the happily overlooked dead. 'Hog's right where that bastard's concerned,' he snarled with indomitable stupidity.

The RSM swivelled majestically to stare down upon the battered co-accused, highly trained moustache bristling with a ferocity seldom observed outside the pit-bull ring.

'I will NOT have nasty wee men interrupt my conversation wi'out my express permission, d'ye hear? Jist crawl back under your green-slimy rock, Fusilier whoever-you-are, so's I dinnae have to disinfect the sole of my boot after I've TRAMPED on ye – ye gleckit wee scunner o' a *sodger*, you!'

'Yessah – gleckit scunner, sah!' Charlie bawled, understanding not a word but interpreting every syllable while stamping to satisfyingly painful attention.

The RSM accorded him a final withering glance before turning back to the CO and raising a respectful eyebrow. 'As I was saying, sir: there's the matter of proof of evidence. In view of the circumstantial nature of the allegations, particularly those you make against the staff sergeant, a corroborating witness will be essential, ye'll understand?'

'Fully understand, Sarn't Major.' Steadman beckoned equably with the cane. 'Corporal Thomas?'

The already edgy Thomas jumped higher than I'd done

when the CO whacked the alleged unstable munition. 'SAH?'

It was his moment in the limelight. I've known corporals make sergeant overnight for a hell of a lot less.

'For the benefit of the record,' the CO snapped impatiently, 'confirm that, before the arrival of Captain Jackson and the RSM, you were witness to the events I've described.'

'Aye, Corporal,' the RSM urged placidly. 'Then I can get on with jailing yon villain, Parrish. Och, and we'll need to move to cancel the staff sergeant's travel warrant for the morning. Maybe, Thomas, you could get on to the transport office and see to that yourself, eh?'

Thomas's eyes opened wide. 'Cancel Staff's flight home, sir?'

'No choice, lad,' Halliday shrugged, pointedly indifferent. 'What with the Commanding Officer making such serious charges, and your own corroborating evidence . . .?'

'Just get *on* with it, Thomas!' Steadman snapped, visibly needled.

'Yessir.' Thomas sought refuge in the vanishing point defence. 'Sorry, sir, but I'm not quite sure of what you're ordering me to confirm, sir.'

The scar began to assume its telltale early warning shade of choleric purple. 'I'm not *ordering* you to do anything, man . . .'

Captain Jackson stirred. So far he'd maintained an understandably discreet silence, career-sensitive as anybody, and probably intimidated by Steadman's already firmly established reputation for intolerance into the bargain. But he was also a good officer, acutely aware that Thomas was being placed in an invidious position.

'Obviously a formality as Major Steadman is the accusing officer, Corporal Thomas,' he nodded reassuringly, 'but essential to due process. Without independent corroboration, there's little the APM's office can do to proceed against Staff Walker.'

I didn't dare look for Steadman's reaction. It seemed he wasn't the only one capable of weighting an argument. Thomas swallowed hard, then said goodbye to his career.

'I can't exactly confirm the Major's recollection of events,

225

sir. There was some confusion. Especially after the CO kicked the prisoner in the kidneys when he'd downed him already . . . SIR!'

It must have come as a body-blow to Steadman to realize he faced climbing another mountain in pursuit of his vendetta. Only this wasn't a sun-washed, isolated place with a child alone and vulnerable: this was a British Army duty room where proof of evidence was everything, the atmosphere was contempt-chill, and those he had elected to confront were big, experienced Redcap bruisers already antagonized by his overweening arrogance.

Not that he foamed at the mouth or bit the carpet following Thomas's bombshell. He didn't even get mad – not *angry*-mad, he didn't. Not so's anyone would detect. He simply shrugged as if having anticipated such treachery all along.

'Following that foolhardy display of barrack-room evasion, Corporal, I won't ask you again to confirm you heard Parrish freely admit to having broken into the base area with the express intention of killing me. No more than I expect you, now, to admit to withholding evidence crucial to prosecuting charges against Staff Sar'nt Walker.'

He reached for the grenade, raising it with the triumphant air of a cardsman snatching a fifth ace from his opponent's sleeve.

'But this is neither speculative, nor reliant on your corruption of the truth. It's an M2A1 fragmentation grenade. Hard evidence, Corporal. It will put you in detention for attempting to interfere with the course of justice, should you persist in your refusal to cooperate with a Royal Military Police investigation.'

I saw Jackson and Halliday's eyes fix uneasily on the grenade. Me, I stepped back a surreptitious pace, for all the bloody good it would do me in such a confined space. But having had ten years to reflect on how psychotic he could suddenly become when thwarted, the prospect of the Mad Major introducing a highly effective anti-personnel weapon as a debating point was worrying to say the least. The two of them together, it was hard to predict which was the most unstable.

Steadman prepared for the – I prayed, strictly metaphorical – kill. Each syllable enunciated with precision: no opportunity offered to his selected soft target to take evasive action. The way he always operated: whether killing children, fitting up admittedly deserving infantrymen or contriving to crush Redcap NCOs under tons of razor-edged wreckage.

'Corporal, you will explain the presence of this ordnance in the duty room,' he said coldly. 'I warn you that failure to do so may well lead to charges of conspiring with others after the fact, to kill or severely injure your commanding officer.'

'*Jesus*,' the Captain muttered, appalled.

'Might I have a wee word with you in private, sir?' Regimental Sergeant Major Halliday urged with ominous calm. 'Before you press this matter further.'

Steadman ignored them both. I don't think he even heard.

'Answer, Corporal Thomas. Or I will order your immediate arrest as well.'

He shouldn't have said that. There's a fine difference between an order, and a threat. The corporal's eyes went blank as a dead man's. He was proving himself a battler, I had to give him that: almost as stubbornly self-destructive as Parrish, but very much smarter. Unlike Charlie who, driven by post-battle rage following the death of his sentry, had blundered into being set up for the Kondoyiannis affair, Thomas recognized he was being used. That Steadman had cynically provoked this conflict with the express intention of manipulating him into giving evidence against us.

'I have nothing more to say, sir,' he said.

I wasn't relieved. I simply felt sick at heart, knowing Thomas had just become another victim. Steadman was right: the presence of the grenade in the duty room was the one unassailable fact that couldn't be countered by evasion on the corporal's part. Five minutes of cross-examination would either extract the truth, or expose him as yet another resentful

NCO prepared to perjure himself . . . and that, in turn, would leave *me* firmly occupying the hot seat in the witness box. Because I was the only other member of the triumvirate who'd been there when Thomas had brought in Charlie Parrish and his pocketful of trouble.

Or dare I take a leaf from Steadman's book of perfidy? Turn events to my advantage . . .? At that moment the only ones who'd elected to place themselves in the frame were Charlie and the foolishly loyal Corporal Thomas. I still retained the option of walking clear by simply telling the truth – that Fusilier Parrish had been apprehended in a restricted area, subsequently brought to the duty room and, on being searched, had failed to offer reasonable explanation for being in possession of an unlawful weapon. Hey, in my fit of childish pique at Charlie's bloody-minded recalcitrance, I'd even formally cautioned and charged him prior to the CO's arrival. Better still – I'd actually got *proof* of having done so in the notes made in my AB466.

Unless . . .?

No, I couldn't – *could* I? Even the thought of the gamble I'd be taking initiated a wave of stomach-churning apprehension.

. . . Then I'd run out of time because Steadman was standing before me holding out the grenade. Walker's Armageddon had arrived. The eyes, devoid of expression, held mine with Captain Jackson and the RSM observing grimly as they, too, realized the crunch was about to come.

'Only one of three men could have brought this into the room, Walker,' the CO said. 'Thomas, you – or Parrish. If the corporal did so for whatever inexplicable motive, then he's a bigger fool than he's just proved himself to be. If you did, then you are clearly deranged . . .'

Me deranged? That comin' from HIM . . .?

'If Parrish did so – which further SIB investigation will prove to be the case, as you well know it will – then my allegation is upheld. In that certain event, both Thomas and you will, in even the most favourable light, be exposed as having conspired to hinder a provost officer in the pursuit of his enquiries into a serious crime.'

228

The grenade lifted fractionally. Now it hovered under my chin: just as he'd held his Browning pistol all those years before. Nothing had changed. The eyes uttered the same cold promise. I would always be the primary focus for his malice.

'For the benefit of Captain Jackson and the Regimental Sergeant Major . . . who smuggled this weapon into the base, Staff Sergeant?'

I stared down at the grey mosaic pineapple and suddenly it turned into a face. A grubby, once-mischievous childish face with enormous black eyes above a threadbare jersey stained by frightened tears. And then the face slammed backwards, and grew suddenly slack and yellowed and waxen as a blood-and-cordite-spattered hole appeared . . .

And I took that image of the always-try-and-do-the-right-thing Redcap of thirty years, and buried it right where my conscience would never hear it.

'You've blown it, Major,' I said. 'Your opportunity to walk away.'

Even Steadman got caught on the wrong foot at that. '*Opportunity?*'

'You can't really expect us to cover for you any longer?' I shrugged. 'There's a hell of a difference between a boozed-up officer and a treacherous bastard.'

'*Sir*, Staff Sergeant.' For once I was ahead and he was struggling to play for time. 'You will address me as *sir* while still permitted to wear uniform.'

I grinned savagely: too late to turn back now. 'Oh yeah, the pleasantries of rank. If I recall, the first time you insisted on those, Steadman, you were grinding a pistol in my temple to make your point.'

'Jesus,' Captain Jackson muttered for a second time. But it wasn't for him to fight the CO's corner. Or maybe he wasn't quite ready to?

The scar throbbed visibly as Steadman fumbled for the only exit strategy he could think of. Retreat and regroup. 'Sar'nt Major?'

The conditioned flash and crash of colliding boots. 'SAH!'

'Place this man under close arrest. The committal charges

229

are uttering false accusation against a superior officer, compounded by gross insubordination.'

Halliday stepped forward smartly: affording me a terrible fierce glance indeed. 'With respect, sir, I believe the Staff Sergeant must be given opportunity to justify his making such a serious allegation against yourself. *Then* I can jail him! Would ye not agree, Captain Jackson?'

'I didn't ASK for the Captain's bloody endorsement!' Steadman snarled.

Just as well, because he didn't get it. Jackson's expression had become bleak now, and uncompromising: mirroring the determination shown by the dead Timms during the Bull's Bum inquiry. Steadman had tried to steamroller *him* with rank, too.

'The commanding officer has chosen not to refer the incident to Brigade, electing instead to pursue what has effectively become a drum-head inquiry. Consequently I feel we have no alternative but to require Staff Sergeant Walker to account for himself.'

Carefully put: totally supportive; beyond criticism . . . and all going to prove the CO had won himself no friend in court by insulting Jackson that first night in the sergeants' mess.

Steadman clenched the grenade tight enough to squeeze juice. 'By God, this is a right bloody Fred Karno outfit I've inherited. But make no mistake, both of you: I'll have it running on a much less democratic basis before I'm finished.'

He couldn't have offended the big Highlander more. The awesome moustache positively exuded outrage. 'Democracy in the British Army is a dirty word to a regimental sergeant major, sir – a dirty, *filthy* word. On the other hand, I'm not a man to see a soldier of Staff Sergeant Walker's integrity ruined wi'out even a chance to defend himself.'

He turned on me, and his stare promised a terrible reckoning if I blew it. 'You will carry on with your explanation, Walker.'

Glancing at Charlie I could see a faint light dawning. I didn't dare risk being seen to catch Thomas's eye for fear of it being interpreted as coercion which, given two minutes alone with him and my truncheon, it would've been. All I could do was pray the corporal would be terrified enough by Steadman's promised alternative to go along with Walker's otherwise-doomed Last Stand.

'You've made play of establishing there were three men in this room when you first entered, Major, any one of whom had opportunity to bring that grenade in.'

Steadman smiled tightly. 'That's your defence? Stating the obvious.'

'Only the way you want others to interpret the obvious. You're wrong in evidential fact, Steadman. There were *four*, not three, suspects in here by the time the captain and Mr Halliday arrived as impartial observers ... me, Fusilier Parrish, Corporal Thomas – and yourself.'

I fervently hoped he'd replace the possibly unstable munition on the table before finally registering what I was driving at. I gathered it was too late when he found voice only as a barely contained snarl. 'Do you actually have the gall to suggest . . .?'

'A simple sum for a court martial board to grapple with, Major. Four present: subtract one lying bastard – carry forward three witnesses . . .'

I took a deep breath and stepped into the minefield.

'. . . each prepared to give evidence that *you* brought that grenade in here yourself.'

Eighteen

It took him time, a very tense time, to respond. Happily it didn't involve pulling pins out of anything. Not right away.

'And why the hell would I bring a grenade into my own duty room, Walker,' he snapped eventually.

That's when I thought: *What the hell, Walker, you're a British soldier. Go down under-valued, under-equipped, under-estimated, but still fightin' vicious as a ferret in a sack.*

'To kill me, as you've threatened to do since Cyprus. Maybe you took a chance on me being in here alone: your modus operandi, Steadman. A tragic accident: an unsuspecting target, no witnesses, or only army witnesses vulnerable to being disbelieved by virtue of your rank . . .' *Don't appear too glib*, I thought anxiously. *Don't over-egg the egg.* 'Or maybe you simply felt pressured to settle for less at the last minute. Provoke me into earning a double-D. A dishonourable discharge for gross insubordination, as you damn nearly did.'

I shrugged. The shrug of a man of probity, totally bewildered by the depths of duplicity to which others can sink.

'Either way, Major, you need to prevent my ever speaking out after I leave the Corps. Because I'm the only man alive who might then be prepared to swear I heard you confess to having murdered a child ten years ago.'

Captain Jackson – to whom this was all news, unlike Jeemy Halliday, who'd at least heard it before – Cap'n Jackson probably suffered the biggest shock at hearing me accuse his commanding officer of child murder. Well, the Captain, and Corporal Thomas: the latter quite genuinely bewildered by the depths of duplicity to which others can sink. Mind you, he could have shown more gratitude than staring malevolently at me with that white-faced look of panic. I'd actually done him a favour: presented him with a choice. Now he could either move straight to detention without passing go, based on the CO's stated threat to charge him with attempting to interfere with the course of justice – or he perjured himself.

And Steadman . . .? Being a psychopath, he betrayed no emotion at all. But then, he was a soldier too, and a battler in his own obsessive way. He didn't surrender lightly, and wore the medal ribbon to prove it.

It was to take the Major some time to conclude that his most effective defence would be to kill everyone in the duty room. A perfectly achievable aspiration given he was still nursing a four-second fused M2A1 fragmentation grenade.

He could have done so immediately, of course. But, being an eminently pragmatic psychopath and thus not inclined to take the *everyone* solution too literally, he probably needed more than two blinks of a dead man's eye to work out how he could contrive to leave the rest of us – especially me – on the lethal side of a locked door while he took off before the grenade did.

In the interim Fusilier Parrish, by then positively wriggling with frustrated resentment at no longer being centre-stage accused, couldn't restrain himself from muscling in on my drama a moment longer. But we were moving remorselessly to the final act of a tragedy and, denied the counterpoint of black comedy without a clown, no tragedy can be judged truly exquisite.

I suppose the outrageousness of it helped take the pressure off: what with Charlie confirming virtuously that the Major had come in a tad boozed up while he, Charlie, was sayin' cheerio mate to me after thirty years, and who would grudge him that privilege? Anyroad, Major Steadman had produced this grenade and shouted how he was going to fix me, Staff Walker, 'cos I, Staff Walker, was plannin' to put the finger on him, the Major, for some killing in Cyprus just as soon as I, Staff Walker, got my discharge . . .

He – *Parrish* – temporarily ran out of breath at that point: a merciful intermission which allowed time for Captain Jackson to collect himself, produce his AB466, and begin to scribble furiously for the record in case he, Fusilier Parrish, didn't do encores.

'*Fix* him, Parrish?'

'Blow 'is fuckin' head off, sir,' Charlie had clarified helpfully.

'Ah,' responded the Captain, looking grimly at the sergeant major, who'd so far elected not to intervene having ominously, it seemed, cast himself in the roles of all three wise monkeys: content to hear all, see all, but say nothing till the court martial. Precisely whose court martial he had in mind, I couldn't begin to fathom. Compared with Halliday's granite-hewn demeanour, that sculpted stone flower girl fronting the house on the Kirchhofstrasse the night Major Timms died had been an extrovert drama queen.

But Jackson hadn't finished. 'Staff Sergeant Walker claims that *we* – meaning, presumably, all three of you – offered to let the commanding officer walk away despite his allegedly having threatened you with a grenade, Parrish. Can you explain such seemingly extraordinary tolerance on your part?'

Shit – THAT bit of the script was the part I still had to work on. So far I'd failed to come up with an even vaguely plausible reason. I *knew* Charlie Parrish would bloody scupper me, grabbing for the spotlight without thinking through the consequences of him being thick as cookhouse mince. I knew that the moment he turned to me in a panic-stricken appeal for support.

'You, ah . . . want to answer that, Staff Sar'nt?' our self-elected counsel for the defence asked.

'I asked you, Parrish, not Staff Walker,' Jackson snapped, very much the bulldog Redcap again.

'TELL the officer,' I growled, salvaging some childish satisfaction from discomfiting him as much as me. It was only when he'd turned back to the captain that I caught the mischievous glint of a deliberately contrived wind-up in the little bastard's eye.

'Hear it from an infantryman, Captain,' Charlie said.

'Threatened by a nutter holdin' a grenade, you got four seconds and two options. Talk to him nice and calm like the Staffie done: persuade 'im to walk away while everyone forgets it – or stick your finger in his eye. Which one would you take, sir?'

I suspect that last from Parrish triggered the start of the Major's descent into overt madness. Mind you, Charlie was inclined to have that effect even on well-adjusted people. But for the first time, Steadman didn't look so sure of himself, so arrogantly in control.

His artificial world was crumbling. Something had gone wrong with the structures of command that had so far shielded him from his actions. He recognized it, but wasn't capable of dealing with it because nothing disturbs an already disturbed mind more than nonconforming opposition to its will. This wasn't the army way. Driven into ever more debilitating pathomania by the wartime event that caused his deformity, Steadman still remained as much a Pavlov's dog as any of us – maybe more so: totally reliant on dealing with people equally conditioned to conform to a disciplined pattern. But now I'd finally succeeded in upsetting the balance.

It couldn't have helped to realize he'd lost Jackson's and the RSM's respect – he'd never had it for that matter, from the night he arrived three weeks before. The crown on his shoulder and Queen's Regulations had long become the refuge for his psychopathy. They also defined the limits of how far his staff were expected to go in support of him. The Major had never attempted to generate loyalty in others because he was incapable of understanding what an elusively precious gift it is. Loyalty is an emotion: it's a personal thing. You can bestow it upon a private soldier or a field marshal . . . a much-put-upon RMP corporal can even feel it towards a hard-bitten Redcap staff sergeant driven by an image.

Maybe it wasn't his fault: just another symptom of his condition. Either way, Steadman suddenly sensed he'd become a man alone, being forced remorselessly towards the Slough of Despond.

Even when he did eventually find voice, he still rounded savagely on those he needed most. 'Jackson: Halliday. You will place these three soldiers in the cells immediately, d'you hear?'

Nobody moved. Not a muscle. I caught a glimpse of Charlie's face in that moment, and hardly recognized him. It gave me a shock to see how abruptly the Clown had changed the moment he'd withdrawn to the wings. I swear he looked as eaten with hate as the Major, maybe as disturbed. So much so I wondered, in that moment, if I'd been wrong in blaming Steadman alone for the Kondoyiannis torture because I sensed, then, that Parrish, too, was capable of such savagery. Or maybe that was only now, maybe ten years in the military sewers had made him that way.

I didn't know it then, but Charlie Parrish hadn't even *begun* to seek his revenge.

Halliday broke the impasse: stepped forward erect as a broom stave to look straight into Thomas's eyes: solid and dependable, a proper soldier. Even while the Corporal braced nervously, you could tell he was grateful for the RSM's being there, bringing order back into a topsy-turvy nightmare world that couldn't be.

'It's always been my contention,' the RSM mused to Thomas, 'that a military policeman's first duty is to seek the downfall of the villain, d'ye understand?'

'Yessir.'

'Your loyalties, Corporal. They're not to the Major, nor to the Staff Sergeant: not even to the Corps. They're to truth, and to the furtherance of justice. Nothing else.'

'I understand, sir.'

I felt inordinately proud of him then: Corporal Thomas. Almost as proud as I'd once been of Foxie all those years ago. If anyone had to destroy me, I was content that it was to be him.

Regimental Sergeant Major Halliday – no, it was Jeemy Halliday in that moment of rare privilege for Thomas – Halliday's voice was soft as thistledown.

'Who's telling the truth, lad?'

236

I caught the slight movement as Steadman clenched one hand. It was the hand holding the grenade, and I bit my lip uneasily. Thomas must've read something sinister from the involuntary reaction too because, all of a sudden, his previously uncertain expression hardened.

'Staff Walker was trying to get the truth out of Major Steadman when you came into the room, sir.'

Captain Jackson swallowed hard. I didn't envy him the responsibility for directing the next act of the tragedy. 'Corporal Thomas. Are you stating formally that the Commanding Officer is lying?'

Thomas examined the vanishing point minutely. 'The Major has not yet told the whole truth, sir.'

And that was when Charlie Parrish smiled. A frightening smile.

Steadman walked very slowly, very deliberately over to Thomas: halting before him with a look of absolute contempt on the ravaged face.

'You stupid *bastard*!' he said in a dead, toneless voice.

Then the cane in his left hand smashed across the side of the Corporal's head and the youngster reeled, sobbing with the shock of it.

Charlie just stood and watched, still wearing that wolfish grin as the rest of us moved to restrain Steadman, but the CO, unpredictable as ever, waved us off with unexpected composure: merely continuing to stare hard at the shocked Corporal. The hand holding the grenade was still tissue-white around the knuckles, though, and I suspect I wasn't the only one feeling nervous by then.

'I'm afraid you shouldn't have done that, sir,' Jackson said. He'd go far if he stayed alive long enough, and didn't do a Timms. For a young officer suddenly subjected to intolerable pressures, he'd laid the foundation for becoming a legend within the Corps by that masterpiece of British understatement.

Steadman stirred: frowned at his deputy as if nothing extraordinary had happened.

'I gave you an order, Captain. Now you will carry it out.'

Jackson came briefly to attention. 'With respect, sir, I must refuse to comply with that order.' He swung. 'Sarn't Major.'

'Sah?'

Captain Jackson's voice faltered only slightly. 'Bear witness, Mister Halliday, that I am relieving Major Steadman of command of this company. This action to be effective immediately as laid down in Queen's Regulations and in accordance with the provisions of the Army Act.'

It was Thomas's turn to mutter '*Jesus!*' at that, and probably wonder too late at what he'd done.

Halliday motioned almost imperceptibly to me to move closer to the Major. 'I stand witness, sir.'

'You will also confirm subsequently, Sergeant Major, that I take full responsibility for this action.'

I'd already begun to sidle round the desk when Steadman smiled. If any warning was needed of his increasing volatility, it was that smile. 'So I have a full complement of mutineers now, eh, John?'

The Captain gazed steadily back, giving nothing away.

'I bear full responsibility for this action . . .?' Steadman mulled on that a moment. 'Neatly put, although I suspect it will come back to haunt you. A concise epitaph to a promising young officer's career.'

I *did* wish he'd avoid using tendentious words like 'epitaph'. It stopped me sidling before I'd crabbed even partway across the room. The RSM displayed a much higher level of resolution, but then, leadership went with the pace stick of office. In this gathering I was more than content to remain as middle-management.

He extended an elaborately casual hand. 'I'd be obliged if you could pass me yon wee grenade, sir. Then maybe the Captain can accompany you to your quarters?'

'Grenade?' The Major blinked from his reverie. 'I think not, Mr Halliday. A mutiny to put down . . .? Hardly the time to surrender arms.'

By then I was eyeing the closed door and trying to figure how many of us would get out once the Mad Major really got mad. Charlie Parrish might make it, him bein' an infantryman like he kept pointing out ad nauseam, and used to having bombs thrown at him. Maybe Thomas would – but me? With *my* bloody luck that last morning . . .? Being farthest away I didn't go much on my prospects of being able to knock Halliday down to beat the rush.

Jackson cleared his throat. 'Pass the grenade to Mr Halliday, sir. If you please.'

He didn't even rate a glance. Why *was* it that Steadman's malice inevitably found focus on me? 'You always were a sedition-monger, Walker. Now you've upped your game. This time you're ringleader of a mutiny. On the verge of retirement, and you've just earned life imprisonment by trying to destroy me.'

'You did that yourself, the moment you struck Thomas.' I jerked my chin masterfully . . . well, more pleadingly, really: it was just the image forcing me to act tougher. 'Give up the grenade, Major, before you kill anyone else. Your war's lasted thirty years and you already executed a child because of what it did to you.'

'He was an armed terrorist, Walker. I acted in self-defence.'

'Self-defence, CRAP! He was ten years old with a pop-gun that didn't bloody work!' I countered, suddenly weary. I'd tried to lead him down that fruitless road so many times before. 'Christ, Steadman, you hadn't even SEEN any so-called weapon before you killed him. You only found it later when you dragged the body from the cleft. Hidden behind him, you hadn't even noticed it by the time I got there . . . but it was a golden opportunity – or more the devil's luck? – to contaminate the scene-of-crime evidence, ready for when O'Feely's section reached the locus.'

'You're pissing against the wind as usual, Walker,' he taunted, cool and collected as ever he'd been in his most reasonable madness. 'Every night when they switch your cell lights out and leave you to rot, you'll scream aloud just thinking about me. You and I, we know he was unarmed – but you'll never be able to bloody *prove* it, Walker! Not without witne—'

'I won't need to prove anything, Major,' I said. 'Not now.'

*   *   *

He could have gone then. Out through the door and away, without any of us in the room risking playing hero – or dead. Our military or the *polizei* would've picked him up later. He didn't have a chance out there on his own in the middle of Germany, no more than Gunners McCafferty J and Irvine P had in the long run.

He *could* have gone.

. . . But Charlie nursed too much hate in him for that.

They'd all eyed the grenade with renewed interest after Steadman slipped up for the first time in his life. All of them except me, that was. I was still revelling in the haunted expression slowly turning the Major's previously arrogant features to wax.

Halliday was the first to find voice. 'Man, ye don't exactly pick the most diplomatic time to extract a confession of murder,' he breathed.

Then, because he was the Regimental Sergeant Major, and a very brave man, he began to move purposefully towards Steadman. 'I will take that off you now, sir.'

Steadman carefully laid the bamboo swagger stick on my duty desk, meticulously squared it parallel with the edge – then hooked the forefinger of his freed hand into the pin ring while raising the grenade for Halliday to see.

'As you were, Sar'nt Major!' he suggested.

Sound advice, coming from a mentally disturbed adversary armed with a fragmentation grenade. At risk of being pedantic, there's a spring lever held in place by the grip of the hand which, when released, automatically triggers the striker which fires the percussion cap which ignites the fuse which activates the detonator which, in turn, explodes the main charge which, in *its* turn, kills you . . . or at least, the razor-edged segmented fragments thus distributed, do.

As a safety measure during handling, the lever is secured in place by a pin with a ring through one end. That was the ring the Major was now holding. If we rushed him and he pulled the pin while freeing the spring lever, we had precisely four seconds left in which to enforce Queen's Regulations before everyone in the duty room reverted to equal rank.

Of course Jeemy Halliday, being a soldier, knew all that. Being an eminently sensible soldier to boot, he halted right where he was. Jackson had taken a half-pace forward at the same time but the grenade vectored sharply, whereupon the Captain embraced prudence too, and confined his heroics to less than subtle persuasion. 'Sir, don't be a bloody fool.'

The scar crinkled. 'I don't intend to be, Captain. Not twice. Which is why I'm leaving now – either alone through that door, or . . .' He smiled tightly then although, to be fair, he wasn't disturbed enough to invest it with a lot of humour. 'Or along with the rest of you, John. Through the roof.'

I became aware of Charlie easing furtively towards the aforementioned door. To me he looked remarkably like a rat at that moment, getting ready to leave a sinking ship . . . yeah, definitely a rat . . . but I didn't dwell on the little chancer's self-serving manoeuvre, more preoccupied by figuring how best I could get to it myself without being rumbled. Then Jackson began to push a bit too doggedly for comfort.

'You won't do it, sir. You're bluffing.'

I stuck my oar in quick before the Major got fed up with being called a liar. 'He can and he bloody will, Captain. He's crazy. He's got a death wish .. . .'

Fusilier Parrish couldn't have heard me though, him being self-absorbed to the core. He'd made it to the door by then, reaching for the handle. I was about to suggest at the top of my voice that he'd upset ENOUGH people's fucking apple carts already when suddenly dawning panic rendered me speechless.

Because Charlie didn't turn the handle – he turned the *key* instead.

Then took it OUT of the lock!

It seemed reasonable to assume Steadman hadn't yet noticed Parrish committing suicide on behalf of all of us. His best ice-encrusted smile was still reserved for me. 'Death wish, Walker? An interesting diagnosis, but then you always did consider yourself a cod psychologist, didn't you? Yet where's the consistency in your thesis . . .? One minute you accuse me of contaminating a crime scene to evade retribution: the next, I seemingly welcome it.'

'That's because you *are* crazy,' I retorted irritably, needled enough by his derision to momentarily forget the grenade. Even better, to forget Parrish.

'Although I don't suppose I mind all that much if I do die,' he mused, fingering the scarred cheek reflectively. 'I believe I told you, Staff Sergeant – a Nazi joke, you know? And I concede there have been times when I would have been content if the joke were to end.'

He spared a sardonic eyebrow for the RSM. 'You could, of course, try and test Walker's diagnosis if you wish, Mr Halliday?'

The big Scot inclined his head politely: he was still being addressed by a major at the end of the day. 'Thank you kindly, sir, but no. You'll be apprehended soon enough, unless you give up this foolishness now.'

Steadman began to edge calmly to the door, the grenade held firmly in one hand with the other still gripping the pin ring. It should have signalled the moment to start relaxing, seeing he was hopefully going out without a bang. Civilized, as you'd expect from an officer. Mutual respect being accorded. Evident in the way we all shuffled hastily aside to let him pass through.

All of us except Charlie. He didn't budge. He was leaning back against the locked door by then . . . just holding the key up mockingly.

'Move, Parrish!' the Major snapped, obviously disconcerted as anyone when he finally clocked where Parrish was. But like I've already said, me bein' a cod psychologist: the unpredictable do have difficulty coping with the unpredictable.

Charlie looked hurt. 'You didn't say that the last time we was face to face in Cyprus. My being in the way came in handy for you. Someone to fit up after you'd beaten the shit out of the Greek.'

'Step from the door, Parrish,' I gritted, sick and fed up with him. 'Don't push your luck.'

Thomas came to life behind me. '*His* luck, he says?'

Charlie unbuttoned the flap of his breast pocket. 'No problem, Staff Sergeant,' he said softly. 'All the Major has to do is take the key off of me.'

Then the mad sod – the smaller of the two – dropped the key into the pocket and buttoned it down, all the while staring challengingly at Steadman. 'Although you might just have a job doing that, Major, what with already having both hands occupied with that little banger there. In fact, unless you let go the pin, you haven't even one hand free, have you?'

It was a crazy gamble. No Redcap would've dared take it simply to prevent a detainee from escaping. It couldn't possibly have come off, not even with a sane prisoner. Hoping to audition for a transfer to Provost, was he . . .? *That'd* be bloody right: the most unfitted soldier ever to be a military policeman – apart from Lance Corporal Tosh, anyway – and anway, I hated Charlie Parrish more than anyone else in the world right then. Hated him for killing me because I knew we were dead when I saw the increasing mania in the Major's eyes.

I whispered urgently to Thomas. 'Down, lad. Behind the desk.'

The Corporal bit his lip, shaking his head stubbornly. He knew as well as I did it was a waste of time in that confined space, but my bloody image kept on pushing.

Steadman's brain weathercocked, volatile as ever. 'It seems I'm not the only one in this room with a death wish. You and I, Parrish: that puts us in a win-win situation either way – if you've the guts to go for it.'

Abruptly he jerked the pin from the grenade and extended it mockingly for Charlie to see. Now the only thing preventing detonation was the compression maintained by his palm on the spring-loaded lever. No one in the room breathed for quite a long time after that.

Apart from bloody *Parrish*, naturally. He'd become as predictable in his stupidity as Steadman was unpredictable. Charlie simply continued to lounge against the door totally unimpressed: arms folded, gaitered ankles negligently crossed like we had all day to die.

I could tell we were approaching end game: the short hairs at the back of Steadman's neck were glistening with perspiration for all his determined insouciance. A further hint came when he deliberately allowed the pin to slip from his fingers. The tinkle when it hit the floor sounded like a cymbal clash in the silence of the tension-stilled room. I bloody near jumped out of my boots, and it was a fair guess I hadn't been the only one.

'And the silence was such one could hear a grenade pin drop – eh, Parrish?' Steadman still spoke softly, still stared Charlie down poker-faced although he must have sensed it was more Russian roulette he was playing by then. Only this game had a round in every chamber. 'Now hand me the key. You have until I count to five.'

My final plea cracked on a low whisper: even the image was terrified. 'DO it, stupid! The bloody thing'll explode quicker'n you can get it outa your pocket.'

'One . . .' Steadman said.

'Ten years of my fuckin' *life* he stole to hide behind,' Charlie snarled back. 'Ten fucking YEARS, mate!'

'Two, Parrish . . .'

I registered the white skin previously taut across Steadman's knuckles colouring with fresh blood as his grip on the striker arm slowly began to ease. Jackson started to move forward ashen-faced, but Halliday held out a restraining hand. 'Ye'll no' get to him, man – prone position NOW for all the bloody goo—'

'Thuree . . .'

Charlie's expression had become sickening to see. That made me feel strangely sad. When he died it would be with a terrible hate in him.

'*Four* . . .!' Steadman hissed tight as a drumskin and the colour of parchment himself now.

I grabbed Thomas, shoved him down behind the desk anyway. He'd been a bloody good soldier. He deserved a chance to try and live, even without all his bits.

Charlie played his final bluff, mouth twisted in contempt. 'You daren't do it, Steadman. You're arrogant, you're a bully, you make out you're a hot-shot Redcap officer, but to me, Major, you're just a sick, vindictive coward – an ugly, scar-faced fucking *psychopath*!'

The RSM committed the ultimate blasphemy at that. He grabbed Jackson's arm – actually laid a hand on an officer – then dragged him down and dived on top of him.

'Ye baw-heided wee excuse f'r a SODGER,' he bellowed – *not*, presumably, referring to the Captain. 'Ye've jist made us heroes, man. DEID ones!'

I didn't join them on the deck. No point to it and, anyway, I couldn't. I just stood hypnotized, watching my mate . . . and thinking very hard.

I was still thinking when Steadman finally went insane. I saw him smile that reckless smile for the very last time: almost as if reminiscing over happier, more promising times. 'I remember telling Walker, Parrish . . .'

He reached out unexpectedly as a striking cobra, free arm embracing Parrish's neck like a steel hawser – like it had gripped me that time ten years ago. Somewhat disappointingly Parrish, for all his boasting of bein' a bloody infantryman and supposedly trained to counter such aggression – Charlie didn't seem to resist at all, so shocked did he seem at finding himself pinned against his assailant's immaculately tailored chest while the grenade lifted to push hard against the side of his particularly thick skull.

Not thick enough, though. Nothing a pound of high explosive wouldn't make an impression on, which would be more than anyone else had managed to do in thirty years of stubborn bloody-mindedness.

'You should never tell a crazy man he IS crazy,' the Major said, winning the game hands down.

I was still standing – *still* thinking – when I heard the striker bite home.

Nineteen

It took a million years for Steadman's arm to begin to tremble. Then the shaking got worse until, finally, the hand opened and the grenade rolled out and fell with a dead thud to the floor. The Major's expression was one of utter disbelief at first while he realized the thing wasn't going to blow, not now, followed by a slowly dawning horror of what the future he hadn't planned for must hold for him as he stared at the grenade lying there like a chequered skull.

Then everybody was clambering awkwardly to their feet with the dull-glazed expressions of reprieved men, while looking a bit embarrassed – *especially* Jeemy Halliday I noted, not without a certain unworthy satisfaction. Thirty years I'd waited to see that happen – a private soldier having achieved the distinction of forcing a Royal Military Police regimental sergeant major to prostrate himself on the ground before him . . . and almost certainly getting away with it.

I was still reflecting grimly on the hard, contemptuous grin on Parrish's face when Steadman sank to his knees. I couldn't avoid the conclusion any longer.

'You *bastard*, Charlie Parrish! You crooked, scheming, evil little bastard,' I breathed so's no one else would hear.

None of us wanted to watch while Steadman lost what little reason he had left . . . or none of us, apart from Charlie. Charlie watched, and I think maybe that purified his hatred too, because he wasn't grinning any longer the next time I looked. Not at all.

We couldn't help but listen though, as the disbelieving voice rambled on. 'A joke – another sick, bloody *joke*! By God, it was a JOKE . . .?'

And the laughter came. A convulsion of semi-hysterical

laughter. Then the laughter died for ever to be overtaken by dragging sobs. The winter sun seemed very bright through the window. Not hot, as it had been on the slopes of that mountain in Cyprus, but infinitely more welcome.

Captain Jackson awkwardly cleared his throat and signalled to the RSM. They went over and gently helped the poor bloody Major to his feet. Jackson saluted smartly. 'Perhaps you would care to go to your quarters now, sir?'

Halliday jerked his chin. 'Corporal Thomas.'

'Sir!'

Thomas came sharply to attention and went to stand beside the Major. I watched quietly: I had a lot to thank that young man for. I hoped he would get over his disillusionment with the system, and become a regimental sergeant major one day.

Steadman stood for a few moments, shoulders hunched, and suddenly he seemed very small and untidy – a lot like Parrish had done when Flint brought him in that first time I'd seen him without his tapes. Then he braced with an effort so the medal and campaign ribbons flashed with colour.

He nodded with great dignity. 'Thank you, John. And you, Sergeant Major.'

The RSM's heels smashed together. Respect the rank, if not the man. It was the army. Nothing bloody changed. 'SAH!'

The Major turned to me then, and we stared into each other's eyes for a very long time. And I thought about a bullet hole in a once-carefree little boy's face, and the bubbling mask that had been the head of a man tormented in a Cypriot duty room, and about a bullet-riddled ambulance and a shrivelled-up little drunk who used to be a bloody good soldier.

Then I looked deeper into the dead eyes, and I saw a once-handsome young Redcap standing proud, like a London bobby, near a shell-torn beach called Dunkirk.

I saw a British soldier. A casualty of war.

Slowly, ever so deliberately I lifted my cap from the desk and placed it squarely on my head, pulling its slashed peak well down. And I came to attention rigid as a stainless-steel bar . . . and saluted.

'Sir,' I said. And I meant it.

A slow smile crept across the now placid face and, in that moment, the purple scar was hidden by the shadow of the hand as it returned my salute.

'Thank you, Staff Sergeant. For acknowledging the pleasantries of rank.'

Then he about-turned abruptly and went out between the Captain and Corporal Thomas.

I never saw him again.

I just stood quietly, lit a Full Strength with still-trembling hands and mulled over a few uncharitable thoughts, while Halliday gingerly retrieved the grenade and examined it.

I wasn't surprised when he held it out me. 'Now there's a peculiar thing, Mr Walker. I would be prepared to swear for certain that the fuse has been withdrawn from this ordnance.'

Charlie blew an innocent smoke ring and stabbed it through the heart. 'Is that a fact, sir?'

Perhaps I was wrong, but I thought I saw a little glint of granite then, in the old wise monkey's eyes. 'Aye, Fusilier Parrish, it *is* a fact. And there was you doing such a brave thing, foiling the Major's escape as you did. In all my years of serving wi' the Colours, I have never witnessed such cold, selfless gallantry . . . I am sure you would concede much the same thing, Staff Sergeant Walker?'

I stared very hard at Charlie. 'More or less, Sergeant Major.'

Charlie shrugged modestly. Don't overdo it, mate, I thought anxiously.

'You know how these things are, sir. Sometimes a man . . . well, he just don't wait to calculate the risk involved.'

Jeemy Halliday nodded gravely. 'Aye, you may be right, Fusilier Parrish. Although I have the feeling that you are a braw man at the calculating.'

I couldn't stick it a moment longer. I examined the crack in the ceiling. I might still have time to get on to public works before retiring . . . or then again, I could get Corporal Thomas to do it, save me the effort. No point in havin' a Pavlov's dog . . .

'I'll notify the sappers on my way past.' The RSM placed the grenade carefully on the table. 'There will be an inquiry, of course, but I suspect the Provost Marshal's office will be more concerned with investigating the Major's wee lapse than in identifying which villain actually did smuggle yon in. In fact, Fusilier Parrish, I'm thinking this would not be a bad time for your own case to be re-examined.'

As he reached the door he turned. 'You'll be away home in the morning, Mr Walker. Ye'd be as well to get your last report made up now, to save time. You'd not be expecting Corporal Thomas to do *that* wee job for you?'

I nodded. I'd make it up, all right. Pretty well every word of it. But then, I suspect we'd both known what Jeemy Halliday had meant when he put it that way.

'I'll do that, Mr Halliday, and . . . thanks.'

He sniffed. It was a sergeant major's sniff: the sort reserved for those who transgressed and got away with it. But as I've said before: this was the army. The gulf between ranks never closes for long.

'Aye. Well, a good evening to ye both – and a long retirement to you, Staff Sergeant Walker.'

The door closed behind him and I stubbed the Capstan in the tin lid. Charlie watched me a bit apprehensively for a few moments then flapped his hands vaguely. 'Well, that's it then . . . innit it, mate?'

I didn't say anything. Just kept staring hard at him till he finally surrendered. 'Well, like I said . . . I mean – hell, I didn't know *you* was to be duty sarge, did I?'

'Like I didn't know you was such a big, brave bloody soldier, Charlie Parrish?'

He started to grin. Shameless and irrepressible, it was. Just the way the old Charlie used to grin. 'I never did get the chance to tell you I took the charge out, did I?'

'Only bloody near an hour of questioning.'

He shrugged. 'I reckoned if the Major found me and a grenade on his stamping ground, well, one way or another he'd blow 'is top, wouldn't 'e? Then the whole story was bound to come out, wasn't it?'

'Was it, Charlie? Or was Steadman just tired, deep down,

249

of being what he was? That death wish I was on about? See, chum, the Major was a brave man . . . not a stupid one.'

Charlie picked up his greatcoat. It would look a lot smarter once he'd sewn his colour sergeant's crown and stripes back on. 'Dunno, mate: you're the cod psychologist.'

Then he smiled broadly, irreverently again, and I knew he really was over the past ten years for ever. 'One thing for bloody certain. He was a bastard Redcap through and through.'

We stood looking at each other awkwardly. It had been a long time since Dunkirk. A whole lifetime, thick and thin. They say old soldiers never die, but they can still pine for what they had. Only eventually did Charlie stick his hand out and I grasped it tight. We held on for quite a while.

'So long, mate,' I said softly.

'Don't fade away too quick . . . Staff Sergeant.'

Then he was gone.

I sat down in the lonely duty room, lit another Capstan and thought about Foxie. And O'Feely. And Major Timms, and the dead child on the mountain and . . .

And as I started to cry I knew the image had left me, along with Charlie. Because it was an army image. A Royal Military Policeman's image.

And I didn't need it any more.